Fire & Rayne

Kate Cann

■SCHOLASTIC

To Stephanie, fellow pantheist,
with love

First published in the UK in 2009 by Scholastic Children's Books
An imprint of Scholastic Ltd
Euston House, 24 Eversholt Street
London, NW1 1DB, UK
Registered office: Westfield Road, Southam,
Warwickshire, CV47 0RA
SCHOLASTIC and associated logos are trademarks
and/or registered trademarks of Scholastic Inc.

Text copyright © Kate Cann, 2009
The right of Kate Cann to be identified as the author
of this work has been asserted by her.

ISBN 978 1407 10703 5

A CIP catalogue record for this book
is available from the British Library.

Printed in the UK by CPI Bookmarque, Croydon, Surrey.
Papers used by Scholastic Children's Books are made
from wood grown in sustainable forests.

3 5 7 9 10 8 6 4 2

www.scholastic.co.uk/zone

Chapter One

Rayne woke screaming.

Gasping for breath, heart drumming.

She'd been burning. Fire had caught hold of her, seized her hands, danced with her. Her hair had flared like a tree hit by lightning. Pain had possessed her.

And, standing in front of her, laughing, St John, the boy she'd thought was in love with her. . .

She let out a long *hooo* of breath, got out of bed, padded over in the dark silence to the tiny kitchen, and put the kettle on.

Don't you start all this, she told herself. Don't you start with the nightmares now. It's over. It was over a week ago, when you burnt out the dungeon. St John's gone. He can't hurt you now.

She made a mug of tea, took it back to bed with her, and propped herself up on one elbow, sipping it. A fox's harsh cry broke the silence but it didn't add to her fear, she liked the sound.

Ten short weeks ago, she thought, I was living on Cramphurst Estate, going claustrophobic and mad hearing the rows and the tellies and the sirens, and now I'm here, in this wild wood...

It was unbelievable to her. When she'd arrived at the ancient mansion house of Morton's Keep she'd had no idea what was waiting for her. There'd been warnings, of course – Becky, who worked in the tearoom with her, going on about the Keep's gory history and its ghosts. Mrs Driver, the elderly housekeeper, warning her to always lock her door at night. Patience, the mad old woman at the Green Lady inn, with her sing-song predictions of danger. And then ... she'd been caught up with St John and his friends. From the moment she'd accessed their weird Hidden History website, they'd tracked her, trapped her, and she'd mistaken it for friendship. She'd mistaken it for love. They were glamorous, seductive, and St John was irresistible. *Beauty is Cruel, Cruelty is Beautiful...*

She put down her mug, pulled the duvet over her head. She was remembering how it had all finished. In her head she was back in the dungeon again.

She saw the black candles cast their lurid light on the low brick ceiling; she felt the smothering miasma of fear and evil. She heard Flora taunting her; saw Abigail terrified and bleeding, and Marcus and Petra like automatons, obeying St John. People she'd thought were her friends, the boy she'd thought was in love with her ... she'd just been their key to Morton's Keep. St John's face was gloating, triumphant, as he goaded her for falling for him, for liking his vampire kisses. She heard him claim ancestry with the sadistic Sir Simeon

Lingwall, claiming the house and its ancient, dark power for himself. . .

She rolled herself tighter in her duvet, willed herself to see Ethan appearing, hurling the flaming torch, launching himself at St John and knocking him out cold as the ravenous fire took hold. . .

Fire. She saw fire scorching through the dungeon, and felt calmer imagining its heat. Her nightmare was wrong. There was safety in fire. Ethan was with the fire festival men and he'd told her they were watchers over Morton's Keep, and somehow their fires kept it safe. Although no one was clear what was myth, what was real, it was all shrouded in a thousand years of uncertainty. . .

It's over, she told herself. Whatever it all meant, what was real, what was unreal – it's finished. I'm safe.

But she couldn't get back to sleep.

Dawn was breaking as Rayne, her short coat over her pyjamas and her wellies pulled on her bare feet, walked out into the medieval garden. She locked the Old Sty door behind her and pocketed the huge iron key.

The birds hadn't started singing yet. She wandered through the trees, towards Morton's Keep. The ancient mansion house seemed to crouch like a great beast behind the woods, its two towers looming.

She stopped in a clearing made by a tree felled in one of the recent storms, half sawn up for firewood, and with a catch to the throat recognized where she'd sat last night, with Ethan. She sank down on to a log, where last night she'd sat half-facing him. She felt like crying.

It had started out so right, with her sudden sense that Ethan liked her, wanted her, with him agreeing to come back to the Old Sty for coffee.

And then it had all gone so wrong.

She covered her eyes with her hands, remembering.

Chapter TWO

Ethan had walked beside her, back through the trees and into the medieval garden. There was very little light from the cloudy moon; the edges bulged with darkness. They reached the door of the Old Sty and as she put the iron key into the keyhole, she could sense him behind her, standing back a tactful distance. She could hear him breathing. He followed her through the door and into her room, which smelt deliciously of wood smoke from the stove glowing sleepily against the wall. She pulled open its glass door and pushed a thick log on to the embers; almost immediately, flames leapt into life. Their flickering light, she thought, was enough to see by. She didn't want to turn on the overhead light. It wasn't . . . intimate enough.

"Well, this is it," she said, turning to him. "This is where I live."

"It's good," he said. "I like it. I don't blame you for not wanting to stay in the Keep."

"No. It's scary enough working there!"

She stared at him as he looked around at everything – the stove with the stag's antlers nailed above it, her bed and table, the red curtains screening her clothes. She thought he looked beautiful; strong, and alive. "Tea or coffee?" she asked. "Or – actually – I think there's a couple of beers in the fridge. . ."

"Yeah? I'd love a beer. Or tea."

She went into the cubbyhole kitchen at the back of the room, yanked open the fridge, and was relieved to see three bottles of Budweiser lined up behind the eggs. She decapped two of them, and hovered undecided over a large bags of crisps lying on the counter. She could tip them in that pretty blue bowl, she thought, put it between them on the table . . . no, that was pathetic, too trying-too-hard.

She marched back to the main room. Her breathing was coming too fast, it was making her nervous. "Beer," she announced.

"Great," said Ethan. He was sitting at the table now, looking out of the window at the dark trees as they swayed and shushed in the wind. She handed him a bottle and sat down opposite him, but his eyes wouldn't meet hers. *Why is this so hard?* she thought. Extraordinary, cosmic events linked the two of them. They'd triumphed together; they'd kept Morton's Keep safe. It had been a long fight, ending in the hateful, hidden dungeon of the ancient house. Where he'd . . . she thought the word carefully . . . *saved* her. On more than one level, Ethan had saved her.

And in the dark woods earlier, they'd had so much to say they'd fallen over their words, but *now*. . .

"So," she said at last, "do you think it's over? Now Lingwall's dungeon's going to be filled up with concrete?"

Ethan shrugged. "Even if Lingwall's been burnt out,

it won't transform Morton's Keep into some kind of holy shrine. If the stories are true, that the house is built on a site of ancient evil. . ." He trailed off, took a gulp of beer, and said, "Sir Simeon Lingwall managed to make something uniquely nasty out of the energy here, but people say the walls of Morton's Keep have always run with blood."

"Shut up," she laughed, "I have to live here!"

He smiled back at her, looking at her at last. "You'll be all right. You're protected, aren't you?"

She knew he meant the green lady, that strange spirit of the woods who skirled through old stories and half-remembered folklore in these parts. Who'd shown herself to Rayne – in leaves, in birds. Who had an old local inn named after her and whose presence Rayne had felt, absolutely. But she couldn't bring herself to talk about all that any more. It seemed insubstantial, silly even – as if it was all slipping away from her.

There was a long silence, the awkwardness between them growing by the second. Rayne looked at him, at his profile half-turned away from her again, and something inside her seized up with how much she liked his face, liked *him*. She had to get through to him again – she had to get close. Almost in a panic she scrambled to her feet, saying, "D'you want some crisps?"

Ethan stood up too. He came round the table towards her and made a kind of lunge for her, getting hold of her arms. Then he kissed her, fast, before she could even focus on his face, but the minute she felt his mouth a violent shudder ran through her, and she wrenched herself away.

"*God*," breathed Ethan, "*sorry* . . . hey, what's *wrong*?"

She was still shuddering, her breath coming in spasms, her legs shaking so much that her whole body trembled.

"Rayne, I'm *sorry*. Shit, I'm sorry. You asked me back here – I thought—"

She raised her hands to apologize, to reassure him. She didn't trust herself to speak.

"You *OK*?" he asked, desperately. His hands were hovering, wanting to touch her, not daring to. "You've gone white. Look, sit down. I'll get you a drink of water—"

"God, I'm *sorry*," she gasped, at last, through chattering teeth, "I'm being an idiot—"

"You're *not*. It's me who's the idiot. It's too soon – it's too soon after everything that happened. . . Look, sit down. Before you fall down. I'll get you that water."

He hurried off to the kitchen and Rayne sat down and tried to calm her breathing, but her hands were jumping on the table, her legs were shaking still. She felt full of anguish. What would he think of her now? That she was some kind of freak who flipped out at a kiss—

He was standing in front of her with the glass of water. She looked up at him and tried to smile. "Any better?" he asked.

"Yes. Shit, I'm so *sorry*—"

"It's OK." He put the glass down on the table warily, to one side of her, as though he was terrified to touch her again. "Listen, I'm gonna go. You should get some sleep." He was acting like he couldn't wait to get away from her, and she couldn't blame him. She wanted to ask him to stay, but she couldn't say the words. She just nodded, smiling, over the rim of the water glass. "I'll call you, OK?" he said. "I'll call you and see how you are."

Then he turned, and almost bolted out through the door into the night.

Oh, *brilliant*, thought Rayne. You get him to come back here, then you freak out. You *wanted* him to kiss you. Ever since you first saw him, if you're honest, you've wanted that. So why act like he's shoved a million volts through you? Shit. *Shit!*

The shaking had stopped. She wasn't even trembling now. She stood up and went over to the door and looked out into the wild, moon-washed garden. It was silent – he'd long gone. In her mind she replayed him saying "I'll call you, OK? I'll call you and see how you are" and she told herself it would all work out, she'd see him again. But then she remembered the way he'd practically run out of the door, and she felt awful again.

He was right, though, it was all too soon. Too soon after somebody else's kisses.

St John's kisses.

The birds were singing now; the sun was growing stronger. It was going to be another mellow autumn day. Rayne felt calmer, somehow, for reliving, for *facing*, what had happened the night before, but she was chilled to the bone. She scrambled up from the log and hurried back to the Old Sty. She kicked off her wellies; then, still with her coat on, she climbed under her duvet, telling herself she'd snatch a few hours' sleep before work. Sleep, she hoped, without nightmares this time.

She lay there listening to the new-day birds, drifting off into a doze, and as she did, she lifted a finger to her mouth, and pressed her lips where Ethan's had been.

Chapter Three

The workmen came at nine a.m. sharp the next morning to start filling in the burnt-out dungeon. The noise of their great, rumbling concrete mixer filled the air. Morton's Keep was closed to visitors for the day but Mrs Driver hadn't given Rayne the day off from working in the tearoom. She said the workmen would need a constant supply of sweet tea, and they'd promised them sandwiches at lunch time too, otherwise they'd have to go off site for lunch and might not finish the job in time. "And it's a chance for us to do some stock-taking," the old housekeeper had said. "We need to count the cutlery – the teaspoons are running really low."

Teaspoons, thought Rayne sourly. She was standing in the kitchen of the old dairy tearoom, staring at the top of Mrs Driver's neat grey head as she bent over the lines of spoons and forks. What was it with Mrs Driver? OK, maybe she didn't want to talk about the dark side of Morton's Keep, maybe she could only cope with living here if she refused to acknowledge the past, but to *so completely* ignore everything that had happened . . . it was bordering on lunacy. She hadn't said one thing about what had happened the night of the fire, and now she was acting like the workmen were just doing a spot of maintenance work . . . talk about denial. *Teaspoons*.

Ben Avebury, the gardener, was just as bad. He'd saved their lives back in the dungeon, coming in with the flaming torch, but now Rayne never saw him, let alone talked to him. He kept to the far parameters of the estate, clearing dead wood, tending the trees.

Even Mr Stuart, the Keep's owner, was avoiding her. When St John had broken in to find the centre of Lingwall's power and twist it to himself, she'd confronted Mr Stuart, and he'd reluctantly told her about the terrible legacy of the place. That it had immense dark power for those ruthless enough to use it; that Sir Simeon Lingwall, alive over three hundred years ago, had been supreme master of the art. Over the centuries, there'd been reoccurrences – evil echoes of Lingwall's crimes. Old mad Patience had been a victim of one such reoccurrence, and now it seemed St John was intent on unleashing another. . .

"And we stopped him," Rayne told herself. "Ethan and I, between us – we stopped it happening again."

Her eye was caught by a pile of photocopied sheets lying on the window sill, next to a little display box of leaflets advertising tours of Morton's Keep. Curious, she picked one up: it was an article from the local paper about the recent apple fair they'd held here.

"Ms Barton did those," said Mrs Driver. "She's *such* a good manager, always having good ideas for promoting the Keep. It was a lovely event, the Fair, maybe people who missed it will make the effort to come next year. . ."

11

The article had a photograph. It showed the four young fire festival dancers during their wildest dance. It showed Ethan. Just the sight of him in the grainy photocopy made Rayne's stomach flip over. He was leaping two feet off the ground, his face was in stark relief from the flames of the bonfire, and alight with energy. He looked supernatural.

"Can I keep one?" muttered Rayne. "I'd like a souvenir of the . . . the Fair."

"Of course, dear," said Mrs Driver, smiling.

As soon as Rayne had made a post-lunch round of tea Mrs Driver told her she could knock off early. "The cutlery inventory's all done," she said. "You've been a great help. I'll make the workmen one more pot of tea before they finish. Now get off outside with you, enjoy this wonderful sunshine."

It was late October, and after the freakish storms that had battered at them over the last few weeks, the stillness and the warm, low sun seemed glorious. Back at the Sty, Rayne stowed the picture of Ethan underneath a pile of tops in her chest of drawers, then went out again. She walked along her favourite route, through the medieval garden and down to the lake. The three white geese were there, hunkered down by their hutch on their little island, safe from foxes. She walked on, following the stream that veered to the right and led into the wood. It was beautiful now the leaves had all turned. Copper, brass and gold, lit by shafts of sun coming down through the branches, flared out at her.

She let the heavy stillness flow into her; she let her mind clear of thoughts. A deep, calm tiredness had taken hold of her. She wandered out from the woods and walked on to the wide lawn at the back of the mansion house. On the terrace, the concrete mixer was churning away; a great pipe chugged upwards through one of the windows, taking up load after load of concrete and slurry. Rayne stood and watched for a few moments. It looked so weirdly – *practical*. A place of centuries-old evil being filled in like a hole in the road. She stared at it and was overcome with wanting to talk about what had happened, to mull it over, come to terms with it, but Mr Stuart, Mrs Driver and Ben Avebury had all in their different ways made it clear that the subject was closed. The only person she could have any kind of meaningful discussion with was Ethan, but there was no way she was going to call him, not yet. Not after what had happened last night.

"I wonder if this is the end," she thought. "I wonder if it *is* laid to rest now." She crossed the lawn, walking over the shadow bars from the great wrought-iron gates, towards the old wall on the far side. A single white dove flapped sadly over her head. "Poor thing," she thought. "Forced to live in that horrible tower. I bet it feels the vibes. No wonder they don't breed properly."

Michaelmas daisies were growing in abundance by the wall, each stalk a mass of small purple flowers. On an impulse she bent down and picked six sprays, then she went through into the garden and stared across the maze of box hedges at the gloomy tower dovecote. She thought of poor Patience, imprisoned there for weeks, maybe months, losing her sanity to one of the last men to be hanged in England. She thought of the three victims from Victorian times who were killed there, then buried here in the maze. She set off, walking into it.

After only four wrong turnings she reached the hexagonal-shaped clearing and stood looking at the three grave markers. They were laid out like an arrow, pointing in accusation at the tower. She remembered how her skin had crawled when she'd first found them, seen the eleven black candle stubs squatting like toads all around them. But the candles had long been cleared away, and the grass had been cut. Slowly, she laid down the sprays of pretty daisies, two to each grave marker, and as she did she wished for peace to come to whoever – child, man, woman – was decaying underneath.

Rayne headed back across the lawn, and saw that the concrete mixer on the terrace had been shut down, and the slurry-pipe was dormant. Mr Stuart was standing talking to the foreman; they were smiling and nodding and there was an air of the job being nearly completed. She went over to join them.

"Rayne!" said Mr Stuart. "How are you, m'dear? Have you been keeping our workers supplied with tea?"

"She certainly has," said the foreman. "We're awash with the stuff. Much appreciated, too. Anyway, Mr Stuart, I'll just do the last check upstairs now, make sure the lads have sealed the infill properly. And as I say, let it dry for two weeks before you board it up."

He walked smartly off, and Mr Stuart beamed rather vaguely at Rayne, as if hoping she'd take herself off too. But she didn't. She said, "Have you ever thought of buying more birds for the dovecote?"

"What?" he asked, bemused.

"The tower dovecote," she said, nodding towards

it. "I think you should get more birds. Those poor few doves – they're never going to breed. They look like they're terminally depressed. If you got some good breeding pairs and they raised some young you'd – you'd tip the balance."

"The balance?" Mr Stuart repeated, sounding irritated. "What balance?" Then before Rayne could answer he went on, "I've given up on them, to be honest. I was just going to let them die out."

"Well, I think that's really *sad*," she said, heatedly. "Birds are great. Birds would. . ." She trailed off. Something had shifted in her mind. She gazed at the huge gates across the lawn, and a shadowy flashback formed of birds flying into a shape, a huge, terrifying, female shape, pointing at her. The green lady, wanting her to *act*. . .

". . . so you can see I have too much else to think about to worry about *doves*," Mr Stuart was saying. "I advertised first thing this morning, but—"

"What?" said Rayne, focusing on him again. "Sorry, Mr Stuart, I missed that—"

"I was *saying*, one has every sympathy for Ms Barton of course, but it lands me right in it—"

"Ms Barton?"

"Rayne, weren't you listening to *anything* I said? Our wonderful house manager has been called away. Very suddenly – two hours ago in fact. Her mother collapsed – she's seriously ill. And she's handed in her resignation because she wants to move back home to take care of her. Admirable daughterly behaviour, of course, but it leaves me trying to find a replacement with *no notice at all*."

Then he turned on his heel and stalked off.

Chapter Four

Over the next few days Mr Stuart got three emails and two letters of application for the vacant position of manager and tour guide of Morton's Keep. Four were from nearby towns and sounded – well, a bit lumpen, Mr Stuart said. Women wanting something to do after retirement, women wanting to fit work round school holidays. Three of them said they wouldn't want to live in, and hoped for an increase in wages because of this. "Ridiculous," he said, briskly. "The one thing we have got – and to spare – is *rooms*. No, they're no good for Morton's Keep. I need commitment. I need *drive*."

Commitment and drive were there in abundance in the fifth application, however. A Miss Skelton emailed from Dunbartonshire, in Scotland. She was currently working as a special events manager, but increasingly felt the desire to be involved in a long-term project that she could nurture and develop. She'd researched Morton's Keep and felt it was ripe for expansion – ripe for the sort of skills she could bring to it. She also said she'd be thrilled to have the opportunity of living in such an ancient and venerable mansion house.

Mr Stuart, greatly excited, invited her for an interview at the end of that same week, then turned up at the tearoom to speak to Mrs Driver about the arrangements for her visit. "She sounds *spot on*," he enthused. "I'm not bothering to interview the others. And I'm not advertising again, not until I've seen her. I tell you, I've got a really good feeling about this one."

"Won't she need to take a drop in wages, if she's been such a high flyer before?" asked Mrs Driver.

"Well – I'm prepared to go up a bit, if she's as right for the job as I think she is. But she mentioned quality of life as being more important to her than money. Seriously, I think we've got a real catch in Miss Skelton."

"Let's hope it works out, then," said Mrs Driver, a touch frostily, and he beamed and left the tearoom.

"Not keen, Mrs D?" asked Rayne, smiling.

"She sounds too much like a new broom to me."

"New *broom*?"

"Don't you know that saying? *A new broom sweeps clean?*"

"And that's wrong?"

"The end of the saying is *but an old broom knows all the corners*," said the housekeeper, archly. "Miss Skelton doesn't *know* the Keep. And anyway, sometimes it's good to let a little dust lie. All this talk of expansion and new projects. What's Mr Stuart want to do – turn Morton's Keep into a theme park?"

"Oh, I don't think so. Just be more professional about everything. Put on more events and stuff. His accountant's always on at him, isn't he – he desperately needs to make more money to keep the place afloat."

"Hm. Well, if *Miss Skelton* thinks she can swan in here and interfere with the tearoom—"

"She'll have you making goat's cheese bruschetta and sun-dried tomato tartlets, Mrs D. Not these old-fashioned scones and sponges."

"Over my dead body," snorted Mrs Driver, slamming the dishwasher shut. "*And* I've got enough to do without cleaning out Ms Barton's flat for that woman to stay the night in, too."

"Oh, come on, you can't expect her to go back to Scotland the same night she comes down!"

"I don't. But why all the fuss? 'Make sure the bathroom's really clean' *in*deed!"

"Is that what he said?"

"It was!"

Rayne laughed. Really, the old girl could almost be jealous.

Ms Barton's flat was on the top floor of what was called the "new building", on the left of the forecourt. Rayne had never been inside, and she was curious to see it.

"I'll clean it," she said. "If you pay me."

"Rayne – would you? Of course I'll pay you! Ten pounds?"

"Done. I can do it early tomorrow morning."

"Don't go overboard. Just a quick whiz round with the Hoover, make up the bed with clean sheets and so on . . . the cleaning cupboard's on the ground floor, and I'll leave the sheets out for you. Oh, that's a relief. Thank you, dear. Now you get off – I'll close up."

Rayne plated up some leftover salad and onion quiche

for her supper, and meandered back to the Old Sty. It was late afternoon, and the extraordinary Indian summer showed no sign of abating. She changed into jeans and a T-shirt, went outside and lay down in the long, warm grass with her plate of food beside her.

All the dramas and horrors of the last few weeks seemed unreal, only the warmth and the shush of the breeze in the grass seemed real. . . "I've got all I need right here," she thought, drowsily. "A bed to sleep in, food – nothing to do but bask like a cat in the sun."

Her mum would say she wasn't normal, not to mind being on her own so much. And she was *really* on her own now. She'd not only lost her boyfriend but all the new friends she'd made here, too, when she'd found out the truth about St John and his twisted crew.

She still had Becky, of course, when she worked at Morton's Keep. And Ethan, she supposed. Perhaps.

A crow landed a few feet away from her and stalked towards her, eyeing her plate of food. She broke off a piece of pastry and tossed it to him, and he collected it in his black beak efficiently and without gratitude, and hopped off.

"I can't be bothered to start again," she thought. "To try to make contact with people again."

Then, into the shushing silence, three shrill beeps – the arrival of a text. She pulled out her phone and her heart quickened because the word *Ethan* was on the screen, like a diamond, like a promise.

How u doing, the text said.

Fine, she texted back, *u OK?*

There was a pause, then another text arrived with

Ethan's name blazoned before it. *Fireworks on Martyr's Hill thurs nyt*, it said. *C u there 7ish?*

She took in a deep breath and texted back: *Gr8. C u there*.

And lay back in the soft grass, arms behind her head, gazing at the trees above her head, feeling her heart beating.

Rayne set her alarm early the next day, so she'd have time to clean the flat before the tearoom opened. She hurried across the forecourt past the ancient wall that surrounded the oldest part of Morton's Keep; the two great towers glared down on her as she ran past. She let herself into the tall "new building" with the keys Mrs Driver had given her. She didn't waste time checking out the offices on the two lower floors, just hauled the vacuum cleaner, clean sheets and cleaning things up to the flat.

When she opened the door, her first feeling was one of absolute envy. The room she'd entered was light and spacious, with luxurious oat-coloured carpeting and a big posh sofa. She went into the bedroom – it was just as fine as the main room. The kitchen and bathroom were small but stylish, all shining surfaces and tiles. The flat made *her* room, she thought sourly, look like what it was – an old sty.

Then, when the envy had ebbed a bit, it hit her that the usually neat, efficient Ms Barton really had left in a tearing hurry. Mr Stuart said she'd been called away suddenly, but this looked like sheer panic. She'd left all kinds of stuff. A cardigan on a chair, shoes by the sofa; an open book on its seat. Unopened post, a mug and a plate with a half-eaten slice of toast on it were on the table; the waste-paper bin underneath it was on its side.

Rayne went into the bedroom. The bed was unmade; a suitcase had been pulled from under it, then abandoned. The open wardrobe showed clothes still hanging inside; wire hangers were scattered on the carpet.

In the kitchen, there was still food in the fridge and tins in the cupboards; in the bathroom, shampoo and toothpaste sat on the little marble shelf above the basin. Rayne pulled open the bathroom cabinet; it was stocked with vitamin pills, two lipsticks, some aspirin. . .

Mrs Driver didn't have a mobile phone, she didn't hold with them. Which was a pity because Rayne was filled with a very strong desire to call her and tell her what she'd found. It unsettled her, as if she was picking up on the panic Ms Barton must have felt to have left the flat like this.

She checked her watch. She'd better get on with it or she'd be late opening up the tearoom.

First she stripped the bed, and made it up with the fresh linen. Then she folded up the clothes from the wardrobe and laid them inside the abandoned suitcase. There were more clothes in the chest of drawers, but they all fitted in the case – even the shoes and the bathroom stuff. The food from the fridge she shoved into two plastic carrier bags.

Then she set about cleaning, working as fast as she could. She was good at cleaning – she'd got a lot of practice at home, her mum had always seemed to leave it up to her. It took her just under two hours to do all four rooms and by the time she'd finished the flat was sparkling and the air of panic that the disarray had created had gone.

But she was starting to sense another atmosphere in the flat, equally as unsettling.

She hauled the cleaning things and vacuum cleaner back down to the cupboard on the ground floor, then ran up again and carried the suitcase, used bedclothes and bags of food outside the flat door and dumped them down, ready to go. Then she hurried back to shut the window she'd opened to air the room – and almost jumped back in fright. The two ancient towers loomed in at her, far too close – for one mad second she thought they'd actually *moved*, they were closing in on her, dark, sombre, threatening. . . Then her brain engaged and she reasoned that the curve of the forecourt distorted the distance, made the towers seem a lot closer than they actually were.

She was still shaken, though. She was filled with wanting to get outside again.

As she hurried to the door she realized what the new feeling in the flat was. It was a feeling of expectancy.

The flat was waiting.

Chapter Five

Mrs Driver was unperturbed by Ms Barton's abandoned suitcase. "You've packed it up beautifully, dear," she said. "I'll send it on to her. I expect she felt she couldn't manage two big cases on the train."

"But she must have managed two *coming* here," Rayne said.

"If you want any of that food she left, you have it," Mrs Driver went on, ignoring Rayne's comment. "Otherwise just throw it out."

"Did she seem very upset, when she left?" Rayne persisted. "Did you actually see her go?"

"I did. I saw her off myself, in a cab to the station. She promised to keep in touch. There were a few tears – she's had a happy three years here. But she knew she was doing the right thing. She knew her first duty was to care for her mother."

Mrs Driver seemed oddly touchy and on edge for the rest of the day. Rayne had to remind her to give her the ten pounds for cleaning the flat, and when she told her she was going to the firework display that night, Mrs Driver rolled her eyes and said, "*Not* the one on Martyr's Hill? Oh, Rayne, that has a terrible reputation. It gets quite wild. Someone was hurt last year, by a banger being thrown. *So* irresponsible."

"I'll be OK. I'll be careful. I'm meeting—" She broke off. She knew it would only add to the housekeeper's alarm if she said she was meeting Ethan Sands, one of the fire festival boys. "I'm meeting up with Becky."

Mrs Driver approved of Becky. Becky helped out regularly in the tearoom and she was bright and cheerful and didn't want to have anything to do with the dark side of Morton's Keep. And she probably *was* going to be at the fireworks, so it was only half a lie, wasn't it?

Mrs Driver's face relaxed a little. "Oh, are you, dear? That's good. Becky's so sensible. If you *must* go to Martyr's Hill, you stick with her, all right?"

It was ten past seven. Acting on Mrs Driver's reluctant instructions, Rayne had got the bus to the west end of Marcle Lees town and was making her way along the roadside to the lane that led up to Martyr's Hill. She'd brought her torch, afraid it would be pitch-black, but a big group of people had got off the bus with her and they all had torches, so she just tagged along behind them.

She had no idea where she'd meet Ethan. She supposed if she didn't see him, she'd phone him. She hoped she'd meet up with him at the bottom of the hill because she didn't fancy climbing it on her own. She could see it ahead of her, an ominous craggy mound, a dark space in the sky with no stars in it.

The group from the bus turned off into the parking area at the foot of Martyr's Hill. Rayne could see a whole crowd of people there, waiting in the dark. Someone shouted something, she couldn't hear what – then the people she'd followed all switched off their torches.

Her heart thudded with the drama of it. It was pitch-black, now. She peered round, trying to focus, but she couldn't see anyone – she could only hear the breathing from the crowd, the odd muttered words. Then there was a rasping sound, and a huge fire torch shaped like a trident flared into life. It was lifted high and in its light Rayne could see that everyone was walking over and lining up behind the man holding it.

He was facing the crowd, his face lit harshly by the flame. Rayne gave a start. She recognized him. He'd been one of the fire dancers at the Apple Fair, one of the men at the strange ritual she'd interrupted in Fleet Woods, who'd chased after her, shouting, *It's her, it's her. . .*

He was one of the watchers. Who believed, because of what mad old Patience had told them, that Rayne had a purpose here, a link with the green lady. . .

She felt her blood drumming in her veins. *All that's over*, she told herself. But she kept her face turned from him as she walked forward, into the crowd.

Then, some way ahead of her, she saw Ethan. He was craning round, scanning the crowd, looking for her. She was sure he was looking for her. She pushed her way through everyone, ignoring their muttered objections, until she was level with him. *"Ethan!"* she called.

He focused on her and his face seemed to open up with pleasure. "Rayne!" he said. "*Here!*"

But before she could reach him, the man with the flaming trident shouted "*Ready?*" and from the crowd came the answering roar "*Ready!*" and they all surged forward. Two men with great barrels of unlit torches were handing them out to people as they passed.

But Rayne wasn't fazed. She shoved her way to Ethan's side and he reached out and grabbed her hand, pulling her through to stand beside him. He'd already got hold of a torch. She could smell the petrol.

When they reached the man with the fiery trident, the people divided, some going to the right, some to the left, and everyone, as they passed, lifted their torches and lit them at the flames. Soon, it was Ethan's turn. As his torch flared into life it seemed to Rayne that the watcher stared down at her intently, examining her face in the firelight. But she shrugged it off.

"I want one!" she muttered. "Not fair!"

"You should've taken one," Ethan said, smiling.

"Too late now."

"You can have a go with this."

The crowd was stretching out now, the crush was over, but he kept hold of her hand. She loved it, she loved the contact. Loved the feeling they were connected.

They walked steadily up the hill, keeping pace with the others. "This must look amazing from a distance," Rayne said. "A procession of fire, snaking up the hill."

"I s'pose it does, but I've never seen it," Ethan answered. "I've always been here, walking with them."

"Even from a baby?"

"Yup. My parents brought me in a sling."

"Weren't they scared you'd get bits of fire dropping down on you?"

"My dad had the sling, my mum carried the torch."

"Ah. Are they here tonight?"

"They wouldn't miss it."

Rayne looked around. There were lots of children in the procession; old people too. Everyone looked intent on the climb, solemn even, as they followed the little winding path through the scrub and the boulders. The atmosphere wasn't like any other firework display she'd been to before.

Then something very obvious dawned on her. "This isn't just early bonfire night fireworks, is it?" she said. "That man lighting everyone's torches. . ."

"Will. Yes. He's a top man in the fire group."

"So this is one of the fire festival marches?"

"Yes."

"When we talked the other night . . . in the woods, before you came back to my room. . ." She broke off, embarrassed. It was suddenly there between them, him kissing her, her breaking away and trembling, shaking. . .

"Yes?" he said again, guardedly.

"I remember you saying that all the . . . all the watchers' stuff – their rituals – weren't real. Like a comfort blanket, you said."

He shrugged. "Yeah, well. The fire festivals are different."

He seemed to want to get off the subject. She felt the same. A deep reluctance to talk about it. To say the word *watchers*.

Or the word *evil*.

She was annoyed by that reluctance.

"So these people," she went on, doggedly, "they're doing all this, taking part, for protection. . ."

"To most of them, it's just a tradition, an event they've forgotten the real meaning of. But it still means something to them – something deep. A while back, the council got all twitchy about health and safety – offered to take over the organization of the fire festivals. Trust me, they backed off pretty soon. No one voted for it. It's got to stay with the people."

"Some people know the meaning still. I met this woman, in the town square, the night of the first festival. . ."

Ethan turned to look at her, and she trailed off awkwardly. That had been an extraordinary night, the night she'd found out about St John and the full extent of his treachery, when he'd turned on her, and Ethan had protected her. Laid St John out with a single blow.

"What about her?" Ethan asked.

"She knew all about protecting the boundaries – going to each corner of the town with the fire, going north, south, east and west to protect the people from 'what's without'. And *then* what got me was she said the braziers on the square, where you all threw your torches, were to protect the people from 'what's within'. It was like she *knew* about. . ."

"St John Arlington?"

"Yes. Him, and Morton's Keep, and the threat that's always there, the reoccurrences, and . . . *everything*."

There, it was out. She'd said it.

Ethan still had hold of her hand. The walkers ahead of

them were slowing a little; the climb had got steeper. Rayne could see the uneven outline of the summit of the hill right ahead of them.

"Maybe she was a watcher's wife," he said, after a moment or two.

"So watchers have to be men, do they?"

"I don't know. They just always are."

"The fire dancers – the ones who were at the Apple Fair, with Will. They're all watchers, aren't they?"

"Most of 'em. Not all the young ones."

"But there has to be eleven, doesn't there? There were eleven at the Fair, and when they came to the burnt-out dungeon – and those candles St John lit, on the graves in the tower maze. . ."

"Eleven's just a number – a number with power for us. St John knew that, he tried to use it against us. But you don't have to dance to be a watcher, and you're not a watcher just because you dance. It's not – *set*. It's not rigid, like a club you sign up to."

"But you're one, aren't you?" she said, in a rush. "Despite your . . . *reservations* . . . you're one."

He didn't answer, and she wanted to ask the question again, *make* him answer, but she couldn't, she stayed silent.

Then he said, "Hey – we're nearly there."

"What happens at the top?"

"You'll see," said Ethan. "Here, you carry the torch now."

She took it, loving the sense of it burning above her head, and they walked on.

Chapter Six

At the very top of the hill was a huge, unlit bonfire. Quietly, the crowd circled round it, spread out all around it, torches still blazing. "I helped build that!" said Ethan.

Rayne smiled to hear the pride in his voice, and said, "God, it must've taken ages."

"I got Hiker to help haul the wood up."

"Hiker?"

"My old horse. He's a trouper. *Shhhh!*"

The whole crowd had fallen completely silent. Will took a step closer to the bonfire, and raised his trident again. "*FIRE!!*" he bellowed.

"*FIRE!!*" came the answering roar from the crowd. "*FIRE!! FIRE!!*" The great shouts seemed to leap up into the blackness, into the huge dark sky. Then, as one, everyone hurled their torches at the bonfire and Rayne, spine tingling, threw hers on, too. Then she clapped her hand over her mouth and turned to Ethan. "God, sorry!" she gasped. "Did you want to do that?"

"It's fine," he laughed.

"I was kind of . . . caught up in the momentum."

"Well, it was a good shot! Look at that *go*."

The huge pile of wood, ignited in a hundred different places, had exploded into life. And with it, the crowd seemed to relax. They started laughing and calling out to each other, and from their bags and backpacks, they pulled out cans of beer, Thermos flasks, and packets of food.

"Did *you* bring a picnic?" Rayne demanded.

"No. That's the girl's job."

"Oh, *what*?" She swiped out at him and he sidestepped, laughing, then pulled two cans of lager from his coat pocket.

"Here. Have one. And don't worry, the food'll get circulated."

As if on cue, a kind-looking woman came over with a huge, lidless cake tin. "Hello, Ethan," she said, cosily. "Here – have a flapjack?"

"Haven't you got anything savoury there, Mrs Lewis?"

"Cheeky monkey! Marjory's got some lovely ham baps, you see her over there? Here – put a couple of these in your pocket for later." Ethan picked up a flapjack, and Mrs Lewis turned to Rayne. "Won't your *friend* have one too?" she asked, smiling.

"Thanks," said Rayne, embarrassed, and picked up a slice. It looked so good she bit into it as soon as Mrs Lewis had gone. "This is *amazing*!" she squawked.

"She's a great cook, Mrs Lewis. Here comes Marjory. We're gonna get stuffed with food – everyone wants to check you out."

"That why you asked me to come? To get offered lots of food?"

"Yup. The only reason."

She laughed at him, drawing closer. They were getting on well, she thought. They were even starting to flirt.

Then there was a sudden zooming noise and a spurt of bright sparkles in the black sky. Three men in a clearing to the right of the blazing fire had started the firework display.

Rayne adored fireworks. The shock and the brilliance of them, the fizzing and crackling and booming. She turned towards the clearing, loving the feel of the hot fire all along her side, and craned her neck back to watch. Marjory arrived, beaming and holding out a tray of baps, and Rayne thanked her and took one, then she opened her lager and swigged. It was all perfect – except for the fact that she and Ethan weren't holding hands any more. They were standing close but not close enough to touch. She willed him to put his arm round her, but nothing happened. Give it time, she thought.

At last, after a stupendous display, the grand finale firework leapt into the sky and filled it with red and silver stars, and everyone cheered and clapped. When the applause had died away Ethan said, "So, how is the old place, now the dungeon's been filled in? Does it seem lighter? Happier?"

"No."

"You mean the corridors aren't echoing with laughter?"

Rayne smiled ruefully. "Not exactly. Mr Stuart and Mrs Driver – they're hardly a barrel of giggles at the best of times, are they. I dunno if it's different. I walked through the Great Hall the other day and it still gave me the creeps, with that one-handed clock upstairs ticking away."

"What about the workmen? D'you reckon any of them . . . felt any vibes?"

"Not a thing. They were so matter-of-fact it was untrue. Cracking jokes when I brought their tea out and filling the dungeon in like it was a collapsed drain or something."

"And Mr Stuart and Mrs Driver – they're still all zip-lipped about it?"

"Absolutely. *And* Ben. It didn't happen, as far as they're concerned. And anyway, Mr Stuart's all preoccupied with finding a replacement manager."

"I heard."

"God – gossip gets around here, doesn't it?"

"Like wildfire. Always."

"He was *so* preoccupied he wouldn't listen to my plan to get some more breeding doves for the tower dovecote. Rude sod."

Ethan turned to smile at her. "That's a nice idea. Bring a bit of life back."

"I know. Anyway, Miss Skelton – the one he's pinning all his hopes on – arrives tomorrow to stay the night. I had to clean out Ms Barton's flat for her." She paused. She was remembering the uneasy feeling in the flat, first of panic, then of waiting, of expectation, and the way she'd been frightened by the Keep towers looming at her. But somehow she didn't want to tell Ethan about that.

The fire was diminishing, sending sprays of sparks into the blackness as the burning logs collapsed. A group of boys on the far side were throwing bangers into the embers; they cracked like whips. A rogue rocket was let off, and a girl shrieked with laughter as it zoomed over her head. This

33

must be what Mrs Driver had warned her against, Rayne thought, smiling.

People had started to drift down the hill again, laughing and talking loudly, carrying the youngest children. It was quite unlike their solemn, measured ascent.

"Hey, they're dishing out parkin over there," Ethan said. "I love parkin."

"*What,*" said Rayne, "is parkin? Apart from when you turn off the engine in a car?"

"God, you really haven't lived, have you?"

"No."

"It's cake, treacly cake. It's ace. You always have it on bonfire nights. Hang on, I'll get us some." He loped off, and she moved closer to the fire, gazing into it as it flickered and flared.

Then everything inside her stopped. Froze.

There was a face in the fire.

It was huge, as big as the heart of the bonfire, and subtle, changing as the flames changed, one second here, one second not, but Rayne knew it was real. It had eyes that burnt deep red, glaring at her, and a great mouth that was open – wide open – gushing smoke and flames.

She screwed her eyes shut against it, but she could still feel the heat on her eyelids.

"*What have you seen?*" hissed a voice right by her side.

She spun round. It was Will, the head fire man, and he was gazing at her greedily. She looked back at the fire – the face had gone. She took a step back, away from him.

"You've seen something, in the fire, haven't you?" he

insisted. "I saw the way your face changed from over there. It was *her*, wasn't it? The green lady. You saw her."

Dumbly, furiously, she shook her head, and then Ethan was beside them, putting his arm round her. "What's going on, Will?" he demanded.

"She's seen something," Will growled. "In the fire. She's seen *her*. Reckon she's the one, like Patience said. No sense hiding from it."

Ethan looked down at Rayne, but she couldn't meet his eye. "I just – the flames were making shapes, that's all," she muttered. "Ethan, can we make our way back? I'm getting really cold."

Chapter Seven

Rayne took one bite from the piece of parkin that Ethan handed to her and said she thought it was horrible. As they set off down Martyr's Hill, she threw it into the bushes. They didn't hold hands on the descent and they walked in silence. She was shaken, truly shaken, by the feeling of terror the face in the fire had stirred in her. Her heart was pounding and her mind was trying to rationalize it, dismiss it. She wanted her mind to succeed.

Ethan turned to look at her, but she kept facing front, kept walking resolutely downwards. "Not going to tell me about it, then?" he asked.

"About what?"

"Oh, come on. You saw something. You looked really scared."

"What scared me was that weirdo! Why are they so *fixated* on me? Just cos some old mad woman thinks I'm. . . *Jumping* on me like that!"

"Yeah, but *why* did he jump on you?"

"OK." She paused. "It was a face – I thought I saw a gigantic face in the fire. It looked – I dunno. It wasn't pleasant. Jesus. I don't want to remember it. It made me feel terrified. I'm probably – I'm still shaken up with everything that's happened. Maybe I'm going mad. I don't know."

There was a silence, then Ethan said, "Rayne, you know you're not going mad. You know it's not your mind."

"Do I?"

"*Yes!* Last week, when we walked in the wood. . ."

She looked at him, remembering his face in the moonlight as they'd talked of unreal things only the two of them understood.

"You told me you'd seen her, then," Ethan went on. "You said you'd seen the . . . green lady." The two words dropped from his mouth like iron, like it cost him to say them aloud.

"Yes," she whispered.

"Three times, you said. In a palm tree, made by the birds, and in the smoke. . ."

She dropped her head. She was thinking that she'd not only seen the green lady, she'd felt her, too. That night she'd gone down into Lingwall's dungeon, it had been *her* behind her, pushing energy and power into her, urging her on. . . It was too terrifying to remember. Her mind closed against it.

They'd slowed right down; neither of them wanted to reach the bottom of the hill because it was easier to talk side by side and moving. "I know I said I'd seen her," she muttered. "And I thought I *had*, then. But we'd just been through this *extreme* thing, hadn't we, and – oh, shit, it's all too *weird*!"

"I know, I know it's weird. But d'you think it might have been *her* again? In the fire?"

"I don't know. It was . . . it made me feel terrible, that's all I know. And if she's meant to be the good one – *why did it do that?*" Rayne stopped walking and took in a deep breath. Her head was spinning, she felt almost faint.

"You all right?" asked Ethan, anxiously, peering at her through the blackness.

"Yes," she muttered.

"But you don't want to talk about it."

"No." She started to walk again. "Look – OK, maybe there are dark energies at Morton's Keep. Maybe St John tapped into them. Maybe I'm tapping into other energies. It's all been really screwed up and creepy. I . . . I thought I wanted to talk about it, I was cross with Mrs Driver for . . . sweeping it all under the carpet all the time. But now I kind of see her point, OK?"

"OK," he said. But he said it reluctantly, as though he didn't really agree with her.

"I just want it out of my head," she pleaded. "It's over, all that weirdness, and I just want to forget it and get my life back, enjoy being here if I can."

"It's OK," he repeated. "I understand."

There was a silence, and they started walking faster. "It's Halloween soon," she said brightly. "Do you have a festival then?"

"No. November the fifth, Halloween – they don't mean much around here. Will and his cronies decide the fire festival dates, something to do with phases of the moon and stuff, and then word gets around."

"You don't do Halloween here? I love Halloween!" Her voice was strident, forcing the conversation along. "I asked Mrs Driver about it, I thought Morton's Keep should have a Halloween dinner – I mean, can you *think* of a better setting than the Old Stone Hall? You'd hardly have to put any decorations up."

"What did she say?"

"She was really sniffy with me. Said Mr Stuart didn't approve of Americanizing our culture, blah, blah. . ."

"Well that's *bollocks*, and she knows it," said Ethan. "Halloween's an ancient pagan festival, an old British festival."

"So what's her problem?"

"I reckon they think Morton's Keep has enough of the grim and the gruesome anyway, they don't want to add to it by hanging up a load of skeletons and witches."

They'd reached the car park at the bottom, where everyone had gathered. "How are you getting back?" Ethan asked.

"Bus," she snapped out. She hated the sound of her voice – it was forced, shrill – but she couldn't seem to change it.

And then before Ethan could say anything a girl's voice yelled, "Hey! *E-than!*" She turned to see Becky, with three other girls, standing there smiling and waving.

"Oh, God," said Ethan, but he was smiling too. "It's that lot."

"Do they go to your school?"

"Yes. I've known them since primary."

Becky and the three others headed resolutely over. A curvy, confident-looking girl led the group. She wasn't pretty but she had sharp, well-cut black hair and she dressed attractively.

"*Rayne!*" squawked Becky. Her eyes flashed sideways at

Ethan, frowning, questioning. "Why didn't you *tell* me you were coming?"

"Yeah, and why didn't *you* tell me *you* were coming, Ethan, you shit?" purred the black-haired girl. "We came down cos there wasn't anything much going on up there."

"I can't believe we didn't see each other up there!" said Becky.

"Er – it was *dark*?" said the black-haired girl. "Unless you were right by the fire. Too hot for you there, ay, Ethan? Who's this?"

"Sarah, I *told* you who it is!" said Becky. "She's the one at Morton's Keep, in the Old Sty. . ."

"*Oh God, oh my Gooo-oood!*" squealed Becky's three friends in unison. None of them seemed to mind, or even notice, that Ethan and Rayne hadn't spoken since they'd joined them.

"God, how *can* you?" said Sarah, turning to Rayne. "I'd rather die than stay there – it's so creepy!"

"Rayne loves it, don't you, Rayne?" said Ethan. "She's a witch. So watch it."

"Yeah, yeah, ha ha," said Sarah, slapping her hand down on Ethan's arm, then leaving it there, fingers flexing. "And you're a warlock, right? When can we see you dance again?"

The girls all burst into laughter at this, and Ethan grinned. "You know when. Saturday after next. The last night."

"God, I *lo-ove* the last night," said one of the girls.

"And I *lo-ove* seeing Ethan flinging himself about," said Sarah, and they all burst out cackling.

"It's a riot, Rayne," said Becky, "it gets completely out of hand."

"Only cos you lot can't behave yourselves," said Ethan, unleashing another tirade of laughter, and then there was more joking and flirting and jeering, and Ethan was all cocky now, confident the four girls fancied him.

And why wouldn't he be, Rayne thought sourly, they're making it pretty obvious. He's more relaxed with them than he is with me on my own.

And something else was niggling at her, something like a realization. . .

She checked her watch. The last bus, the bus she planned to get unless Ethan had any better ideas, was due any minute. She looked back along the road and saw headlights approaching.

"I have to go," she said. "There's my bus coming."

And she ran across the road to get it, barely hearing Ethan shout after her.

On the bus, she settled back into the worn seat and watched the country roads stream past, the hedges and trees lit starkly by the bus headlights, and the niggling thought became clear. It was that maybe Ethan wasn't interested in her for *her*. Maybe it was all this green lady stuff. He claimed to think the watchers and their rituals were daft, he'd warned her not to open up to them about what she'd seen, but she knew a deep-rooted part of him was with them. He met with them, he danced with them – maybe he wasn't so different from Will and the other watchers after all. Wanting her for her link with . . . *her*.

She hated her thoughts. She was sick of thinking. Sick of all the weirdness and tired, bone tired. She looked out into the night and longed to get back to her bed, to sleep.

Chapter Eight

The next day was the keenly anticipated date of Miss Skelton's arrival. Mr Stuart met her at the station and showed her round the house. By the time he got to the tearoom, he was like a dog with two tails – Miss Skelton was clearly an enormous hit.

She was certainly stunning. Around thirty-five years old, she had pearl-white skin, dark hair curling on to her shoulders, and a beautiful mouth lipsticked in red. She was dressed in high heels and a dark suit with a nipped-in waist, and looked a bit like a film star from the 1940s.

Mr Stuart introduced her proudly, as though he was personally responsible for her existence.

"I'm so pleased to meet you both," she said. She had a pretty, lilting Scottish accent, and her dark eyes flickered as she talked. "I've been hearing great things about you from Mr Stuart. And this is the tearoom. Well, it's lovely."

"It is," said Mrs Driver, stiffly. "It would be a shame to change it."

"Oh now, *come*, Mrs D – why so defensive?" said Mr Stuart. "We're not talking about changing anything. Not yet."

"*Utilizing* is a word I prefer," purred Miss Skelton. "Utilizing the wonderful things we have here – *building* on them. This tearoom, for example. It's perfect, and it could serve maybe twice, three times the customers it does already, if we can persuade them to come here."

Mrs Driver sniffed. "You'd need more tables," she said. "For more people. More staff, maybe, too."

"That's easily arranged. Now. Can I see a menu?"

"Um – we don't have a menu *as such*," said Mr Stuart, with a nervous glance at Mrs Driver. "It's just fresh, good, home-cooked food. . ."

"Perfect," smiled Miss Skelton. "But it should be displayed on a menu, to show its worth."

Then the two of them left, still smiling and talking about utilizing all the great things at Morton's Keep.

"Looks like she's got the job," said Mrs Driver, gloomily.

Rayne didn't answer. She still felt tired, defeated. She'd hoped for a text from Ethan checking she'd got back OK, but none had arrived. She'd baulked at sending him one. Maybe that was childish, but too bad. She felt childish.

The day seemed to go on and on, but when it was finally over and Rayne was back in her room, she couldn't relax. She wound herself up in her duvet on the bed and read for a while, thinking she might doze off, but she couldn't settle.

She went to make herself some hot chocolate, and found she'd run out of milk. Well, she thought, at least it would be something to do, fetching some more. She got the keys to the Tudor kitchen and let herself out of the Sty.

Dusk was settling in over the trees as she walked through the medieval garden.

When she reached the back door to the kitchen, her eyes were drawn to the lighted window beside it. With a shiver of alarm, she saw someone sitting hunched over at the old refectory table, working at something, *carving* something – she could see a knife glinting. . .

Then with a sense of relief she realized it was Mrs Driver. Weird, she thought, that she hadn't recognized her at first. She tapped – too loudly – on the door, and let herself in with her key.

Mrs Driver was on her feet when Rayne walked into the kitchen, looking flustered. "It's you, dear – you startled me!" she cried. She was standing in front of the table – Rayne couldn't see what it was she'd been doing.

"I ran out of milk," Rayne said. "Is it OK to take some?"

"Of course it is, dear, take a pint from the big fridge."

There was a strange awkwardness in the room with them. "Thanks," Rayne muttered, and hurried through to the utility room to get the milk.

When she came back, a malevolent little face was staring at her from the table. Its eyebrows were twisted and its eyes were cunning slits – but its mouth was wide open, streaming light at her.

She stared at it, and her pulse raced.

"I made it for you, dear," said Mrs Driver. "It's a turnip lantern."

"A turnip lantern?" echoed Rayne, trying to hide from the housekeeper the fear she'd felt . . . was still feeling. "What – like a pumpkin lantern, for Halloween?"

"That's right. Except turnip lanterns go back a lot further in time and they're a lot harder to carve."

"But Mrs D – you said you had no time for Halloween!"

"Well, I don't. Not for trick-or-treating and all that nonsense, dressing up in black plastic capes and pretending to be vampires. But this old tradition I like. On Halloween night, you put out turnip lanterns and they scare away the evil spirits. It's an old bit of nonsense, but I . . . I like it. I always do it."

There were three more turnip faces on the table, but Mrs Driver hadn't lit the candles in them. "Who are they for?" asked Rayne.

"Oh, Ben always has one, for his front window. And I'll have one for my room, and Mr Stuart if he'll take . . . if he wants one. It's just a bit of fun."

But Mrs Driver's face suggested it was anything but fun. She still seemed awkward, embarrassed. She picked up a large bowl, held it level with the table and started to sweep the scraped-out turnip flesh into it with her hand. "I'll put this in with the mashed potato tomorrow," she said. "When I make Mr Stuart's dinner. It's lovely with sausages."

"Sounds delicious," said Rayne. "Waste not, want not, eh? Well – thank you for the lantern."

"It's Halloween the day after tomorrow," said Mrs Driver, "but put it out tonight. Facing out to the woods, in your window. It's tradition. Here – take these extra tea-lights too."

"OK," said Rayne, dubiously, pocketing the tea-lights. She was taken aback by Mrs Driver's intensity. There was an awkward pause, then she asked, "Any news on Miss Skelton?"

"Yes. She got the job, of course. Mr Stuart came to tell me, about an hour ago. He's *delighted* – he's put her wages up by twenty per cent. I asked him if we could afford it and he said with the improvements she planned, we could easily afford it. In fact he's looking at giving her a raise in six months."

"Oh. Oh, don't look so gloomy, Mrs Driver. It'll be good if Morton's Keep makes more money. And I'm sure he'll give you a raise, too."

"I'm dreading it, though, dear. All that upheaval. And it starts tomorrow. She's not going back, now – she's moved in already."

"*Really?* She doesn't waste any time."

"Apparently she said she was so sure she'd get the job – she was so *sure* she'd be right for it – that she got all her stuff ready before she came to the interview, to be sent down after her. Mr Stuart – well. He's so happy. He's taking her out to dinner, to celebrate. He got me to book Barkers, in town."

"Barkers? That's that dead posh place, isn't it – by the town square?"

"That's right. He got me to book a taxi back, too. For eleven."

Rayne picked up the turnip lantern and balanced it on her left hand, then with the milk in her right, she made her way back to her room. The lantern stayed alight all the way back to the Sty, despite a soft wind blowing. She put it on the table in the window, face out as Mrs Driver had said she should. She could see its reflection in the window, in the gap where the curtains didn't meet, which meant it was looking in at her as well as looking out. It made her uneasy, but she didn't blow it out.

Twenty minutes later, she was snuggled up in bed with her book and a mug of hot chocolate, and soon she was drowsy, falling asleep. She turned off her bedside light, promised herself she'd do her teeth in the morning, and let herself drift. . .

When she woke hours later, an owl was shrieking and the little face reflected in the window was still staring at her, shimmering as the candle flickered. How, she wondered, could it still be alight, how could it burn that long? The face reminded her of something, a statue or something she'd seen, maybe a carving . . . something in the old house?

And then it hit her. It was the face in the bonfire. The mouth was open just like the face in the fire.

Her face.

Chapter Nine

The next day was Saturday, and as there were no events planned for that day or evening, Rayne had a full day off.

But it didn't feel like a holiday. She still felt weary and anxious. When she took her laundry over to the utility room, Miss Skelton was in there with Mr Stuart, analysing the efficiency of the cooking arrangements. "Of *course* you want to keep the Tudor kitchen unspoilt," Miss Skelton was saying, "but we could do a lot more in *this* room to maximize the space. Move that washing machine and dryer out for a start." She shot an irritated glance at Rayne, who was loading her clothes into the drum. "Put them in an outhouse, create a proper laundry room. Then you can have a real working kitchen out here to cope with the increase in guest numbers. Remember we discussed a second table in the Old Stone Hall? Think banquet, not dinner party!"

"Excellent, excellent," enthused Mr Stuart. "A banquet – I'm sure it will be excellent. But you still have to convince me about the musicians up in the gallery. I mean – it was the *dock*. Endless people have been sentenced to death, standing up there. It just seems a bit. . ."

"What? Morbid?"

"Irreverent."

"It needn't be. They won't be playing boogie-woogie, you know. Only *reverent* music."

"Ah, now you're teasing me," said Mr Stuart – and they both laughed, heads close.

Oh, throw *up*, thought Rayne. Don't say they've taken a fancy to each other.

She stomped outside, started walking back to the Sty. And stopped dead, as her heart jumped. Ethan was standing at the top of the steps to the medieval garden. At his feet was a large cage with something white moving inside it. He had a backpack on and an embarrassed expression on his face.

"Hey," he called, "I was just making my way down to see you!"

She smiled at him. He looked gorgeous, standing there by the trees.

"What on earth have you got there?" she asked.

"I brought you a present," he mumbled.

"Really? What is it? A cat?" The cage was shifting on the ground – something squawked. Rayne dropped on her hunkers and peered in, to be faced by eight – then twelve – beady eyes, and six bright beaks.

"Doves!" she cried. "Oh, Ethan, that's great – doves for the tower dovecote!"

"They're pigeons, actually," he said. "I thought pigeons might be a bit hardier than doves. Three breeding pairs – well, we hope they'll breed. I got them from my uncle, he's overrun with white pigeons at his place. Someone used to keep 'em nearby, and loads escaped and now they just kind of hang around."

"Ethan, that's brilliant! How did you catch them?"

Ethan shrugged. "How you catch most things. A trap with food in it. I got a lot of brown pigeons too, and they ended up in a pie. My mum was well pleased – she makes great pigeon pie."

Rayne grimaced. "They look really squashed in there," she said.

"Yeah, well, it's a ferret cage, my uncle lent it to me."

"Oh, *sweet*!" she said – then, without giving herself time to think, she rose up on her toes and planted a kiss on his cheek, right by his mouth.

"Careful," he said, grinning. "I thought kissing was out of bounds."

Rayne stepped back. She could feel herself going red. Ethan, looking at her, went a little red too. "Sorry," he mumbled. "Just – you know what happened last time—"

"*Yes*, thank you for reminding me!" she said, waspishly.

"Sorry," he said again.

"I only kissed your cheek! To say thank you!"

"I know. Not a vampire kiss."

"Look – don't joke about it, OK?" Rayne said, and she felt her throat tighten with the memory. "It was horrible. Not at the time, obviously – St John was *amazing*, he kissed better than anyone I've ever *met*, *miles* better, that was why I was so stupid over him, he kissed like an *angel*. But—"

"He wasn't an angel. He was the reverse. I know. Sorry." And he bent down and picked up the cage by the ring at its top. "You're right," he said, "they want to be let out. Shall we take them over to the tower?"

They started walking, glad of something to break the clog of embarrassment between them. "Won't they just fly off?" Rayne asked. "When we let them out?"

"I've got some corn with me. If we give them a bellyful now, and then you bring food every other day or so – they'll stay, I reckon. Do the doves get fed?"

"Now and then. There's a big tin with bird seed in it in the utility room. I don't think Mrs D bothers much, though."

"Well, there's been lots of berries around. But now winter's coming, you need to feed them."

They reached the old wooden door in the wall to the dovecote garden. Ethan went through first, and Rayne shut it behind them. The sun was behind the tower and it cast a dark shadow over the maze of bushes, making strange shapes. "Weeurgh," she shuddered. "It's such a sinister place sometimes."

"The pigeons won't mind that," he said. "Come on."

Ethan didn't even try to navigate the maze. He just stalked over the top of the waist-high hedges towards the tower, and Rayne followed him. The door to the tower was standing ajar. Ethan pulled it open further and they stepped inside.

It was the first time Rayne had actually been inside the dovecote. It felt dank, unfriendly. The floor was broken brick, covered in old straw and birds' droppings, with a derelict table in the corner. She looked up. There'd been an upper floor, once, but it had collapsed and now all that was left was a wide, uneven ledge. A few rungs of a stairway still clung to the far wall. She tried not to think about mad old Patience, tried not to wonder if, when she was a girl, she'd been held prisoner up there, or down at ground level.

"See that ledge?" said Ethan, pointing. "That's where they'll roost and make their nests. It's perfect, with all those old floor struts – gives them something to wedge the twigs up against."

A couple of doves flew in through one of the entrance holes and settled on the ledge, peering down. "Let's get the food out," Ethan said.

From his backpack, he pulled out two large tin dishes, a bag of corn and a bottle of water. He laid the dishes out on the rickety table, and filled one with the grain. Rayne picked up the water bottle and filled the other. Then he stooped down, opened the ferret cage, and seized hold of a pigeon. He plonked it unceremoniously down by the food dish and it started to peck, ravenously. "I kept 'em hungry," he commented.

Rayne thought about picking up one of the other birds, but she didn't want to. And anyway Ethan was there ahead of her, seizing two this time, one in each hand, and dropping them down by the food dish. Then he picked up the cage and held it over the table and the other three birds tumbled out and all of them started to eat.

"So far so good," he said.

A dove had circled down and landed on the table. It eyed the pigeons nervously, then it began to peck up grain that had been scattered away from the dish. "Oh, good," said Rayne. "Won't it be good if they integrate?"

Ethan smiled. "They will. Birds know when they're safe and well off. You keep this bowl filled, and I reckon they'll settle. And in the spring, they'll nest here, if we're lucky. . ."

He picked up the empty cage, and they turned to go. One of the pigeons had flown upwards and was investigating the ledge. Already the atmosphere in the gloomy tower seemed lighter, somehow.

"Ethan, thank you," she said. "Seriously – it's great you did this."

"It's OK," he said. "I'm glad you like them."

"I promise to take care of them," she went on. "Oh, it'll be lovely if they nest and the eggs hatch and everything! Wouldn't it be wonderful to have a whole flock of birds here?"

"Yeah," he said. "It would." He said those three short words with such intensity that she suddenly felt stupid for thanking him – stupid for acting like he'd brought the birds just for her.

Because you're not doing this for me, are you? she thought. You're doing it for the green lady.

Chapter Ten

As they walked back across the wide lawn behind Morton's Keep, Rayne didn't say a word. Her mind was full of images of white birds flying in the tower; torches trooping up a dark hillside; a mighty face in the flames, roaring at her.

Get out of my mind, she thought, angrily. *Leave me alone. It's over.*

She glanced sideways at Ethan. He was frowning, his profile set.

I don't trust you, she thought. *St John was after me because I was here, at Morton's Keep – are you any different?*

They walked on.

I'm sick of all this. I need to get away. She hated her thoughts but she couldn't stop thinking them. *I need to get away from you.*

I'm not getting used again.

They said goodbye, quickly and awkwardly, and she tramped on through the trees back to the Old Sty. A note, written on thick white paper, was tucked into the jamb of the door. She pulled it out and read:

Rayne – can you come to a meeting at the library at midday?

It was signed – *Louisa Skelton*.

Rayne felt like a dog with its hackles rising. It's *Saturday*, she thought, indignantly, who the hell does she think she is, ordering me about on a *Saturday*? She pulled out her phone and checked the time. It was ten to twelve.

"I'm not hurrying," she told herself, stubbornly. "She can wait. I want a cup of tea."

She marched through to the kitchen and put the kettle on, defiantly. But once she'd made her tea, she found herself gulping it down. She wanted to get there, to the library. She wanted to find out what this was all about.

The easiest way for Rayne to get to the library was to go through the Tudor kitchen and along the ancient flagstoned corridor to the Great Hall. As she crossed it, passing the huge carved outer doors you could ride an army through, her heart quickened. The monstrous cherubs over the fireplace sneered down at her as she opened the door to the library corridor. This place will never, *never* not scare me, she thought, hurrying along.

She knocked on the library door. "Come in!" called Mr Stuart, and she stepped inside.

A fire was blazing in the fireplace; the room was fragrant with wood smoke and the smell of fresh coffee. Mr Stuart and Miss Skelton were sitting together on one sofa; Mrs Driver and Ben Avebury, the gardener, were on the other. A coffee pot and white china mugs were on a low table in between them.

"Rayne, at last," said Miss Skelton. "Now we can start."

"I only just got your note," said Rayne, more rudely than she meant to. "I was out . . . um, walking."

"It's OK, it's OK," said Miss Skelton, in her lilting voice. "But while I think of it – can I have your mobile number? Then we can avoid me having to trek out to your wee *sty* in future."

Rayne's hackles rose again. And she was caught off guard. Something in her didn't want to give Miss Skelton her number. *Really* didn't want to. But how could she refuse? Miss Skelton had already pulled a trim mobile from the stylish bag beside her on the sofa and was looking at her, pointedly. Reluctantly, she mumbled her number, and Miss Skelton efficiently tapped it in. "Thank you!" she purred. "The next step is to persuade Mrs Driver and Ben to get a mobile. Then we can really become efficient here."

Mr Stuart laughed, nervously. "All in good time," he said. "Rayne – do sit down." He indicated the space to the other side of Mrs Driver. "Help yourself to coffee."

Rayne sat down. Neither Ben nor Mrs Driver, she noted, had a mug in their hands. She didn't take one either.

"And don't look so worried," he added. "Louisa has got some lovely plans for you, for us *all*."

Louisa, thought Rayne, acidly.

"Now, this is just an informal meeting," said Miss Skelton, taking over from Mr Stuart as though it was the most natural thing in the world. "Since I've been here, Harry and I –"

Harry! thought Rayne, even more acidly.

"– have done nothing but talk about this place." She glanced sideways at him, smiling; he returned her smile.

"What Morton's Keep needs – and I hope everyone agrees with me here – is a thorough overhaul. I don't mean the fabric of the building – although there is huge work to be done there, which is why we have to start making serious money. I mean what it *does*. How it funds its existence. There is *so much* we could do with this place."

She paused. Mr Stuart was gazing at his three employees opposite like a father hoping his offspring would behave. "We need to – *reach out*," she went on. "Advertise. The first thing I'm going to do is set up a website."

Rayne felt her mouth downturning in a sneer. What would *Louisa* think if she found out about St John's twisted group's Hidden History website, with its plea for lost stories of Morton's Keep's murderous past and its logo *Beauty is Cruel, Cruelty is Beautiful*?

"The website will be linked to a travel company," Miss Skelton went on, oblivious to the stony faces in front of her. "We will market aggressively – arrange tours from all over the country. In two weeks' time, the house and the tearoom will open at weekends – we'll close on Mondays only."

"Only one day a week off?" cried Mrs Driver.

"For now, yes. Don't worry – your pay will be adjusted. And I'll be employing more staff. But for now – we all need to pull together to make this work." She paused, and smiled at the three opposite her. They stared stonily back. "The upgrading of the tearoom will be a priority," she went on. "I'd also like to begin overnight stays, in the three formal bedrooms on the first floor. . ."

Ben Avebury snorted. "No one'd pay to sleep in them," he said. "Unless they were ghost hunters."

"Well, thank you, Ben!" gushed Miss Skelton. "You've brought me to one of my main points. We must stop ignoring Morton Keep's grim and ghastly past. Instead, we must capitalize on it."

There was a heavy silence. Maybe she *would* like the Hidden History website after all, thought Rayne. The silence was broken by Miss Skelton's fluting laugh. "Don't look so alarmed!" she said. "Mr Stuart has already started to do this, with his wonderful grand dinners in the Old Stone Hall. Candlelight, firelight – intriguing stories of the past. Perfect. I propose to increase them – improve on them – enlarge them. And put on other events that . . . shall we say, *tie in* with the history of this place? Musical concerts, for example. Forget Mozart, forget pretty blandness . . . we need drama, Gothic darkness. In other words, we *specialize*. That's where the money lies."

Mrs Driver shifted on her seat. "I don't like it!" she blurted out. "The Keep is dark enough without making it darker still!"

"Oh, Mrs *D*," murmured Mr Stuart, softly.

Miss Skelton looked at the old housekeeper icily. "So how do you propose making revenue then, Mrs Driver?" she demanded. "Birthday parties? *Wedding* receptions? That's how a lot of stately homes make extra cash. But I ask you – who'd want a wedding here?"

Mrs Driver was looking down at the floor ahead of her, as if she was trying not to cry. Rayne wanted to put a comforting hand on her arm, but she didn't move.

"No," Miss Skelton went on, brightly, "we have to utilize what we have. That's what makes financial sense. We stop papering over the past – instead we expose it. We reach out to a specialist market. That's the way forward."

Then she reached over to refill her coffee mug, smiling. A delicate jade bracelet on her left wrist clinked against the china as she lifted it to her lips. She's pretty pleased with herself, thought Rayne, angrily. Sitting there all dolled up in her lipstick and heels. On a *Saturday.*

"But we're *making* money," said Mrs Driver. "We made a good profit from the Apple Fair this year. . ."

"Well, that's relative," smirked Miss Skelton. Rayne glared at her.

"Look," murmured Mr Stuart. "We just called you all in to give you an idea of the lines we're thinking along, and to tell you the more immediate decisions we've made. . ."

"Like cancelling the Advent Craft Market," rapped out Miss Skelton, as Mr Stuart winced.

"You *can't*," said Mrs Driver, aghast. "I've already done the leaflets! It's – it's all planned!"

"Well, I'm afraid it's going to have to be unplanned, Mrs Driver!"

"But I've had seven bookings for stalls already – the Women's Institute want three this year—"

"Women's Institute. That's a perfect example of what we *don't* want associated with Morton's Keep. Think dark style, Mrs Driver. Dark glamour. Not stalls full of knitted socks and jars of home-made chutney—"

"*Louisa!*" murmured Mr Stuart.

"I'm sorry, Harry, it needs to be said. Either you move on – or you stay floundering, just about making the books balance. You've got something special here, unique – you can

59

really capitalize on it. If you want me to help you with that, fine. If not. . ." She trailed off, and gazed icily into the fire. Her perfect mouth looked very red against her pale skin.

There was a nasty silence. Then Mr Stuart smiled, all desperate enthusiasm, and said, "The Grand Christmas Week Dinner, on the other hand, is not going only ahead – we're expanding it. Superb food, a yule log in the grate—"

"But this time focusing on the old pre-Christmas tradition of telling ghost stories," interjected Miss Skelton. "And it won't just be for local people this time – my website will see to that."

"We have other dinners planned, too. Lots of waitressing work for you, Rayne! We'll be looking at a rise soon!"

"When the profits start to show," murmured Miss Skelton.

"Well," said Mr Stuart, into the frigid silence, "are there any questions? No?" He got to his feet, and his three employees sitting opposite him stood up too. "Thank you for coming," he went on. "And please don't worry! Early days, early days, nothing's set in stone. But I need to take Morton's Keep *forward*. I really have no choice."

In the narrow corridor outside the closed library door, Mrs Driver, Rayne and Ben Avebury stood and looked at each other. Anger and unsaid things sparked between them. Then Mrs Driver murmured, "I think we all need a nice cup of tea, don't you?" And she led the way to the Tudor kitchen.

"*Profit*," snarled Ben, as he sat himself down at the ancient refectory table. "*Exploit. Capitalize. Financial sense*. It's all she's about, that one. It's all she can see."

"She doesn't know what she's doing," muttered Mrs Driver, unhooking three pansy-printed mugs from the dresser. "All this talk of utilizing the Keep's dark past. She doesn't know what *harm* she could do."

"Local people have always been the main ones coming to Morton's Keep. It's important. If she starts getting in outsiders. . ."

"Opening at the weekends. We'll be exhausted. And I can't believe she wants to cancel the Advent Craft Market. I know it hardly turns a profit but it's a tradition. It . . . it promotes goodwill in the town."

"Well, *she's* not interested in goodwill in the town, is she?"

"Or with us."

"No. I'm not taken in by her easy compliments."

They grumbled on, while Rayne's gaze went from Mrs Driver to Ben and back again, like a spectator at a tennis match. She could understand why they were so upset but she couldn't share it, not completely. She cleared her throat and said, "I just think she's a lousy choice as the new manager. She's got everyone's back up. She's not so much a new broom as a new – I dunno – *sledgehammer*."

Ben chuckled. "You're right there, girl. But Mr Stuart can't see it. He's getting his head turned."

"Oh, I spotted that right away," said Mrs Driver, primly. "*And* she knows it and is playing on it. Bright red lipstick on a Saturday morning – I ask you. Still, there's nothing we can do, is there?" She poured the tea out, and everyone took a first, soothing sip.

"Not unless we all go and resign, no," said Rayne.

Both Ben and Mrs Driver turned to look at her, as though she'd said something unthinkable. "We can't do that," said Ben, simply, and returned to his tea.

Rayne spent the rest of the day in a state of restlessness. Her thoughts were like a dark marsh; she had to skim over its surface or she'd be drawn down. She went for a long walk, and dozed in the afternoon. She was glad when dusk started to fall and she could legitimately light the stove and curl up on her bed with her book again. Soon it grew too gloomy to read. She switched her bedside lamp on, and the window turned black.

Saturday night spent all alone with a mug of Ovaltine, she thought, miserably. And no plans for Sunday, none at all. It was Halloween tomorrow and she knew that back on Cramphurst Estate there'd be parties and trick-or-treating, great gangs of kids in masks roaming around looking for trouble. . . "Maybe I'm in the right place," she told herself.

But she still couldn't relax. After a while she got up to switch the kettle on again, then went over to draw the curtains. The turnip lantern on the table glared at her, its dull eyes a reproach. She picked it up and for a moment she considered opening the door and hurling it out into the trees, but something stopped her. She sighed, tipped the old tea-light out, replaced it with one of the new ones, and lit it. Then she set the lantern down before the gap in the curtains, and stood watching the menacing little face as it leapt into double life again, its mouth streaming light.

Chapter Eleven

Sunday and Monday passed, thundery and overcast with sudden fierce flurries of rain. Everyone was talking about winter setting in. Rayne hadn't been back to check on the pigeons. She felt resentful and suspicious of why Ethan had brought them, and she didn't want to go to the sinister tower dovecote all on her own, especially when the sun had vanished. She told herself they'd be all right.

Miss Skelton's presence hung over the mansion house like some kind of modernizing, toxic cloud. She'd already arranged for the creation of a new, gravelled car park to the side of the house. They had to be ready, she said, for the influx of visitors. Mrs Driver was tight-lipped, anxious; Ben kept out of sight, on the far edges of the estate.

Then, on Tuesday morning, it was Becky's turn to come up against the new manager. She burst out of the tearoom door with her quiche-tray swinging and practically collided with Rayne. "*Oh my God*," she breathed, "my mum is going to be *so pissed off!*"

"Why, what's up?" asked Rayne.

"I've just met the *new manager*." She glanced over her shoulder, checking Miss Skelton was still inside. "*What* a *cow*. She criticized my mum's pastry. Said could I ask her to *ensure* it was *uniformly lightly baked* in future. Just cos two of them got a bit overdone."

"Don't tell her."

"I'd better. That cow is capable of firing her if she overcooks them again. She said it like it was no big deal, just a little comment, but my mum'll go mad – she's dead proud of her quiches."

"So she should be. They're ace. Seriously, Becky, don't let Miss Skelton get to you. Everyone hates her. Apart from Mr Stuart."

"Yeah? I bet he fancies her. That's why he gave her the job. *God. Hey* – talking of fancying – you don't let the grass grow, do you?"

"What?"

"You and Ethan! What happened to St John?"

For a moment Rayne felt completely disoriented. St John? How could Becky not know what had happened with St John? He was way, way back, back in the past before the night of the fire in the dungeon. . . But of course Becky believed the newspaper report, that the fire in the dungeon was "due to careless use of candles while exploring a cellar room". She knew nothing of what had happened here, and Rayne couldn't even begin to tell her.

"I finished with him," she said. "You were right – he was a snob and a creep."

"Told you so!" crowed Becky. "Hey – well done! *You* dumped *him?*"

"Yes." Rayne shrugged. The truth was so bizarre that that would have to do as an explanation.

"*God.* I bet that's the first time anyone's ever finished with *him*. Has he gone back to Flora?"

"I don't think he ever left her."

"*Told* you!" repeated Becky, eyes gleaming. "*Told* you I'd seen them together! So – if you dumped St John, you're not with his creepy group any more?"

"No. All alone."

"Except you got with Ethan."

"No. *No!* He just – he just invited me along to the fireworks, that's all."

"Oh, come on. Why would he invite you if—" She broke off.

The tearoom door swung open; Miss Skelton high-heeled out. She was dressed in a black trouser suit with a rope of pearls round her neck. "Rayne!" she said, and looked at her watch. "What time are you supposed to start?"

"Around ten," Rayne said, sullenly.

"There's no *around* about it. You start at ten and it's a quarter past now." And she stalked elegantly off, in the direction of the house.

Rayne and Becky stuck their tongues out at her back, then grinned at each other.

"I'd better go in," Rayne said. "Before she comes back."

"OK. But I want *all* the details about Ethan."

"There aren't any details!"

"Just as well. Sarah's fancied him for ages."

"Your mate? Yeah – she made that pretty obvious!"

"He fancies her too!"

Rayne made herself smile.

"She'll kill you if you pull him," Becky went on. "Hey – you going to the last night?"

"The fire festival thing?" said Rayne. She felt a surge of fear, just saying the name. An image of a bonfire came into her mind, the flames shifting and surging, forming shapes. . .

"You've got to! It's brilliant. Hey – give me your mobile, quick." Becky pulled her phone out of her pocket and Rayne rattled off her number. She felt flattered, pleased – maybe she and Becky could be proper friends now St John was out of the picture.

"Got to go," said Becky. "Mum's in her car at the end of the drive. Dunno *what* I'm going to say about the quiches! I'll call you to arrange about Saturday!" And she ran off.

After work that day, Rayne decided she really had got to check on the pigeons. The low autumn sun was out, it was a good time to go. She was ashamed of herself for leaving it so long. "If they've finished all the grain and disappeared," she told herself, "it's your fault. You should've gone yesterday. *God*, I hope they're still there."

Carrying a large bag of seed she'd scooped out of the tin in the utility room and a bottle of fresh water, she ran over the lawn behind the mansion house. Once again she felt that sense of someone watching her from one of the high windows in the house – someone who didn't want her there. But she ignored it, and hurried on.

As she pulled open the decaying door to the tower, a white bird flapped out through one of the holes in the side and flew away. "Don't you dare be the last one left," she muttered, and walked in.

She looked up, but there were no birds on the ledge that had once supported the upper floor. The tin dish on the table, she saw to her dismay, was quite empty. But there was still water in the other dish, and a sprinkling of grain on the table. She went over and poured seed into the dish, filling it to the brim and beyond. Then she chucked out the stale water on the brick floor, and refilled that dish.

Sun was coming through the dovecote holes, great shafts of it gleaming down on to the curved, crumbling brick walls, and on to her. It made the place far less dank and sinister. A clattering noise from above made her look up.

Four white pigeons had flown in and were settling side by side on the ledge, shifting from foot to foot, peering down at her. She stepped back carefully, quietly, and waited against the tower wall, as far away from the table as she could get.

One of the pigeons cooed, long and loud, then it launched itself from its perch and floated down, crossing a shaft of sun, and landed on the table. And then the other three birds followed, wings shining in the bars of light. Rayne smiled with pleasure. There was another soft clatter of wings overhead; two more birds appeared through the holes and landed on the ledge. These, she thought, were the doves; they were more delicate-looking, their chests less puffed-out. They too floated down, and then another pair of birds flew in through the holes, followed by a single one. The tower seemed transformed by sunlight and the beautiful, floating white birds. They all settled on the table and started pecking, nine of them now. Six pigeons – all of Ethan's pigeons – and three doves. "I promise," she whispered, "to feed you every other day now, at least. OK?"

As she stood watching them feed, she remembered what she'd said to Mr Stuart the day the workmen were there, filling up the dungeon with concrete and slurry. She'd said that more birds would "tip the balance" in the tower. She hadn't really understood what she'd meant then, but watching them now, pecking away happily, she could almost believe that some kind of balance had been tipped. The tower was no longer filled with such menace, such darkness.

But something had spooked the birds. A dove flew upwards – the others flapped after it, circling.

And just for a second, Rayne could see a huge shape in the birds as they flew upwards, a shape as tall as the tower itself. A head, shoulders – two arms held wide.

Fear filled her.

Then joy, somehow more terrifying than the fear.

The birds settled back on the table to feed.

Chapter
Twelve

Back at the Old Sty, Rayne sent a text to Ethan: *Birds r fine, well settled, v greedy.*

Almost immediately, he called her back.

"That's great!" he said. "They're all there, then? No escapees?"

"None!"

She was waiting for him to ask if she'd only just been back to feed them, wondering if she'd lie if he did ask, but all he said was, "Well, you keep them fed and watered all winter, and they won't be going far. Pigeons know when they're well off."

"Three doves turned up, too. I bet that's all there are left, poor things."

"Well, you're looking after them now. Come spring, maybe we'll have baby doves as well as pigeons."

"Oh, I hope so. It made such a difference to the tower, having the birds there – the sun was coming in and. . ." She trailed off. She wasn't going to mention what she thought she'd seen. The fear and joy had been intense, but short-lived – her mind was already dismissing it, like it tried to dismiss the huge open-mouthed face in the fire. "Thank you for getting them," she said.

"No problem. Fingers crossed they last the winter. Listen – are you going to be there, Saturday?"

"Saturday?"

"The last fire festival."

"Oh, right!" Rayne stalled for a second or two, panic circling her. Then she said, "Yes, I think so. Becky said I can go with her."

"Oh, God – Becky and the rest of them?"

"Yes, I guess so. You'll be busy, won't you? And I don't want to go on my own."

"No. Course not. No, that's good."

There was a pause. She thought of saying something about Becky's friend Sarah fancying him, find out from his reaction if it was mutual, but just the thought of saying the words made her squirm.

"It's a really good night," he went on. "You'll love it. Loads of musicians turn up. It gets wild."

"And you'll be dancing?"

"'Fraid so!"

Another pause, and this time it was too long for the conversation to be salvaged. "OK, then, I'll see you there," said Ethan, and she said goodbye, and they rang off.

I'm spending every evening on my own, Rayne thought, self-pityingly, as she got ready for bed that night. She could have done with some company in that long stretch of time between finishing work and going to bed; she couldn't seem to shake her gloomy state of mind.

She was working harder now, too. Miss Skelton's new website, full of dark imagery and Gothic scrolls, was already up and running, and the travel company was very efficient. More coach loads were coming in, with many more booked for the future, especially for after mid-November when the Keep opened for the weekends. Extra tables had been moved into the tearoom, and arranged in "random blocks", as Miss Skelton termed them, some flush against the walls, some in the centre, with exotic pot plants (that looked quite out of place in the old dairy) as screens between them.

Mrs Driver hated it. She thought it looked untidy. She was quietly subversive, slow to make the additions to the menu that Miss Skelton asked for, rearranging the tables "more tidily", and "forgetting" to increase prices. She was tense, on edge, often snapping at Rayne and Becky. A lot of the pleasure had gone out of their working day.

Rayne sighed as she got into bed, too early, before she was tired. She'd lit the little Halloween lantern again. It was beginning to collapse in on itself now, and there was a smell of cooking turnip in the room. But she kept lighting it, on Halloween night, and the next night, and now tonight. Something compelled her.

On Friday, around closing time, she got a text from an unknown number.

Louisa here! it said. *Are u free for supper 2nite at my flat?*

Rayne was taken aback. The text was so pally, so unlike Miss Skelton with her autocratic ways. Maybe, she thought, *Louisa* has finally got the message that she's causing a lot of bad feeling, and maybe she's getting Ben and Mrs Driver round too, on a damage limitation exercise.

She was intrigued. She couldn't bring herself to be too enthusiastic and say she'd love to come or anything, but she texted back, *Yes thx what time?*

8? the reply came back. *Give me time 2 cook.*

Blimey, thought Rayne, and texted back: *C u then.*

At five past eight Miss Skelton opened the main downstairs door of the "new building" in jeans, bare feet, and a rust-coloured silk blouse. Her hair was loose and the bold red lipstick was missing. She had a glass of white wine in her hand and she looked infinitely more approachable.

"Come on up," she cooed, and sashayed on ahead up the stairs. Rayne followed, thinking that she couldn't blame Mr Stuart for being seriously attracted to her. In the main room, the curtains were drawn; low table lamps gave a soft light. Jazz was playing and there was a mouth-watering garlicky smell in the air. The ominous, waiting atmosphere that Rayne had felt when she'd cleaned the place had disappeared. The flat was now entirely inhabited by Miss Skelton.

"White wine?" asked Miss Skelton, gliding over to a silver wine cooler on the table and pulling out a bottle.

"Oh, yes, please," said Rayne, adding, "Oh, lord, sorry. I should've bought a bottle."

"Och, don't be daft, darling," said Miss Skelton, pouring. "Not on your pay. Here. Cheers!" And she clinked Rayne's glass, smiling. "That's one of the reasons I've asked you here," she went on. "To say thank you for all the hard work you do on what aren't exactly fabulous wages."

"That's OK," said Rayne, guardedly. She took a sip of the wine. It tasted flinty, subtle, delicious.

"Come – sit down. When we're ready to eat I'll put the pasta on." Miss Skelton subsided elegantly into the cushions on the huge sofa, and patted the space next to her. Rayne sat down at the other end of the sofa. "Help yourself to olives," Miss Skelton said, indicating a little green bowl on the low table in front of them.

It was pretty clear, Rayne thought, that she was going to be the only guest. It made her uneasy. But she picked up an olive and put it in her mouth.

Miss Skelton turned to look at her, and smiled. "That meeting I held," she said, "with you and Ben and Mrs Driver – it didn't go very well, did it?"

"Um. . ."

"I was *so cross* with Mr Stuart. We'd agreed he'd make the major announcements – opening at weekends, cancelling the Advent Craft Market and so on – but he left it all to me."

Rayne blinked. That wasn't how she remembered it at all.

"The thing is, Rayne – I'm so excited about the possibilities for Morton's Keep that I let my mouth run away with me. I wanted everyone to share my vision, and get excited too, and I was just *too* untactful. Are Ben and Mrs Driver *very* cross with me?"

"They're anxious about too much change," Rayne said stiffly, "obviously."

"Of course they are. Old people are always anxious about change. And maybe we did pile in too hard. But we

73

need to start *now* – not dissipate energy on a cosy wee craft market that is quite at odds with the direction the Keep needs to go in. . . You do see that, don't you, Rayne?"

Rayne took a sip of wine to avoid answering. *You might be able to manipulate Mr Stuart*, she thought, *but it won't work with me*. And out loud she said, "The thing is, Mrs Driver hates the idea of anything that emphasizes the awful history of the Keep—"

"Then she quite simply shouldn't work here," broke in Miss Skelton. "Sorry, but that's ridiculous. It's like working in a zoo and not liking the animals. Morton's Keep *is* its darkness, its history! Look – *Rayne*. Mr Stuart didn't want to go into it too much at that meeting, but Morton's Keep is in very dire financial trouble. The roof on the west tower needs major repairs *now*, before the winter really sets in, or the weather damage it sustains could cause the whole thing to collapse – as it is, the brickwork is completely saturated—"

Aghast, Rayne turned to look at her. "But if the tower collapses, won't that damage the side of the house it's attached to?"

"You said it."

"But – why didn't you talk about this at the *meeting*?"

"Because Harry – Mr *Stuart* – can hardly bear to acknowledge it to *himself*, let alone announce it at a meeting. He feels he's failed the Keep, letting it get into this state. And in a way he has. He should have grasped the nettle ten years ago, before the deterioration really escalated. He made me promise not to speak about it in front of Ben or Mrs Driver – he doesn't want them to know how bad things are. He's so acutely aware that this is their *home* and has been for decades – he feels he's failed *them*, too. Lamentably."

Rayne stared into her glass. She felt deeply shaken – she'd had no idea that things were that bad. It put a whole different complexion on things – on how she saw Miss Skelton, and the way she'd behaved at the meeting. She took in a breath and said, "Can you make enough money in time, though? Just from the tea shop and a few dinners and things?"

"I'm determined to. I've *got* to. Opening at weekends will bring in the cash, and I have grand plans for the dinners. We can institute overnights here quite easily, and they'll be money-spinners. Rayne – I'm aiming to *double* the Keep's revenue by the end of December, and then the thing is, we can *borrow* money on the strength of that." She leant towards Rayne eagerly. "Once the bank sees that our plans are working, they'll *lend* us enough for the emergency repairs."

"I see," Rayne said. If anyone could convince a bank to loan money, Miss Skelton could, she thought. Maybe she wasn't such a bad choice for the manager after all.

"I know it seems brutal," Miss Skelton said, "on the surface, changing so many things at Morton's Keep – but the worse brutality is to just let it go on unchanged. Because then it'll go under."

Rayne turned to meet her gaze, feeling strangely flattered that she'd chosen to confide in her. "I think. . ." she began.

Miss Skelton smiled encouragingly. "What? I want your opinion. That's why I asked you here."

"I think you should be honest with them, with Ben and Mrs Driver. Tell them about the Keep's finances. They know the place needs money, of course they do – but if they knew how *bad* things are, maybe they'd be more understanding, more likely to cooperate—"

Miss Skelton put a manicured hand on Rayne's arm. "No. I can't. I've absolutely promised Mr Stuart I won't – he sees it as sparing them. And – he's *ashamed*. I must ask *you* to promise not to say anything to them, either. Rayne – do you *promise*?"

Again, Rayne felt that silky sense of being flattered. "Of course I won't," she said. "If Mr Stuart's against it."

"When we've got the loan, when the west tower's being fixed – maybe we can tell them then. But not now. It's too alarming."

"I understand."

"Wonderful," said Miss Skelton, warmly. "Now! Shall we eat?" She got to her feet.

Dinner was a delightful meal of ribbon-shaped pasta and prawns in a garlicky sauce, a herby salad, and more stony white wine. While they ate, Miss Skelton asked Rayne questions about where she'd come from and if she liked working at Morton's Keep and seemed so genuinely interested in the answers that Rayne was quite disarmed.

When they'd cleaned their plates, Miss Skelton went off to the kitchen to get the next course, and Rayne found herself thinking about a teacher she'd once had, Mr Leek. Miss Skelton, she thought, reminded her of Mr Leek. For the first week or so he'd been an absolute nightmare – fanatically strict, determined to get control. Then, having got control, he relaxed – and became one of the best teachers at the school.

Miss Skelton came back out of the kitchen with two fluted glasses full of ice cream dripping with hot toffee sauce, with two feathery wafers in each.

"That looks fantastic," said Rayne. "I haven't had such a treat of a meal for ages!"

"Good, I'm glad," purred Miss Skelton. "Eat up – I've got another treat for you afterwards. At least I hope it's a treat. I hope you'll like it."

"What?" asked Rayne. "What is it?" The wine had got to her, a bit. She was enjoying herself. She smiled across the table at Miss Skelton, who smiled back, murmuring, "Wait and see."

When the ice cream was all eaten, Miss Skelton led Rayne through into her bedroom. There, hanging on the outside of the wardrobe, was a marvellous dress. Gothic black, like something a vampire princess might wear. Long, with a swishing, uneven hem, low-necked, very fitted. Glittery coppery-coloured beads traced a mysterious, beautiful pattern down its front.

"That's stunning," breathed Rayne.

"It's for you," said Miss Skelton. "Try it on."

"You're joking!"

"Not at all. The next grand dinner is a week tomorrow, and I'm scheduling in two more after that – and then there's the Christmas Feast. You're our chief waitress. You need to be dressed for the part." She went over and took the dress down from its hanger, held it out to Rayne. "It's all about theatre, Rayne. I'm making Mr Stuart wear a fabulous new dinner jacket."

Rayne reached out for the dress. It felt silky and slippery in her arms. "What will you wear?" she asked.

"Oh, that's in hand. It's red, ruby red, and it's gorgeous."

"But – I thought you said there was no money!"

"In business, you need to spend a bit of money – even if

you're broke – before you start to make it. Now come on, try it on!"

Rayne put the dress down on the bed, kicked off her shoes and jeans, and peeled off her top. Then she stepped into the dress. It had lacing up the back. Miss Skelton came up behind her, and started to lace her up, quite tightly.

"Oh, it's a perfect fit," she said. "I guessed your size well. And lacing, of course, ensures the best fit – *there*. Look at yourself." She opened the wardrobe door – there was a long mirror on the inside.

Rayne walked over, the dress shushing round her ankles, and looked at herself.

She looked stunning. Even with red socks and her hair all messed up.

"Make-up," said Miss Skelton, coming up behind her again. "You need lots of drama and colour in your make-up."

"If I'm serving, though, shouldn't I wear more of a . . . a servant's dress?"

"Oh, pooh. We're not going for usual stuff here. We're not going for a horror film look, either – too ordinary. Just decadence, and class. And you've got it."

"Have I?" laughed Rayne, still gazing at herself. "This dress is amazing, but I'm not sure I can carry it off!"

"Oh, you can, Rayne. I've watched you move. You have a kind of – inborn elegance."

Rayne felt herself blushing. "How many people have you got signed up?" she said, quickly. "For the dinner?"

"Twenty-five, so far, but there'll be more. It's gathering

momentum. I'm hiring another big table to set against the stone table, and more chairs."

"And more waitresses, too, I hope?"

"Oh, don't worry," smiled Miss Skelton. "I'm taking care of that too."

The evening had come to an end. Rayne got changed out of the dress and Miss Skelton folded it carefully and gave it to her. As she left, Rayne thanked her hostess for a brilliant evening, and Miss Skelton smiled and said it was her pleasure. "Don't mention our wee conversation about money, will you, Rayne?" she said again, as she unlocked the door downstairs to let her out. "To Mrs Driver, or Ben. Or indeed Mr Stuart. He'd be devastated if he thought we'd been discussing it."

"I promise," said Rayne, and left, with her dress.

As soon as she got into the Old Sty, Rayne fetched a hanger, shook out the dress, and hung it on the antlers that were nailed above the wood stove. But the hanger slipped off and the dress slithered to the ground. So instead she hooked it over the curtain rail in front of her clothes. She didn't want to tuck it away out of sight, she wanted to be able to keep looking at it.

The turnip lantern had finally collapsed in on itself; black, feathery mould was growing out of its eye sockets. She picked it up, carried it outside, and laid it down to rot under an apple tree.

Chapter Fourteen

Becky was very efficient. Late Saturday morning Rayne was heading back from the Tudor kitchen with her clean laundry in her arms when she got a text: *Meet u market sq 7pm we get bus on frm there bex xx*

Rayne texted back that she'd be there. She told herself she'd mastered her fear about the fire festival – after all, she didn't have to look *into* the fire again, did she? – and it was all going to be fine. As she put her tops away in the chest of drawers, she pulled out the photocopied newspaper article of Ethan jumping high in the dance, and stared at it, smiling. The way she'd been thinking before – it was silly. Ethan couldn't use her if she didn't let him. He didn't have St John's power. All that was over. *Over.*

She started getting ready to go out at about five-thirty. The evening, she thought, was perfect for a bonfire. It was clear, cold, just the lightest of winds blowing. She dressed in her newest jeans and a jumper that flattered her; she put on eye make-up and lipgloss. Then she put on her short coat and wound a bright scarf round her neck. Her reflection in the bathroom mirror pleased her.

She wasn't sure how she'd get back – a bus back to the market square with the others, then maybe a taxi if the last bus had gone. She wasn't as worried about it as she'd once have been. But she still switched on her bedside light before she left, and put her torch in her bag. The Old Sty might have started to feel like home, but you didn't want to come back to it in the dark.

When Rayne got off the bus in the market square, Becky was already there, standing chatting with two other girls. With a flip of jealousy she recognized Sarah. When Becky saw her, she rushed forward, flung her arms round her and kissed her. Rayne was taken aback – it was the first time they'd ever really touched. It had to be some kind of scoring gesture over the other girls. Which – if it meant she had some kind of status – was OK by her.

"You've met Sarah and Chloe, haven't you?" Becky said. "We're just waiting for Lisa."

"The bus goes in a few minutes," said Chloe, anxiously. "If she's not here by then we're not waiting, are we?"

"No, we're not!" said Becky. "I'm not missing the beginning. That's so great, when they light the bonfires and everything."

"Where is it we're going?" asked Rayne.

"It's called the Devil's Tankard," said Sarah. She'd been assessing Rayne, casting cold, appraising glances over her face and clothes, ever since she arrived. "It's to the south of Marcle Lees."

"It's a local beauty spot," Becky said. "The Tankard itself is this weird pit, this huge, deep bowl shape in the ground.

They build one fire at the bottom of it, and another on the little hillock above it. Don't ask me why, they just always have."

"It's so cool," said Chloe, fervently. "No fireworks – but dancing and music and barbecues and – God, *everything*, instead."

Lisa and the bus turned up at the same time. The five girls clambered on, with a lot of other people too. The bus was jam-packed; they stood close together at the back.

"So," said Becky, chummily, leaning in close to Rayne, "how's scary Miss Skeleton then?"

"*Skeleton?*"

"Well, she's scrawny enough, isn't she!"

Rayne laughed. "Same as ever. She dragged us all in for this awful meeting. She's changing so much about the house, it's really upsetting Mrs D. Although. . ."

"Although what?"

"I dunno. I sort of see her point. We *do* need money."

"Blimey, *we* already!" crowed Becky. "On *her* side now, are you? She gonna promote you to assistant manager, then?"

"*No!*" laughed Rayne, and she turned to look out of the window. "How long before we get there?"

"Not long," said Becky.

Along with just about every other person on the bus, they got off at a bus stop by a car park set in a field. The car park was full of tightly parked cars. Walking with at least thirty others, all ages, they went through a gate at the end on to a dirt track and started trekking up the side of a hill. There was no need for torchlight; the moon was almost full, and shining down on them.

You could see where the Devil's Tankard was by the crowd of people lining its edge. Their heads were bent; they all seemed to be looking down. It gave Rayne a weird feeling, like they were all looking down into a fighting pit or something.

"We're in time," panted Becky, close beside her. "No fire yet."

When they reached the top, Rayne pushed her way through everyone, and looked down into the Tankard. At the bottom was a great pile of logs and brush wood. And just as Becky had said, twenty metres or so beyond it was a small mound, with another bonfire set on top of that.

"What do we do now?" asked Rayne.

Becky grinned at her. "We wait."

About five minutes later, there was a strange shout – a loud, deep ululation – cutting through the chatter of the crowd. It came from a clump of trees growing some distance beyond the mound. Instantly, the crowd divided, so that there was a clear pathway from the trees to the mound and on to the Tankard. Then some of the crowd started to ululate, weird and deep, and some to cheer, everyone yelling together.

"What the *hell*—" muttered Rayne.

"Just wait!" Becky said, excitedly, and she started to yell too.

Out from the trees came eleven flaming torches, moving at speed towards the pile of wood on the mound. The people drew back further and the cheering grew louder.

The torches got closer, and Rayne could see that they were carried by six young men, running hard – the last boy, who looked like the youngest, had a single torch. The runners reached the mound; they divided and ran round it, straight at the crowd.

Ethan was right at the front, laughing, arms braced to hold the torches, face bright with firelight. It was a race between him and the lad next to him. They sprinted towards the lip of the Tankard, ran over it, and began the descent, hurtling sideways down the steep slope, earth and stones spraying from their feet.

"That's Cory in front," cried Becky. "He's so *fit!*"

"Oh my God, do they ever *fall?*" breathed Rayne.

Becky clutched her hands to her mouth. "No one has yet!" she squealed, through her fingers.

Cory was still ahead but, two metres from the bottom, Ethan skidded to a halt, drew his right arm right back and hurled one of his torches. It roared past Cory and shot straight into the heart of the bonfire, which caught, flickered, and flamed into life. Then Ethan, grinning in triumph, turned and raced up the steep slope again, passing the last two boys who were still heading down.

Cory threw one of his torches and charged after him; at the top, he almost caught up with him. Together, torches guttering, they raced towards the bonfire on the mound and, once again, Ethan braked, hard, and threw his torch like a spear. It soared in an arc, hit the bonfire, and flamed it into life, and the crowd exploded into applause.

"What a hero!" said Sarah, lasciviously, clapping furiously. "Cory hates him doing that."

Cory hurled his torch on, followed by all the others, then he let out a roar and ran full-tilt at Ethan, landing on his back, both of them laughing. A drumbeat started up, fast, urgent, from somewhere in the crowd, and a woman in a long purple coat stepped forward into the surging firelight and began to play a fiddle. The man with the drum and another woman with a fiddle joined her. The music they played sounded magical, elemental, on top of the hill in the night. Ethan staggered round with Cory on his back, almost in time to its beat. Two other boys playing piggyback ran at them, and Ethan charged like a bull, Cory waving his arms, urging him on faster.

Rayne, staring, realized she hadn't taken her eyes off Ethan since he'd first appeared from the trees, running with a torch in either hand.

Becky nudged her. Five men were walking up to the bonfire, two of them with an armful of long wooden staffs. Cory slid from Ethan's back in time to catch the staff that was tossed to him; Ethan, too, caught his, as did the other two boys. Two more lads ran up and were thrown staffs; then eleven of them formed a ring.

Eleven, thought Rayne. Always eleven.

The dancing began.

Rayne, watching, thought it was wilder and even more mesmerizing than the Morris dancing she'd watched at the Apple Fair. One of the older men was the leader, that was clear, and the others had to follow him, but there was no set form to the dance. There couldn't be, with an uneven number of men. It was thrilling, always threatening to break down into anarchy, but never quite doing so. The leader would shout out commands, names like *blizzard!*, and change the pattern, and there'd be confusion and laughing – but the circle was always restored again. The dancers swung the wooden staffs and then, holding both ends, clashed them together so hard that splinters flew. And all the time they were grinning, and swearing if they got hit.

Rayne thought she recognized Will and some of the other watchers, but she barely glanced at them. She saw only Ethan as he jumped and landed and fought.

Then the older men drew back, leaving the six boys. The drumbeat quickened, the fiddlers stopped. Cory shouted something out and they leapt in the air; then as they fell, each boy reached for the end of the staff of the boy to his right, and they came together and made a star shape with their staffs, a six-pointed star. The speed of it was thrilling. They broke away, leaping and bounding in a circle – then Cory yelled again, and they jumped and made the star again. Rayne remembered the star from the Apple Fair, remembered St John telling her it was a witch sign and being offended when she told him it wasn't. But the making of that had been more orderly – this was wild, dramatic.

Then the drummer slowed his beat, and the fiddlers joined in again. People came from the crowd and made a second circle around the eleven, and began to dance too, some jigging wildly, some swaying calmly, and the air of festivity increased.

"Coming?" said Becky.

"Not yet," said Sarah. "The lads'll be out in a minute."

"But I want to dance!"

"So go! I'm waiting, that's all."

Rayne glanced at Becky's face – it was set, hostile. There was tension between the two friends; Rayne knew this was why Becky had been focusing so flatteringly on her. Becky slipped her hand through Rayne's arm, tossing her long brown hair back behind her shoulders. "You'll dance, won't you?" she asked. "Everyone joins in. It's just – it gets you, that beat."

"It does, doesn't it," said Rayne. She was practically dancing already, her head moving in time. "Come on, then, let's go."

Together they moved towards the crowd that was dancing under the bright moon, in front of the roaring firelight. It looked to Rayne like some pagan revel, some ancient rite. She'd lost sight of Ethan now; he was in the centre. Half turned towards Becky, she started to dance, letting her feet and arms do what they wanted to do.

The music grew louder. Two more violins and three high-pitched pipes had joined in; then a group of five women started singing, no words, just a high, rhythmic keening. Rayne, grinning, raised her arms high, moved her head forward and back – Becky laughed, and copied her.

Then after a while the drumbeat changed, grew more rapid, and the crowd parted, and the six boys ran out, laughing and shouting, their staffs held high like spears, and started to jig along the lip of the Devil's Tankard. Soon, people were following, swaying and hopping in one long line all along the edge of the pit. The flames from the bonfire at the bottom leapt high and sent sparks at their faces.

"Does this always happen?" Rayne asked. Something in her wanted to join in, to snake round the edge of the pit with the others. They looked like they were dancing round a ravine in hell, defying it.

Becky shook her head. "They've never done it before," she said.

A woman to the left of them turned, smiling, and said, "It never follows a set pattern. There's nothing set on this night, that's the point of it. If you start to do the same things year after year, it gets stale – the life goes out of it."

Cory had stopped at the far end of the pit. He held his staff high over his head, and roared, yelling like a berserker before battle. Then he hurled it down at the fire. Immediately, the other lads did the same, raising their sticks high and spearing them down, as everyone shouted and cheered. Ethan hurled his staff right up into the air, where it spiralled impressively, then nosedived right into the centre of the bonfire.

"Oooh, Will'll be annoyed at that," said the woman, grinning. "He took the best part of two hours finding and chopping those staffs."

"Will they get into trouble?" asked Becky.

"No. Course not. Not on this night."

The music had changed again; it was slower, softer. Everyone started to drift away from the edge of the Tankard. Some people carried on dancing, others sat on the long, soft turf near the bonfire on the mound and held out their hands to it. The fire in the pit sent a strange glow upwards; its light met the moonlight.

And Rayne looked up and saw Ethan heading straight for her.

Chapter Fifteen

"Hey, girls!" he called out. Cory and a couple of the other lads were right behind him.

"Hi, boys!" Becky called back.

The four boys were in front of them now, Ethan glancing at Rayne, glancing away again. Cory was grinning, and the other two were hanging back and acting cool. "Like the show?" demanded Cory.

"Brilliant," said Becky, smiling, the dimple in her left cheek showing prettily. "Have you met Rayne?"

"I know who she is," said Cory, and he turned to her and said, "Hello, Rayne."

And then Sarah appeared beside them, slightly out of breath, with Lisa and Chloe in tow. "Hey, Ethan," she yelped, "hey, Cory – that went a bit wild tonight, didn't it, round the edge of the Tankard?"

"Blame him," said Ethan, shoulder-barging Cory. "He was so pissed off about *losing the race* he had to think up something new to do, didn't you, you idiot?"

"It was a stroke of genius," said Cory. "Come on, you all copied me, it must've been."

"That was *pity*, mate! We knew you'd look a right prat just chucking your stick down on your own, we had to make something of it!"

"Aw, don't bully Cory," said Sarah, putting her arm round his neck, "it was great! Especially the *roaring*!"

The boys all laughed at that, and Cory cursed happily, and Sarah shoved him backwards, and the girls laughed too.

They're so easy together, thought Rayne, enviously. Easy and jokey – and I can't think of a thing to say.

She was standing next to Ethan now, and everyone else was occupied talking to each other, but she still couldn't make conversation, not like Sarah with her teasing and innuendoes.

"Having fun?" asked Ethan.

"Yeah," she said. "It's great. Off the wall, but great."

"Glad you're liking it. Are the pigeons still OK?"

"Yes. They're fine."

There was a long, difficult pause. Then a topic to talk about dawned on her. "Are the people here all local?" she asked.

"Most of them. Why?"

"Just – I thought these fire festivals would attract outsiders. You know, like the Lewes fireworks do, in Sussex. Miss Skelton – the new manager at Morton's Keep?"

"I've heard of her," said Ethan. "The gossip's started up."

"She's got all these plans to make money. To keep the manor house going. I was thinking – if she could harness an event at the house to one of the festivals, advertise it on that new website she's got—"

"It won't happen," Ethan said, sharply.

She was taken aback by his fierceness. "Why not?" she said. "I'm not saying *change* anything at the festivals, just let a few extra people come—"

"From outside. No. It won't happen. She's not suggested it, has she?"

"No, but I thought I might."

"Don't. Why d'you want to think like her?"

"*What?* All she's trying to do is get the bills paid. . ."

"And turn on its head the way things have always been done here."

"E-*than!*" A pair of yellow-mittoned hands crept over Ethan's shoulders. Sarah's face appeared behind them. "Aren't you going to come and dance?"

Ethan got hold of Sarah's hands, pulled her up against his back, then shot Rayne a look almost of dislike. "Yeah," he said, "I think I will."

Rayne felt wretched after that. The fire boys and Becky and Sarah and the others formed a great, shifting group, dancing on the edge of the pit, messing around by the fire, and Rayne, tagging along, had to pretend to be having fun while Ethan ignored her and Sarah got more and more up-close and flirtatious with him. If she'd been braver, she'd have walked off on her own down to the bus stop, but the great expanse of empty, moon-flooded hillside was too intimidating for her.

Although she was feeling increasingly nervous up on the hilltop, too. She kept away from Will and the other watchers, but she'd sometimes look up and see one of them staring at her. She kept away from the bonfires, never looking into them. She tried not to check her watch too often, and all the time she was willing Becky to want to leave soon.

But it didn't look likely. Someone had laid a large grill over the embers at the edge of the bonfire on the mound and now several long rows of sausages were sizzling, smelling delicious, and Becky dragged her over to wait for one. Parcels of food and bottles of drink were coming out, just as they had done at the fireworks on Martyr's Hill. Rayne took a piece of cold chicken from an enormous plastic box that was circulating, and said, "It's amazing, the way people do this here. Just handing out free food to everyone – even us lot!"

Becky shrugged. "They want us to come. Hey – look at that." Sarah had got hold of Ethan's arm and was towing him over to the other side of the fire. He was laughing, allowing himself to be led. "She's gonna pull him tonight, trust me," Becky went on, and she glanced slyly at Rayne, to see how she'd taken this announcement.

Rayne didn't trust herself to say anything. Her throat had suddenly got tight with wanting to cry.

A man and a woman with sacking wrapped round their hands lifted the rack of sausages from the fire. "Quick," Becky said, as two more women started to fork up the sausages and put them into rolls. "Get in line! Grab one!"

An hour and a half later, Rayne was wearily making her way up the long drive to Morton's Keep, trying not to dwell on Becky's story about the spectral horseman who rode along it – and who'd dismount and come lurching towards you if you saw him. There was no need for her torch – the fat moon lit her way. Halfway up the drive, she made her way into the bushes, through the gap where St John once used to conceal his motorbike.

St John. She hardly thought about him now, she'd buried all that horror and manipulation deep down, where she thought it couldn't touch her. But it was still all there, it had to be, and it had to have something to do with how nervous she often felt, all anxious and full of foreboding, as though more bad things were going to happen. . . She hurried on, across the medieval garden. The night was rustling around her.

She reached the Sty and let herself in – and her heart wrenched in terror. A thin woman in black was floating towards her, hovering above the floor. . .

Then she saw it was her dress, her lovely new dress, hanging on the rail, and she gasped out a curse, amazed at how terrified she'd been just for that moment. She stamped off to the tiny kitchen, heart still pounding, berating herself for being such an idiot.

She made a mug of tea, came back into the room and hunched up on her bed, thinking over the events of the night. Nothing – *weird* – had happened. That was quite a relief. But it was probably the only good thing about the night. Ethan had ignored her, he'd been all over Sarah. She was pretty sure they'd got off together, even though his mates had been around all the time. And if they hadn't it could only be a matter of time.

She'd messed it up with him, that was clear. By being

edgy and hostile and suspicious and distant. She'd wanted to talk about it all with Becky, on the bus – but she didn't trust her enough. Becky was "off" Sarah for now, complaining about how up herself and bossy she was, but next week they'd probably be best mates again and she couldn't risk telling Becky any confessions about Ethan that Sarah might get to hear. And anyway, Becky had pretty quickly switched from bitching Sarah to slagging off Skeleton, as she called her – complaining that she nagged and criticized and wouldn't confirm she needed her for the grand dinner next Saturday. Rayne had thought about the wonderful supper she'd had with Miss Skelton and the present of the black dress, and stayed silent.

Her eyes were drawn to the dress, now. Horror of the sight of it when she'd opened the door still seemed to cling to it – as though the thin woman she thought she'd seen still inhabited it. After a while, she got off the bed, and took the dress down. It was silky and beautiful in her arms, and for a second she thought of trying it on again, just for the sheer pleasure of it. But she didn't. She hung it behind the curtain, where she couldn't see it, and went to get ready for bed.

Chapter Sixteen

The next day, Rayne, sick of the thoughts whirling in her brain, sick of the undercurrent of doubt and anxiety she felt, decided to write it all down. If everything was laid out, she thought she might make sense of it. She found an old notebook in one of her bags and started to write a list, marking each with an asterisk.

* The awfulness is over. The dungeon is filled up, St John has gone.
* But I can't expect to get over it just like that. I'm going to feel weird still, and shocked. <u>I must stop worrying about feeling weird</u>, or I'll feel weirder.
* I fancy Ethan. REALLY fancy him.
* He fancied me once but now he's gone back to fancying Sarah.
* He probably never really fancied me, he was just after me because of the watcher stuff.
* The watcher stuff does my head in. It's so freaky I don't even want to think about it.

She paused, wondering if there was anything else she should add to her list. It had helped, writing it down. As though writing it was naming it, and naming it meant she knew it, she'd started to come to terms with it. Then she wrote:

* Miss Skelton might not be as bad as I first thought. At least she's part of the twenty-first century. <u>Focus on the here and now.</u>

She read the list through, slowly, thinking about it all, doodling on the asterisks, inking them in, so they turned into little six-pointed stars. Like the shapes Ethan and his mates had made with their sticks. When she saw what she'd done she shut the notebook and put it back in her bag again.

Plans for the grand dinner that Saturday night dominated the following week. Mrs Driver was purse-mouthed with disapproval at all the upheaval but Rayne decided she liked the distraction. When the wonderful local lady cooks had a panic attack at cooking for over twice the number they usually cooked for, she was the one who calmed them down, told them how much more money they'd be making, and convinced them they could do it. When Ben Avebury baulked at raking the forecourt gravel and clearing it of weeds, she was the one who persuaded him that the Keep had to look its best on the night. She checked reservations, made phone calls about orders. Miss Skelton kept telling her how marvellous it was to be able to rely on her. And on

Thursday night, when it was clear everything was coming together, Miss Skelton took hold of her hands, looked straight into her eyes, and told her that she quite honestly couldn't have done it without her. Rayne squirmed a bit, but all the same it was sweet to hear.

"Mr Stuart's delighted with you, too," she went on. "Things are working out, Rayne. We recognize you're doing more work and as soon as we can afford it, your wages will reflect that."

Rayne raised her eyebrows at the "we", but it didn't really bother her any more – it just seemed to show how committed Miss Skelton was to the Keep.

"By the way," Miss Skelton went on, "I've solved the waitress problem. My niece Tara is coming to stay."

Rayne, taken aback, managed to say, "Oh, right! Well, *good*!"

"It's not good, really. She's in dreadful trouble at home – she's just dropped out of university, her parents are furious with her – it's all been ghastly. I suggested she came here for a cool-down period. I think you'll like her, Rayne. And she's done waitressing before, she'll be perfect."

"So there'll be three of us, with Becky?" Rayne blurted out. "Only she was saying – you haven't told her she's working on Saturday yet."

"Haven't I? Oh, don't worry – I need Becky. Now – I must get on." And with a brisk smile, she high-heeled away.

Saturday arrived, but Tara still hadn't. Miss Skelton said another row at home had delayed her, but she would be here for the night – she'd promised. Rayne said that if the worse came to the worst, Becky and she could manage, and Miss Skelton had smiled lopsidedly and hurried off again.

At five o'clock, Rayne pushed open the thick oak door to the Old Stone Hall, carrying a heavy tray of silver cutlery, and gasped.

The Hall had been transformed by flowers.

Four great stands, piled high and overflowing with vine leaves and exotic purple blooms, had been set between the standing candelabras. The pagan fireplace, that Mr Stuart told her had been built as a kind of altar, a source of power to balance out the ancient evil, was crowned with vines, grapes and dark flowers. They tumbled luxuriously over the mantelpiece and fell on to the strange, goat-legged men that held it up. Most impressive of all, the gallery where prisoners used to stand had great swags of greenery and shaggy purple dahlias hanging from it in sweeping, decadent abundance.

A huge gilt-framed mirror had been hung below the high windows opposite the fireplace, so that everything was dramatically doubled. There was a fragrant, spicy smell in the air.

Dazedly, Rayne set her tray down on the new, dark-wood table. It had been positioned at right angles to the ancient stone table, to form a T shape. Where the two tables met there were yet more flowers – a low, dramatic display of deep red blooms and wide exotic leaves. She began to lay out the complicated sets of cutlery as Mrs Driver had shown her. There were forty-two place settings, over twice the number of the last grand dinner.

She was halfway through when Ben Avebury arrived, carrying on his shoulder a huge wickerwork basket full of logs and kindling.

"Hi, Ben," she said, smiling at him. "You forgiven me yet for making you rake the forecourt?"

"Not your fault, miss," he said, dumping down the basket beside the massive grate. "I know you were just carrying out orders."

"What d'you think of all this, then?" she asked, indicating the abundance of flowers. "Stunning, isn't it?"

"That's one word for it," he grunted.

"Don't you like it? I wanted to put flowers in here for that last dinner, but Mrs Driver said flowers were never used in the Stone Hall—"

"She's right, they're not."

"Yes, but *why*? I think they really brighten the place up." It was a stupid thing to say, and as soon as it had left her mouth she regretted it. It would take more than flowers to brighten up the Old Stone Hall. Its very air was ancient and chill, clotted with all the suffering that had taken place within its walls.

Ben, laying out kindling in the grate, didn't answer her. She went back to laying the tables, and soon she could hear the crackling of the fire, and smell the delicious scent of burning apple wood, mingling with the flowers. She turned, to see Ben standing looking at her. "Things have always been done a certain way here," he said. "Changing them – it's not a good idea."

"Oh, *Ben*. I know Miss Skelton's come in like a bull in a china shop but – I dunno. I think we might've misjudged

100

her. Her one aim is to increase revenue and God knows Morton's Keep needs that. . ." She broke off. She knew she couldn't say any more about the Keep's dire financial situation – she'd promised Miss Skelton.

"She's turned the Stone Hall into a film set," said Ben disgustedly. "Flowers – they aren't *right* here. And she's getting *musicians* in. To stand on the gallery. Three of 'em, two with lutes, one with a pipe. They sing as well."

"Well, I think that's lovely!"

"It won't be lovely. Remember what she said she was after? *Dark glamour.* It won't be lovely."

"Well at least it'll bring in a bit of energy!" Rayne retorted. "It's what the place needs, don't you think? Some new energy?" She looked at him, challenging him to talk. "Oh, come on, Ben – she might be changing things, but you of all people should want this place to move beyond its *past*?"

But Ben had turned his back on her, turned to face the fire again. He heaved four logs on to the flaming kindling, nudging them into position with his boot. The flames leapt up as the logs caught, and Ben stood back from the grate. Then with furious movements he swept away the loops of vine leaves that were hanging down obscuring the faces of the goat-legged men. "Fire risk," he grunted, and stamped out of the Hall.

Chapter Seventeen

Lifting her skirt free of the damp grass, Rayne made her way over to the Great Hall. Miss Skelton had told her to report at seven o'clock sharp, as the first guests might turn up before the arrival time of seven-thirty.

Her dress felt sensational. From the tiny mirror in the bathroom, she knew she looked fantastic. She'd made her eyes up dramatically, all bronze and glittery, to match the strange tracery of beading on the front of her dress. She was dying to see the full-length effect.

The great baronial double doors already stood a little open. Rayne slipped through them and was faced with an image of herself from which all the colour had been leached.

A girl of her height and like her, slender, was standing on the wide wooden stairs. She had pale skin and white-blonde hair hanging straight down her back and her dress was like Rayne's but it was bone-white, with darker ivory beads.

If I'm the vampire princess, Rayne thought, *she's the bride.*

She took in a deep breath. "Are you—"

"I'm Tara," said the girl, gliding down to meet her. "And I hope I look half as sensational as you do."

There was peal of laughter from the doorway, and Miss Skelton came in. She looked stunning – her dress was ruby red, with broad, dramatic sleeves and a low front. Her dark hair was piled up, with many drifting, curling strands; her lipstick and her beautiful drop earrings matched her dress. "You *both* look sensational," she cried.

"So do you!" said Rayne.

Miss Skelton smiled. "Come. I want you to see yourselves." And she swept over the flagstones to the library door, the two girls following. The fire had been lit in the fireplace; its flame-light flickered upwards on to the two hefty cherubs perpetually crowning the mad-smiling woman. Rayne felt its heat as she passed.

They hurried, skirts swishing, down the corridor with its oil paintings and arrowslits, and into the library. Miss Skelton turned on all the lights and stood them in front of a long mirror on the wall. And she was right – they did look sensational. Like two otherworldly spectres, light and dark, balancing out each other.

"Do you mind?" murmured Miss Skelton, coming up behind Rayne, taking hold of the laces at her back and pulling them tighter. "I've already done my niece."

"Right," groaned Tara, "I can barely breathe!"

"It's worth it," crowed Miss Skelton, "to look this good. Now come! To work!"

"Now," Miss Skelton said, as the three of them swept back into the Great Hall, "Tara, I want you to stand on the stairs. Elegantly. You'll be the first thing people see when they enter. This is theatre, remember. Rayne – you take the coats, and hand them up to Tara. Tara – nip them up to the half-landing and dump them. Harry and I will greet everyone and hand out champagne –" she indicated the long side table, already set with sparkling glasses – "and as soon as it gets too full out here, we'll move into the Old Stone Hall. At *that* point, I want *you*, Rayne, to come through and hand round the canapés and *Tara*, you'll deal with the remaining coats on your own. Late guests will get their champagne in the Stone Hall. All clear?"

Tara rolled her eyes at Rayne, grinning, and said, "All clear." Rayne nodded, smiling. She was beginning to like Tara, and beginning to feel excited about the night.

Then the heavy green curtains that screened the kitchen corridor parted, and Mrs Driver and Becky came through. Becky was in jeans and a T-shirt, and her expression was sullen. "Ah, there you are!" cried Miss Skelton. "Now – Mrs D and Becky are our food carriers. They convey food *from* – and dirty plates *to* – the kitchen. The four of you will meet here for the changeovers. Becky and Mrs D are back-room staff. The Stone Hall is the stage and they do *not* cross on to it. Understood?"

Rayne could feel the indignation coming off Becky like heat; she couldn't meet her eye. But then a car's wheels sounded, grating across the gravel drive, and Miss Skelton shot to the bottom of the staircase and shrieked out *"Harreee!"*, and Mr Stuart came running down, handsome in his black dinner jacket, and the first guests came through the great doors. . .

And the play began.

Miss Skelton made a scintillating hostess, far more gracious than poor, awkward Ms Barton had been. Once everyone was seated, she stood at the head of the ancient stone table and spoke feelingly of the dark history and mysterious power of Morton's Keep. Tonight, she said, they were all privileged to experience it. She called for a toast; forty-two glasses chinked together, once to the left, once to the right. The musicians began to play, haunting, romantic music that transported the listener. The fire roared; the sumptuous flowers released their scents.

Rayne and Tara served the first course, a rich salad with walnuts and crumbled blue cheese. Rayne held the huge, brass-handled tray; Tara swiftly laid a plate down in front of each guest. Then Rayne hurried over to the door to swap her empty tray for another full one and soon, all the guests were eating. As they moved about the tables, keeping wine glasses full, Rayne caught delicious, theatrical glimpses of herself and Tara in the wide mirror. The sound of conversation rose and, as each course arrived, the sense of success of the evening grew.

Rayne was kept too busy to feel bad about Becky now, and the changeovers of used plates and fresh food were so fast there was no time to find out how fed up the "back-room staff" were. Towards the end, as Rayne took hold of a tray of cinnamon custards, Mrs Driver said, "Only the cheese after this. There's not as many courses as we used to do. She's charging more, for less."

"Well, the punters seem happy," said Rayne. "The music's wonderful. Great acoustics in there."

Mrs Driver sniffed, and didn't reply.

It was nearing the end of the evening. Glittering cut-glass decanters of port were put on the tables with cheese, grapes and oat biscuits; the pitch of conversation rose further. Mr Stuart had relayed a few stories about his childhood at the Keep and its dramatic history but now the guests seemed content to relax and talk amongst themselves. The fire devoured logs and the mirror reflected its flames; the flowers shimmered in the candlelight, and the music soared.

There was nothing for the girls to do for a while. They stood either side of the fireplace, waiting, and Rayne moved a little nearer to the gallery, to hear the music better.

There was something behind the flute and the singing. At first she wasn't sure she'd heard it, but she stood stock-still and listened, and then she became sure. It was a rhythm, a regular rhythm, it fitted with the music like a drum but it wasn't a drum. . .

Then she realized what it was. She felt as though her heart had stopped.

It was feet, she was sure of it. The sound of many pairs of feet, dancing, dancing in unison.

It was the dancing Mr Stuart had said he'd heard as a boy, it had to be. He told Rayne it had filled him with dread.

She glanced in terror at Mr Stuart now, to see if he'd heard it too, but he was chatting and laughing with the woman next to him, calm, oblivious.

But dread was filling her.

It was ghosts dancing. Ghost guests at one of Sir Simeon Lingwall's evil parties, all unaware of the fate that lay in wait for them.

Fearfully she looked around the room, at Tara and Miss Skelton, at all the guests one after the other, but no one seemed to hear it. The musicians in the gallery played blithely on. They finished one melody, and after the light applause was over, Rayne could hear that the dancing had stopped too. But then the musicians started up again, a new tune with a faster rhythm, and then Rayne, cold with fear, heard that the feet had started up again too, in time with the beat.

They were responding to the music.

They were here.

Chapter Eighteen

Rayne fetched the guests their coats, accepted tips and thanks and compliments on how well she'd served and how wonderful she looked, all in a dream, in a coma of fear. Her blood was thudding through her veins; she felt as if she might faint with it.

She kept shooting looks at Mr Stuart, but he didn't look at her. When the last guest had gone he turned to Miss Skelton and bowed like a cavalier in front of her, and they both laughed, intoxicated with the triumph of the evening. He picked up her left hand and pressed it to his mouth. "Let's go back in," he said, feelingly. "Let's drink the last of the champagne by the embers of the fire and . . . *enjoy our success!*"

He looked happier, more animated, than Rayne had ever seen him – he was shining with it. And Miss Skelton seemed to glimmer back at him. He kept hold of her hand and they went back into the Old Stone Hall together; Rayne watched as the door swung shut behind them.

She turned. Tara had disappeared; she was alone in the hall. She could hear footsteps heading off to the Tudor kitchen. She pushed the heavy curtain aside, and hurried along there too.

At the long refectory table, the wonderful lady cooks and Mrs Driver were cling-filming bowls of leftovers. They looked white and exhausted. Piles and piles of dirty plates stood around them. "Oh, there you are, dear," said Mrs Driver, wearily. "Have they all gone?"

"Yes," Rayne croaked.

"We're just doing what needs to be done tonight. It'll be all hands on deck tomorrow to clear this lot up, but we're leaving it for now. Is Mr Stuart. . .?"

Rayne stared at the old housekeeper helplessly. Mrs Driver was clearly expecting Mr Stuart to come to the kitchen, to thank everybody. As indeed he should. But he'd been so absorbed in Miss Skelton, it hadn't seemed to have crossed his mind. . . "He's just in the Stone Hall with Miss Skelton," she muttered. "I'm sure he'll be along soon."

"But he thought it went well?"

"Oh, yes. Oh, he was delighted. Honestly."

"It was hard to get a sense of it out here. Not like the old days, when we were more involved."

"Everyone thought the food was fantastic. Honestly."

The lady cooks looked up at that, and smiled tiredly, but they didn't say anything.

"I've sent Becky home," Mrs Driver went on. "Her mum came for her. She was nearly in tears by the end. She said if she'd known she was just going to be a *runner* – that's what she called it – she wouldn't have worked tonight. And I must say it did seem unfair of Miss Skelton – choosing her niece Tara, who's only just got here, over Becky."

Rayne licked her dry lips. She couldn't think of a response to this – she felt implicated, guilty. "Where is Tara?" she asked.

"No idea. She didn't come in. Wanted to avoid the clearing up, no doubt."

"Can I help?"

"Bless you, dear, that wasn't a hint," said Mrs Driver. "No, you look exhausted too. You get to bed and we'll do this tomorrow."

Rayne hovered for a moment, then left by the door in the corner that led straight outside. She'd gone to the kitchen out of some jumbled sense that it would comfort her, but it hadn't. She couldn't talk to Mrs Driver about what she'd heard.

On the steep stone steps outside, she hesitated. She could go back to the Sty, try to sleep. . .

Sleep. She wouldn't get to sleep. She kept hearing the feet, all in unison, in time with the musicians. The feeling of dread was still with her.

She ran down the steps and over to the great cauldron of the forecourt, her way lit by the harsh spotlights on the ancient wall and the two towers. She headed for the low building in the centre, where Ben Avebury lived, and knocked on the door.

There was no answer. She knocked again, more loudly. She told herself she didn't care if he was in bed, she didn't care if he was asleep, she had to talk to him.

After a few moments' ringing silence, a bolt was drawn back on the other side; a key turned. Then the old gardener peered out at her across the door chain.

"Ben, can I come in for a moment?" she cried. "*Please*. I need to talk to you."

Ben slipped the chain off, and drew her inside into a narrow, red-tiled hall. "What's happened?" he asked, hoarsely. "Is *he* back?"

"He? Who?"

"St John Arlington."

"No – no, of course not!"

"What's wrong, then? What's happened?"

"It's – it was at the dinner. I heard . . . *dancing*."

"What?"

"Dancing. *Ghosts* dancing."

Ben shrugged, turned away, and walked through a doorway on his right. Rayne followed him into a little old-fashioned room, with two upright armchairs on either side of a stove. "Sit down," he said. "You've had a shock. Will I make you some tea?"

Gratefully, Rayne nodded, and sat hunched in one of the armchairs, gazing at the glow of the fire, until he returned. He handed her a mug; she took a sip, and screwed her face up. "It tastes weird!" she exclaimed.

"I slipped a bit of Scotch in."

"*What?*"

"Don't fret. It was barely enough to fill a tooth. You looked like you needed it. Now – describe what you heard."

Rayne took in a shaky breath and explained about the sound of the dancing: how it had followed the music as though the ghosts were there, in the room with them; how she was sure it was the sound of one of Sir Simeon Lingwall's twisted parties.

"It may well have been," said Ben, darkly. "There are ghosts all over this place. I see 'em myself sometimes, at the edge of the woods, in the mist . . . and there's a little serving girl Mrs Driver keeps seeing on the stairs."

"Mrs Driver told me she'd *never* seen a ghost here! Just after I started working here, she told me that!"

"She wouldn't want to talk about it. But you don't need to worry about the ghosts, they don't do any harm."

"But this was about *him*," said Rayne, leaning forward. "Lingwall. Don't you think it's creepy that I heard it after we *defeated* him? Burnt out the dungeon, broke up St John's hideous cult? Don't you think that should have made the ghost presence weaker, not stronger?"

"You're being too logical. Ghosts aren't logical."

"But I felt – I felt *so scared* when I heard it. And all kind of filled up with horror, dread. It just seems – it seems. . . Ben – you do think we *have* defeated him, don't you?"

There was a silence, just the sound of the burning logs clicking in the stove.

"I can't say," Ben said at last. "We did what we had to do at the time, that's all I know. But I can't say if it's over."

Rayne felt her chest constrict with panic. "Something's happened, hasn't it?" she croaked. "You've seen something – you know something—"

"No. Now don't go getting in a state. Drink your tea."

"*Why did you ask me if St John was back?*"

"I don't know. No reason."

Rayne stared at the old man, eyes wide. He looked at the fire, refusing to meet her gaze.

She didn't trust him, she didn't believe what he'd said. It

hadn't done any good to reach out to him. It had just made her feel more scared. She put her mug down, stammered goodbye, and ran out into the night.

Five minutes later she reached the Old Sty.

There was a light shining in the other bedroom, and a shadow of someone against the curtains.

Chapter Nineteen

Rayne stood stock-still staring at the shadow and the light, as though it might be a mistake, as though if she looked long enough it might suddenly not be there any more.

The other bedroom was never occupied. The only way into it was through her room.

Her impulse was to run back to Ben's home, but she couldn't make herself move. She stood there, one hand on the branch of a nearby tree to steady herself, staring at the shadow as it crossed the room.

She felt like she stood there for hours, staring until her eyes were raw, and in the end her fear made her angry. She was sick of feeling fear – first the ghosts, then Ben's bleak hints, now this – she was sick of how weak it made her. She marched forward, rammed the ancient key in the lock, turned it, and shoved the door open.

To be faced by Tara, emerging from the bathroom in a long emerald-green kimono. "Hi, you," she said.

"How did you get in?" Rayne demanded. "There's only one key to this door."

"The window," said Tara.

Rayne glanced at the old pine table beneath the window. She'd done her make-up for the night sitting at it. Her lipgloss, mascara and bronze eye make-up were all still lying there, undisturbed.

"Not *your* window," said Tara. "*My* window. It's neat, there's a lock in the frame, I'm going to use it like a front door. Well, a back door."

"The window by the kitchen? It's not wide enough."

"It is. Or I wouldn't be in here, would I?"

Dazed, Rayne followed her through the bathroom and into the other room. The second window and the absence of a door were all that stopped this room being a mirror image of Rayne's. The bed had a yellow-covered duvet on it, and clothes had been hung up on the rail; a gaping suitcase was on the floor.

Under the window between the kitchen and the bed was a block of wood. "I'm using that as a step," said Tara. "I've got another lump of wood on the outside."

Rayne was silent. In her mind was an image of Tara clambering through the window in her bone-white dress. A kind of shiver ran through her.

Tara stared at her. Then she groaned, "Oh, *no*! She didn't *tell* you, did she? Aunt Louisa? That I'd be staying here?"

"No," said Rayne. "She didn't."

"God, you must've been *freaked* when you saw the light on!"

"I was."

"That is so *typical* of her! Though I suppose she *has* been run off her feet with this posh dinner. I was going to stay in the main house, up on the third floor, but she said she'd be

115

needing those rooms for the next grand dinner because she was going to do overnighters – so I'd be better off settling in out here, with you. You don't *mind*, do you?"

Rayne sat down heavily on the end of the bed. "I don't know," she muttered. She was remembering with sudden vividness the first morning she'd woken up in the Old Sty, how magical it had seemed as she'd walked barefoot on the cold, wet grass of the medieval garden, snuffing in the fresh earthy air, eating her first-ever apple straight from a tree. How, when she'd come back in, she'd danced into this room and out again through the kitchen and then back again, winding round and round like she was casting a spell, making it safe, making the whole Sty hers.

And now it wasn't all hers, not any more.

"Aunt Louisa said you'd like the company," said Tara, looking at her sympathetically. "Out here all on your own."

"Yes, but – she might've *asked* me!" Rayne burst out.

"She should've done. That's her all over – she's like a steamroller. Oh lord, I feel awful about this now."

Rayne looked up at Tara and smiled. "Sorry," she mumbled. "I don't mean to be rude. It's just—"

"No one told you. *Asked* you. I do understand."

"I . . . I came here because I wanted to get away from people. From being crowded all the time. I've kind of loved being on my own."

"Oh dear. Look – I won't cramp your style, you know. And I won't hog the bathroom. Honestly." Tara's face split in an enormous yawn. "God. 'Scuse me. I'm knackered."

"Me too," said Rayne. "It's been a long night, hasn't it?"

116

"Especially as I had to travel all the way up from Kent today."

Rayne felt a jolt of guilt. "God, I'd forgotten. Look – I'm sorry. You get to bed, OK?" She stood up, and walked towards the kitchen. When she reached it she turned and said, "Tara?"

Tara looked up at her, sleepily.

"Of course it's fine for you to be here. Of course it is."

When Rayne woke the next morning she remembered immediately that she wasn't alone. She couldn't hear anything from the room next door – she hadn't heard anything all night – but somehow she was aware of Tara's presence.

It was still very early, only just getting light. She got up and went to the bathroom to pee, locking the door to Tara's room as quietly as possible, and remembering to unlock it again afterwards. She made herself a cup of tea to take back to bed, and lay there, brooding.

She'd got on all right with Tara at the grand dinner, she thought. There hadn't been much chance to talk but they'd worked well together, taking it in turns to carry the huge trays, smiling at each other. One woman had been a real pain about her food, always complaining in a high-pitched voice, and several of the men had got very drunk and flirtatious. Over the guests' heads, they'd giggled about it together.

Maybe it would be good to have Tara here. Maybe it would be fun, and they'd end up friends. It was great for a start that she seemed to take the Old Sty and the mansion house in her stride, with none of Becky's hysteria. Maybe she'd take ghosts in her stride, too, and laugh about them.

Rayne put her mug down, and jumped out of bed again. She didn't want to think about ghosts.

She went back into the bathroom and showered, then she dressed in jeans and a jumper. There was still no sound from Tara. So she let herself out of the main door, and set off to the Tudor kitchen to help clean up.

Mrs Driver was already there, with Mrs Brooks, Becky's mum; the dishwasher was humming and half the table was cleared of dirty crockery. "Blimey," said Rayne, "what time did you get here?"

"Eight o'clock," said Mrs Driver. "I had to let Mrs Brooks in."

The clock on the wall said it was ten to nine. "Sorry I'm late," mumbled Rayne.

"You're not, dear," said Mrs Driver, briskly. "Start drying those glasses, if you would, and putting them back in the boxes. I'll sign your hours sheet from now until we finish in here."

Mrs Brooks had her arms in the sink, scrubbing roasting pans. She'd barely glanced at Rayne. No doubt Becky had complained bitterly about her subservient role last night, and described Rayne's and Tara's beautiful dresses, and now Mrs Brooks was implicating Rayne in the poor treatment of her daughter.

Well, too bad.

"Did you see Mr Stuart last night?" Rayne asked, as she picked up a tea towel. "Did he come to the kitchen?"

"No," said Mrs Driver. "He did not."

No wonder she's in a bad mood, Rayne thought. But it's too bad about that, too, and not my fault, no more than it's my fault Becky's pissed off.

The three of them worked in near-silence. It took another hour and fifteen minutes until everything was washed, dried and put away. "Is there anything to do in the Old Stone Hall?" asked Rayne. "What about all those flowers and everything?"

"You'll have to ask Miss Skelton about that," said Mrs Driver, tartly, as she bundled linen napkins into the washing machine.

Rayne shrugged. She went over to the bin on the floor where the bird seed was kept, and scooped out a big bagful. Mrs Driver made no comment, although usually she'd ask how the pigeons were doing – she liked the idea of the tower dovecote being repopulated.

Rayne called out goodbye, and went out of the door before she could hear if she'd been answered or not.

A few minutes later, she was slipping in through the old door in the wall to the tower garden, and crossing the maze of hedges. The sun was scudding in and out of the clouds; the place didn't feel so ominous when the sun shone, even briefly.

She was just about to step over the last but one hedge, when she stopped. The sun had disappeared but there was a dark shadow, a shape, on the door to the dovecote. Even from that distance, it looked unbearably sinister. She remembered a photo she'd seen once, of a dead fox nailed to the door of a hen house, to warn the other foxes away. It looked a bit like that.

Then the sun came out from behind a cloud, and the darkness vanished, but the shape didn't. Now it was white.

Something deep in Rayne knew what it was even before she saw the beaks and the feathers, streaked with blood.

One pigeon was nailed up by its foot; the other, underneath it, had a nail driven low through its throat. Their necks hung limp and hopeless, as though they'd been twisted. A long stain of blood had congealed on the door, soaking into the wood. The brutality of it made Rayne feel sick.

This isn't ghosts, or suspicions, or shadows against a curtain, she thought.

This is real.

Chapter Twenty

Rayne made herself put her hand low on the door, as far from the crucified birds as she could, and push it open. Then she went in and hurriedly refilled the food dish and changed the water. When she'd finished she glanced up. Three birds were peering down at her from the ledge, but they wouldn't fly down. She felt near to tears. Maybe that was how the two pigeons had been caught, by someone bringing food to the table.

She knew she ought to call Ethan. She didn't want to, though – she didn't want to tell him what had happened to his birds.

She left hurriedly, pushing the door open hard, not looking at the dead birds. She told herself she'd come back and bury them but she couldn't do it yet, not while she was so upset. She sped across the great lawn behind the house to the safety of the wood again.

When she let herself into her room, she could smell bacon frying. "Want some?" called out Tara. "You're just in time. Aunt Louisa came over with a peace offering about ten minutes ago. She was full of apologies for forgetting to ask you about me moving in and she brought bacon, mushrooms, eggs—" Tara's head appeared round the kitchen curtain. "*Blimey*," she said. "Whatever's happened? You look ghastly."

"Thanks," croaked Rayne. "I feel pretty ghastly. Something – oh, God."

"Sit down. Go on, Rayne, sit down, you look white." Tara took hold of her arm, steered her to the chair by the table under the window.

"Something horrible's happened," Rayne said.

"Let me turn the bacon off, and get some tea," Tara said. "Then you can tell me, OK?"

Sitting opposite Tara, Rayne explained about the birds Ethan had given her for the dovecote – and what she'd found this morning. Tara let out a low whistle. "God, that is sick," she said. "God, there are some *sick* people about."

"I know," muttered Rayne. "I can't bear to think . . . who did it. *Why* they did it. . ." She trailed off. She couldn't explain to Tara what she feared – that it was somehow connected to St John, and his ancestor Sir Simeon Lingwall – because if she did she'd have to explain the whole immense story, about the ancient evil and the reoccurrences and what had happened in the dungeon. . .

"You know who did it, don't you?" Tara suddenly said.

Rayne felt cold. "No?" she whispered.

"One of those weirdos from last night. Seriously. They get all tanked up, all pumped up listening to the history of this place – wasn't Mr Stuart going on about murders in that tower at some point?"

"Yes, he did mention it – he talked about the gravestones in the maze. . ."

"Then on their way out, they do a detour to see the tower – and get high on a bit of barbaric sacrifice. Perfect end to a perfect evening."

"But . . . that's horrible."

"No more horrible than that rocker who used to bite off live chicken heads on stage. Or was it bats' heads? Anyway, I bet that's what it was."

Rayne wanted to believe her. She wanted to think it was just a twisted, isolated act of brutality. That was bad enough, but what was squirming about in her mind was far worse.

Tara stood up. "I'm making brekky now. Full English. And more tea. Then I think we should take a trip into town. Aunt Louisa said most of it's open on a Sunday. You need to get *out* of this place!"

Tara was fun to go into Marcle Lees with. And she was right – it was just what Rayne needed. They wandered up and down the little arcades that fanned out from the market square, going into the most upmarket shops, trying things on, trying out new looks. Tara persuaded Rayne to splash out on a baby-blue top that was expensive but really flattered her. Then she insisted they get milkshakes – big strawberry ones – and as they sat drinking them Rayne got out her phone to text Becky, something conciliatory about last night, but she couldn't think of what to say. Then a group of lads came into the café, sat near them and started chatting them up, and Tara gave as good as she got. Rayne laughed, egging her on, and put her phone away.

After that Tara offered to cook supper, and they went into a small supermarket and bought all the ingredients she needed to cook her "*amazing* spag bol sauce". As they split the bill at the till, Rayne realized she wasn't feeling so scared and anxious any more. She realized she was enjoying herself.

"D'you think you'll stay here long?" Rayne asked, as they meandered back to the bus stop.

"Dunno," said Tara. "To be honest, I'm not thinking about it. It was so dire at home, before I left – all the long silences and disappointed looks and lectures about 'throwing away my place at uni' – I'm just glad to be out of it. What about you?"

"Same," Rayne shrugged. "Just taking it a day at a time."

"Aunt Louisa told me a bit about why you were here. Needing to get away from urban hell and a possessive boyfriend?"

Rayne flashed with indignation that they'd been discussing her – then decided it was fine, even quite flattering. "Something like that," she said. "I just flipped, decided I had to get out."

"It's not for ever, though, is it?" said Tara, as they arrived at the bus stop. "It can't be. Stuck out here in the sticks. You'd go mad."

"I suppose so," said Rayne – and was surprised at the rush of grief she felt, at the thought of leaving the woods and the fields, the open spaces and the silence.

Then the bus arrived, and they climbed on board.

*

When they got back to the Old Sty, Tara announced she was starving and headed for the kitchen. "How long will it be?" asked Rayne.

"At least an hour and a half," Tara said. "Really, it needs two hours to simmer and be totally brilliant. But I'm too hungry for that, aren't you?"

"Getting that way," said Rayne. "Anything I can do?"

"Nope. Even if there was, there's only room for one in this skinny little kitchen."

"In that case, I'm just gonna wander out for a bit."

"Really? You got the energy? I thought you'd want a nap."

"Maybe later. I won't be long." And she slipped out of the door again before Tara could say anything else. There was something she had to do.

When Rayne reached the door to the dovecote garden, Ben Avebury was just coming out. He had a tool box in one hand and a spade in the other, and he looked at her shiftily, barely meeting her eye. "Ben!" she exclaimed. "Have you . . . have you seen the pigeons?"

"I've seen 'em," he said, gruffly. "I just been burying 'em."

"Oh, *thank you*. I – that's what I was coming to do. I saw them this morning, and it *freaked* me, I didn't want to deal with them then. . ."

"You told Ethan yet?"

"No. Not yet."

"You want to tell him."

Rayne stared at Ben, wondering how he knew they were

Ethan's birds, then she said, "Tara – Miss Skelton's niece – she reckons it was someone from the dinner last night. Someone a bit off his head, some ghoul, who got drunk and wanted a nasty thrill. . ."

"Could have been," grunted Ben. "Did you see the adverts that woman did for the dinner?"

"No. Did you?"

"Mrs Driver showed me. Morbid, they were, like the whole of that damn website she's set up. Going on about murders and death trials and the dark side of the Keep. Mrs Driver said no good would come of advertising like that."

"Maybe she was right!"

"Maybe. Stands to reason adverts like that would attract a rum load of guests."

There was a silence. Then Ben said, "I put a padlock on the door."

"A *padlock*?"

"Here's the key to it. If you're feeding the birds, you'll need the key. I shored the door up too, with an extra piece of wood. . ."

"But Ben – it won't happen again! Not if it was just some idiot from the dinner. . ." She trailed off. She was trying to persuade him, she realized. As well as persuade herself.

"We don't want to take any chances," Ben grunted. "It was a nasty mind did that." And, head bowed, he stomped off across the lawn with his tool box and his spade.

Chapter
Twenty-one

The following days passed more or less uneventfully. Rayne made herself go back every other day to the dovecote, to feed the birds, but she hated doing it. The thick piece of wood nailed on to the decaying door and the heavy iron padlock hanging from it disturbed her. The birds, when she went in, seemed anxious and sad, never flying down to her now when she refilled their dishes.

She didn't phone Ethan to tell him what had happened. After three days had gone by she told herself he'd know by now anyway; Ben would have got the news to him, or he would have heard it filtered through the local gossip.

Underneath, though, she was longing to talk to him; she wanted to tell him about the ghost dancing she'd heard, discuss her fear that Sir Simeon Lingwall's influence was still alive in Morton's Keep. But then she'd remember the last fire festival, how he'd got hold of Sarah's hands and pulled her up against his back, throwing Rayne a look that was almost dislike. And she knew there was no way she'd contact him first.

*

By the middle of the week, it became clear that Tara had replaced Becky in the tearoom. As soon as she saw Miss Skelton, Rayne challenged her about it.

"There's work for three waitresses now," she said, heatedly. "We're so much busier."

"Would you say you're not *managing*, you and Tara, then?" asked Miss Skelton, smoothly.

"Yes, just about," retorted Rayne. "But we're pushed – and it's so *unfair* on Becky, just to get dumped like that. . ."

"Rayne, Becky was paid a higher hourly rate than I'm paying you or Tara, because she's not living here. Tara is saving us *money*. This is a *business*. And also – frankly – Tara fits our image better. I don't have to spell it out for you, do I?"

Miss Skelton didn't have to spell it out. Rayne and Tara were both slim and graceful, they balanced each other beautifully, the light and the dark. Becky was much more solid and earthy, more matter-of-fact.

"I hope you're *on board*, Rayne," Miss Skelton went on, silkily. "I hope you support what we're trying to do here."

"Of course I do," said Rayne. "I just think . . . I just think it's unfair, that's all. Becky's really nice, and she's worked here for ages."

"Hmm," murmured Miss Skelton, and she looked at Rayne, her dark eyes flickering. Then she turned on her heel, and walked off.

Rayne knew there'd be no persuading Miss Skelton, and she texted Becky, saying how lousy she felt about it all, asking if they could meet up. But she got no reply.

She missed Becky, but she was getting used to sharing the Old Sty with Tara; in fact, she was taking more and more comfort in her presence. They were like two refugees camping out together. Rayne loved Tara's flippant sense of humour, and the way she seemed so unaffected by the grim energy of Morton's Keep. Tara didn't share Rayne's love of walking in the wilds, but the two girls went out shopping again at the weekend, and to a pub in the middle of Marcle Lees on Saturday night.

They often made an evening meal together, eating well on food scavenged from the kitchen. Tara was a creative cook who could look at random ingredients and make something delicious out of them. Rayne picked a bowl of russet apples still clinging to the little trees at the end of the medieval garden – they glowed on the table where the two girls sat to eat and chat.

That weekend the first of Miss Skelton's Gothic concerts were to be held, on two consecutive nights. She'd booked the musicians from the grand dinner again, along with a pianist, and a soprano from Wales who'd begun, Miss Skelton said, to make a real name for herself. They were all staying on the top floor of the Keep and their rehearsals in the library filled the courtyard with music.

With all the extra bustle about the place, the atmosphere should have been lighter, more vibrant. But to Rayne it was as dark as ever, like the dark weight that seemed to be inside her so much of the time.

And then something happened that broke everything apart.

*

It started as an ordinary day, an ordinary Thursday. The weather was terrible. Rain was sheeting down, blowing in great gusts against the Old Sty. Rayne, as usual, had to wake Tara, who would sleep till noon if you let her. She made her a cup of tea, went through into her room, put the mug down beside her bed, and drew the curtains back at the windows.

"Oh God, Rayne, *don't*," groaned Tara. "It's the middle of the *night*!"

"It's not. Clue – it's light outside. It's eight o'clock. Here's your tea."

"You're an angel," muttered Tara, rolling over.

"Come on, or you'll have your aunt round here. Don't you remember what you've got to do today?"

"Wuuuurgh. Yes. Get the spooky state bedrooms ready."

"Got it in one. And *I've* got to work twice as hard in the tearoom cos your aunt won't give Becky a call."

Miss Skelton had been very firm on the matter. The special overnight packages for the concert had all been taken up, but she still insisted they could manage with no extra help from Becky or her mum. Tara and she would prepare the bedrooms, she said, and they'd just have to cope in the tearoom.

"She's just thinking of the bank balance," yawned Tara, propping herself up on an elbow and taking a sip of tea.

"Have you ever been in those bedrooms?" asked Rayne.

"Yes," she mumbled. "No big deal."

"Rather you than me. They're creepy."

"Not in the day."

"Well, they're certainly *worse* at night. I just hope the people who've booked them know what they're letting themselves in for."

"Like Aunt Louisa says, they're people who get off on that kind of thing. Maybe the four posters'll see a bit of action."

"*Gross*," said Rayne, grimacing. Then she hurried off to get dressed for work.

When Rayne walked through the door to the tearoom, she knew immediately that something had happened. Ben, who never usually put a foot inside for fear of trekking mud on the floor, was heading out, face grim. Mrs Driver was seated at one of the tables, her head in her hands, a cup of tea in front of her.

"What's up?" Rayne asked.

"She'll tell you," Ben muttered, as he passed by her.

"Tell me what?" asked Rayne – but he'd already gone through the door.

She hurried towards the elderly housekeeper. "Mrs Driver?" she called, anxiously. "Mrs Driver, what's wrong?"

Mrs Driver looked up, her face pudgy with shock and grief. "Oh, Rayne," she muttered. "Dear, it's you."

Rayne pulled out a chair and sat beside her. She wanted to put her arm round her, but somehow that didn't feel right. "What is it?" she said. "What's happened?"

"There's been . . . there's been a murder," Mrs Driver sobbed out. "Oh, dear me, I – I still can't take it in. A girl. A girl's body was found. She was lying . . . she was lying at the bottom of the Devil's Tankard."

Chapter
Twenty-two

The air in the tearoom seemed to shake. *The Devil's Tankard*, Rayne thought, horrified. *A girl's body*. In her mind she saw an image of the fire boys lined up round the edge of the pit, hollering and laughing and throwing their staffs into it, like spears.

"A dog found her," Mrs Driver said, her hand trembling as she lifted her cup of tea to her lips. "It was an old friend of Ben's, Martin Rochdale, out walking his dog on the hills. The dog went crazy, Martin said, racing round the edge of the pit and barking. He said he stared down and at first all he could see was the remains of the bonfire they'd had there, on the fire festival night. But then he noticed something white sticking out – it just didn't look right to him, he said. So he and his dog went down to investigate." The teacup clattered as she returned it to its saucer. "It was the poor girl's foot. Martin's still in shock about it. He said he kept slipping back as he tried to climb out of the Tankard, he was in such a state. And who can blame him."

"Who is it?" whispered Rayne. "Who's the girl?"

"We don't know. Martin got to the top and phoned the

police on his mobile, right away. They're local bobbies, they know everyone hereabouts, they didn't recognize her."

"Was she . . . how badly. . ." Rayne took in a deep breath. "How had she been killed?"

"Her throat had been cut, they said. Like a goat, like an animal. She was clothed, no sign of . . . you know."

"Rape."

"They don't think so. Just this terrible, slit throat."

"Who – do they have any idea *who*. . ."

"None at all, from what Ben told me. But they've called in all the fire festival people for questioning."

"The *fire* people?"

"Well, it was their place, she was found in the remains of their bonfire. They've got to start somewhere, I suppose."

There was a long silence. Rayne thought about Ethan being hauled in for questioning about the murder of the strange girl. Then the old housekeeper sighed and sat up straighter, smoothing her greying hair back with the palms of her hands. "We've got to open up, dear, tragedy or no tragedy," she said. "Get the scones made up and in the oven, will you? The first coach load has already arrived."

The rest of the morning and lunch time disappeared under sheer hard work, with only the two of them to cope. At around three, there was a lull, and it looked as though they'd served the last of the visitors. Rayne's mobile sounded just as she was closing the dishwasher on a full load.

"Rayne!" cooed Miss Skelton into her ear. "Can you bring a tray of tea and some nice cakey goodies up to the Spanish room, please? I feel we've earned a break. Bring a cup for yourself too, OK?" Then before Rayne had a chance to say anything, she rang off.

Mrs Driver was stony-faced when Rayne told her what she'd been asked to do, but she put three coconut cakes and three scones on a large plate printed with ivy leaves and handed it to her.

"Will you be all right on your own?" Rayne asked. "I feel mean, leaving you to close up. . ."

"Off you go, dear," said Mrs Driver, firmly. "Don't let the boss's tea get cold."

As Rayne climbed the wide, wooden stairs of the grand staircase, she heard laughter. Shrill, happy laughter, coming from the Spanish room. *They haven't heard the news yet*, she thought. She trudged on with her tray. The door to the Spanish room was ajar; she pushed it open with her foot, and went in.

Miss Skelton was perched, legs elegantly crossed, on the end of the great four-poster bed with its shroud-like hangings. Tara was sprawled in a low velvet-covered chair, opposite her. Both had smiles on their faces.

"Rayne!" Miss Skelton cried. "Lovely, darling – put the tea over there, on the table."

Rayne put the tray down beside a large vase of hothouse yellow roses. "Don't you think the room's *sparkling?*" demanded Tara.

Rayne looked around. The ancient, tooled Spanish

leather covering its walls still looked repulsive to her, like the skin of a rotting lizard. "It's great," she lied.

"*I* had to do all the work," Tara went on, "while my aunt swanned around doing tours."

"Tara, you wee brat! *You* got to take a break whenever I led the tour into one of the rooms you were making up. *I* didn't get a break at all. Now pour the tea out, there's an angel. I'm parched."

"I'll do it," said Rayne. "Don't move." It seemed a shame to have to tell them the awful news. They were so pleased with themselves, with the hard work they'd put in.

"We thought of coming down to the tearoom," Miss Skelton said, "but we knew Mrs Driver would be in full mourning mode. We thought it would be more fun up here."

Rayne, carrying a cup of tea and the ivy plate towards her, stopped dead. "You've *heard*?" she exclaimed.

"About the murder?" said Miss Skelton, accepting the tea and lifting a coconut cake straight to her mouth. "Harry told us."

"He kept on giving us bulletins throughout the day," Tara said. "Discreetly, so the visitors wouldn't hear."

"Although they'd probably have loved it," added Miss Skelton. "A murder, on the outskirts of Marcle Lees! Exciting stuff."

Wordlessly, Rayne went back to the tray, picked up Tara's cup, and took it over to her with the ivy plate.

"So tell me, is our worthy housekeeper devastated?" asked Miss Skelton.

"Yes," said Rayne. "She's really upset."

Tara peered at Rayne as she handed her her cup.

"You think we're awful, don't you?" she demanded. "We don't mean it. It's . . . it's kind of hysteria. It's all been . . . *surreal*!"

"You said Mr Stuart was giving you updates," Rayne said, stiffly. "Do they know who . . . the victim . . . is yet?"

"They do," said Miss Skelton, mouth full of cake. "I've forgotten her name, but she was some kind of druggie, on the run from home – she'd been living rough for several weeks."

Rayne wanted to snap out *So that makes killing her OK, does it?* but she stopped herself.

"They've hauled in all the fire festival weirdos for questioning," Miss Skelton went on. "Let's hope they pin it on one of them, fast, and don't feel the need to overrun this place."

"Aunt *Louisa*!" cried Tara, her eyes on Rayne's face. "You really are the limit – don't be so *callous*!"

"Sorry!" Miss Skelton cried. "But we've done so much work for this concert – I don't want it ruined by police investigations! Och, *look* –" she turned to Rayne – "*ignore* me. I'm so tired I'm raving. Of course it's dreadful. But it's bound to hit Mrs Driver harder – she's from round here."

"Aren't you going to sit down, Rayne?" said Tara. "Go on – have a break."

Rayne, who'd been thinking about just walking out, took her tea and a scone and sat down at the table by the yellow roses. They gave off a sultry, slightly sickly, scent.

"Rayne, do you think it was one of the fire people?" asked Tara.

"No," said Rayne, flatly. "I know it wasn't."

"Oh, come on, sweetheart," said Miss Skelton, "you can't *know* that – nobody can. You can't *know* your own *child* isn't a murderer. Not absolutely."

There was a silence. Rain lashed against the windows. The ancient leather hangings lowered down at them; the four-poster bed was gloomy with shadows. But no one got up to turn a lamp on.

"Let's change the subject," said Tara, curling her legs up beneath her on the velvet chair. "It's all too grisly. Let's talk about the concert. Do you want us to wear our dresses again?"

"Of course," said Miss Skelton. "You both looked so wonderful at the dinner."

"What do we do? Apart from show people to their seats?"

"Oh, hand out the programmes – be *charming*! And then in the interval, hand round drinks and refreshments. . ."

"Oh, goody – food. What's it going to be?"

"Lovely sophisticated wee canapés," cooed Miss Skelton. She leaned forward; her black hair brushed past the bed drapes. "Caviar, smoked salmon on blinis, asparagus rolls – nothing naff."

"You think Mrs Driver and her ladies are up to all that?"

"Probably not. I may well order them in."

Rayne stared at the profiles of the two women as they talked together. The shadows in the room made their noses and cheekbones sharp. Abruptly she stood up, and said she had to go.

Miss Skelton turned to look at her. "Goodbye," she said. The single word seemed to hang in the air, like breath in the cold.

Chapter
Twenty-three

Rayne was halfway down the grand staircase when her mobile went. She stopped and pulled it out of her pocket, expecting another command from Miss Skelton, then with a kind of excited panic saw that it was Ethan calling her. "Hello?" she said.

"Hi, Rayne." His voice sounded loud in the dark vault of the Great Hall. "Just to let you know they haven't arrested me."

"Have they arrested anyone?"

"No. Were you expecting them to?"

"No, of course not."

"Where are you?"

She paused. "Why?"

"I'm outside the Sty. I need to see you."

"Why?" she said again, and her blood was racing.

"I found something out. We need to talk."

"I'm just at the house," she said, and hurried down the last few stairs. "I'll be there in a minute."

He rang off.

*

When Rayne got to the narrow stone steps that led down into the medieval garden, Ethan was waiting there, sheltering from the rain under a stubby tree. "Thought I'd come and meet you," he said. "Seeing as there's a murderer on the loose." He was trying to sound flippant, but his eyes were tense.

"*Don't!*" exclaimed Rayne. "Oh, God, I hadn't thought of that."

They started walking towards the Sty. "Sorry," he said, "I didn't mean to scare you. But the police were talking about issuing a warning. To women and girls – not to go out alone after dark. Till they've caught him. *It.*"

"Great," she muttered. "*Brilliant.*"

"Yeah. As if it isn't scary enough here, right?"

"At least I'm not alone at night now."

She wasn't prepared for the effect her words had on Ethan. He stopped dead, said, "*What?*"

"Miss Skelton's niece," she said. "She's working here now – she's moved in."

"Oh," he said, and walked on faster, so she couldn't see his face. They reached the door; she unlocked it and they went in. If Ethan remembered the last time he'd been in her room, when he'd tried to kiss her and it had turned out so disastrously, he didn't show it. Without being asked he sat down at the table and looked at her, steadily.

"Was that what you came to tell me?" she asked. "That the police are issuing a warning?"

"No. Look – why didn't you tell me about the birds being killed?"

She dipped her head, embarrassed. "I don't know. It just seemed so horrible. . ."

"It is. You're still feeding them, though, right?"

"Of course I am. It's creepy, though – Ben's put a padlock on the tower door. . ."

"It's just as well. Especially now this murder has happened."

She took a sharp breath. "You think they're connected?"

"I don't know. How can I know?"

There was a silence. Fear was in the room with them, skirting round the edges, in the dark corners, in the unsaid things.

"Look, are you going to sit down?" he said, abruptly. "Or are you just going to stand there?"

She slid into the chair opposite him. There was still enough light through the window for them to see each other's face, but only just. He crossed his arms, looked down at the table. "My cousin's in the police force. I got hold of him afterwards, after they'd questioned me. I wanted to find out. . ." He took in a breath. "You know the girl's throat was cut."

"Yes," Rayne breathed. "Horrible."

"There was something else."

"Oh, God. Mrs Driver said she hadn't been . . . she said it was just the throat."

"It was. I mean – it was the throat that did for her, and there weren't any other signs of mutilation, except when they did the autopsy they found that some of the blood round her mouth . . . *came* from her mouth."

Rayne's hands shot to her own mouth. In an instant,

she was back there. Back in Sir Simeon Lingwall's cellar with St John crowing and his band of slavish followers, Flora and Petra and Marcus, all around him . . . and Amelia whimpering in terror, her mouth drooling blood.

"There were two little cuts to her mouth," Ethan went on, grimly, "and a tiny stab wound on her right arm. Made by something short and sharp, my cousin said. Like a dagger."

Rayne was still in the cellar. She saw St John with Lingwall's dagger in his hand, saw it glinting. . . "Cruelty is beautiful," she muttered.

Ethan leant towards her across the table. "Rayne – when we burnt out the cellar . . . when I knocked St John down. . ."

"The dagger shot across the floor. I saw it."

"Did you see where it went?"

"It burnt. It must have burnt."

"Flora . . . she could've picked it up. She could've picked it up and hidden it in her clothes, in a pocket, before she got out."

"No. They were all, like . . . mesmerized. Her, Marcus, Petra – they didn't move."

"*How can you be sure?* I was kicking that burning chest up against the roof strut. You and Ben were heaving that old table on to the fire. We were busy building a *fire*. She could've just ducked down, scooped it up."

There was a long silence. Then Rayne said, "Yes. I s'pose she could."

"Flora's still with him. I saw them together the other day, in town. He looked – he looked kind of done in, like he was ill or something. But they were wound round each other, as close as ever." Abruptly, Ethan pushed his chair back from the table, stood up, and glared at her. "If your Mr Stuart wasn't so keen on hushing up what happened that night in the cellar," he said, "we could put the finger on St John. Get the police to take DNA swabs from him, like they did from us."

"But *why* would he murder a complete stranger? Far away from the Keep?"

"I've no idea. I'm going to see him – try and find out."

"What? *Now?*"

"Yes."

"He lives miles away!"

"I can take the old man's car. He doesn't like it cos I've only just passed my test, but he's out at the pub tonight and when he goes there he always leaves his keys on the dresser. . ." Suddenly he spun round, and stared wide-eyed at the curtains that screened the narrow kitchen from Rayne's room. "What was that?" he breathed.

Rayne, listening, heard a scraping, shuffling, slithering noise. She felt cold at the sound of it.

Then she suddenly laughed, shot to her feet, and ran through the kitchen, Ethan following.

Tara was squeezing herself through the back window, head and shoulders first. Her arms were stretching long, fingers splayed, trying to make contact with the block of wood on the floor. She looked weird, like a pale witch diving into another dimension.

"Want some help, Tara?" Rayne asked. Her voice was brisk; she was trying to shake off the spasm of fear she'd felt at the sight of her. "Are you stuck?"

For answer Tara gave another shunt forward on her stomach and her hands reached the wood; then she pulled her legs up and clambered through. "Not the most elegant of entrances!" she announced, grinning.

"You should've come in through the door!" said Rayne.

"Oh, I saw you had a *visitor*," purred Tara, her eyes slewing sideways to Ethan. "Didn't want to interrupt." She forked her long white-blonde hair back from her face with her fingers, then smoothed down her clothes, passing her hands slowly down her thin body, eyes still on Ethan.

"Tara, this is Ethan," Rayne said, "one of the. . ." She broke off. She didn't want to tell her he was one of the fire boys, not after what had happened that day. "Ethan, this is Tara, Miss Skelton's niece."

"Pleased to meet you," said Ethan, not sounding in the least pleased. "Rayne, I gotta go."

And Rayne took in a deep breath and said, "I'll come with you."

Chapter Twenty-four

"You don't have to come," Ethan insisted, as they hurried down the drive in the dusk. "I would've thought *St John* was the last person you'd want to see again."

"He is," she panted, "that's why I've got to see him."

"Great logic, Rayne."

"I want to face him, face him *down*, prove to myself he hasn't got any power over me any more. . ."

"Right."

And I want to be with you, she thought, as she cried, "*Jesus*, Ethan, can't you slow down a bit?"

"Sorry," said Ethan, slowing so little she barely noticed it.

"I think two is better than one, don't you?" she went on. "Kind of – present a united front and also – just spot if he's lying. Pick up on stuff. You know."

"Female intuition?"

"Maybe."

They reached the great entrance gates, and turned left on to the track beside the road. "How long was that girl there for, outside?" he suddenly asked. "How long was she listening for?"

"What, Tara? I don't suppose she was listening at all. Too busy squirming in through the window."

He let out a short laugh. "I'm getting freaked. Suspecting everyone."

"Well, I wouldn't worry. Tara wouldn't know what you were talking about, even if she had heard. She's kind of – oblivious."

"Ah," said Ethan, and they sped on.

Before long they reached the grey outbuildings on the edge of Ethan's family's farm. Rayne was surprised by how close it was to Morton's Keep. "Wait here," he ordered. "I'll bring the car round." She stopped and watched him as he ran towards the farmhouse and disappeared inside, ignoring a couple of collie dogs who bounded out to greet him. Then she heard a car growl into life from the other side of the house and soon an old Land Rover was careering across the ground towards her, headlights glaring. It came to a grating stop beside her and she opened the passenger door and jumped in.

Ethan ground the gears hideously as he drew away again. "You sure you can drive this?" Rayne said.

"Yes. Belt up."

"*Don't you tell me—!*"

"Put your seat belt on!"

"Oh. Right." They turned out of the farm gates and on to the road.

It only took ten minutes to drive to the other side of Marcle Lees. "This is his road," muttered Ethan, as he swerved left, cutting the corner. "He's down at the end. His house has got some of those phony stone columns out the front . . . there it is." He stopped the Land Rover by the wide kerb, a bit jerkily, and killed the engine.

St John's house said *money*. It was new, built to impress, with grand, wrought-iron railings. Soft spotlights illuminated statuesque shrubs and the wide, curved drive up to the columned porch. A sharp black sports car was parked halfway out of a double garage alongside the house. "Are you just going to knock?" Rayne asked nervously.

"Yeah, what else can I do? It's good you came, actually. Looks more like a friendly visit."

Together, they crunched up the drive and Ethan pushed the expensive brass doorbell. There was a few moments' silence, then the door was wrenched open. A tall woman in a business suit held her left hand, palm out, towards them; in her other hand was a mobile, clenched to her ear. "I'm on my way," she said. "Tell Greg it's booked for seven. These are important clients, Sally. If he screws up *again*. . . No. . . No, OK. . . Right. . . Right. See you."

Then she lowered both hands and rapped out, "Yes?"

Ethan smiled winningly. "Mrs Arlington?" he said. "We were just wondering if St John was in?"

"Oh *God* – has he turned his phone off again? I'm surprised he's got any friends left. . . Oh, you are sweet to visit him! I've got to dash, but—"

"That's fine," smiled Ethan, taking hold of Rayne's arm and stepping into the hall. "We'll go on up, shall we?"

"Bless you. You know where his room is, don't you?"

"Yes . . . first door. . ."

"On the right. That's right. Try and talk some sense into him. Well – bye!" Then, pulling out her mobile again, she shot past them and slammed the front door shut behind her. They heard a car start up, and roar off.

Rayne and Ethan were alone in the cream-coloured hall. "Have you been here before?" Rayne hissed.

"No."

"So how did you know his room. . .?"

"*Male* intuition."

"Oh, *what*?"

"OK, I guessed. If I'd got it wrong she'd just've corrected me, wouldn't she? She was so keen for him to have someone visit."

"What's going on with him?"

"Let's find out. You sure you want to do this?"

"Yes. But you do the talking."

"OK. Come on – let's go up to his . . . *lair*."

They climbed the stairs with their deep-pile cream carpet, and stopped outside the first door on the right. "You knock," Ethan said, quietly.

Rayne took in a breath, and rapped softly, three times, on the glossy wood.

"Flora?"

It was St John's voice, unmistakably his, but it sounded weak, complaining.

Ethan took hold of the door handle, turned it, and pushed the door open. Then he stepped smartly into the room, Rayne following, and pushed the door shut behind them.

The room was in darkness apart from a small bedside

light. St John was lying on the bed, arms behind his head. Rayne felt her stomach seize with revulsion at the sight of him; anger pulsed inside her.

St John sat straight up, his handsome face contracted with suspicion. "What the hell—?" he snarled. "How the *hell* did *you* get in?"

"Your mum let us in," said Ethan. "She's just gone out. She was pretty pleased we'd come to see you, St John. Haven't you been well? We'd've brought *flowers*."

"What are you here for?" St John said, swinging his legs off the other side of the bed and standing up. He was silhouetted against the dark window now; it was hard to read his face. The bed with its dark purple duvet was a barrier between them.

"Have you heard about the murder?" Ethan rapped out.

"Some scrubber with her throat slashed? Yes – it was on the radio." His teeth gleamed in the half-light – he was smiling. "She was found on one of *your* special sites, wasn't she?"

"What else d'you know about it?"

"Not much. Why should I? It's *you* lot who are under suspicion."

"How d'you know that? That wasn't on the radio."

"Oh, *Ethan*. You aren't the only one with contacts in the police force."

There was a silence. Rayne was standing half behind Ethan; she could sense his tension, his suspicion. And she could feel St John's eyes on her, seeking her out.

"Have you been up to the house again?" demanded Ethan. "Up to Morton's Keep?"

"No."

"In the grounds? To the tower dovecote?"

"No. Ask my mother, I hardly ever go out. She can provide me with an alibi for anything you're trying to pin on me. I only see Flora. I've been missing school. My mother's quite worried about me. When she thinks about it."

"Hit you hard, did it?" said Ethan, loudly. "What happened in the dungeon?"

"Very hard." The teeth gleamed again. "But I'm getting over it. And now I'm tired of you firing questions at me. You should go."

Ethan took a step closer to the purple bed. "You know it's over, don't you?" he said. "Lingwall, your inheritance, all that shit you were spouting in the dungeon? It's over."

"Oh, yes. Like you, I'm sure he's all been burnt away," said St John.

And then he laughed.

It was a horrible noise in the dark room. It made the skin on Rayne's spine crawl with loathing, and fear. "Let's go," she whispered.

"Eager to go, are you, sweetheart?" said St John. "Well, it was lovely to see you again. Till next time, ay?"

Chapter Twenty-five

Rayne and Ethan didn't talk until he'd parked by the ivy-choked fountain in front of Morton's Keep. "Are you OK?" said Ethan, quietly.

"Yes. No. I wish we'd left him to burn."

"*Rayne. . .!*"

"Sorry. D'you still think he's got something to do with the murder?"

"I don't know," muttered Ethan.

"He was pretty clear about never going out, and his mum being an alibi."

"Except – to judge by this evening – she's out a lot herself."

"Yeah, but you saw him – he's like an invalid, the way he moves."

"What was it he said? *Like you, I'm sure Lingwall's all been burnt away.* Except the way he said it – he didn't mean it. Not the way he laughed afterwards."

Rayne looked out at the ancient walls and towers, and shivered, remembering St John's laugh. Remembering the way he'd called her "sweetheart".

"He was so sarcastic," Ethan went on. "Kind of . . . smug. Maybe he knows it hasn't all been burnt away. If he's got the dagger. . ."

"Oh, so what if he has?" snapped Rayne, as fear beat away inside her. "It's not *magic*, Ethan, it's not some bloody thing with magic powers like in a film or something. . . Look. He wasn't the one who killed that girl, or the pigeons. He's just not *up* to it. I'm sure of it."

"OK," said Ethan, shortly. "D'you want me to see you back? Only I ought to get the Land Rover home, if my dad sees it's gone he'll go on at me and. . ."

"I'm fine," said Rayne. She felt hurt that he wanted to get away so fast. It was all about the fire men and Morton's Keep, she thought, bitterly – it wasn't about her at all. She pulled open the car door and jumped out and the sound of them saying goodbye was drowned out by her slamming it shut again.

When Rayne walked into the Old Sty, she smelt a delicious savoury smell and realized how hungry she was. "Hey, you!" called Tara, from the kitchen. "Hungry?"

"Starving!"

"Sit down, then. I'll dish it up."

Tara had made a casserole. Beef, onions, potatoes, carrots and leeks, all in a wonderful rich gravy. She plonked it down on a mat on the table, fetched plates and cutlery, and served Rayne up a generous portion.

"You're a star, Tara," said Rayne, mouth already full. There's nothing spooky about Tara, she thought. It's just me getting freaked out by everything. I've got to *calm down*.

"Wasn't sure you'd be coming back," purred Tara, "thought you might be eating out with your *man*."

"No chance," said Rayne. "And he isn't my man."

"Oh, that's a shame. For you, anyway – maybe it's quite good for the rest of us girls, ay? He's gorgeous. Really fit. Is he local?"

"Very. He's one of the fire boys." It was out before Rayne could check herself and then she thought – *oh, what the hell*.

"My God, is he?" exclaimed Tara. "So he'll have been dragged in by the police, then?"

"Yes. No charges, of course."

"No. I heard from Mrs Driver – the police are widening the search now. They think someone from outside Marcle Lees did it."

"Aren't there any clues or leads or anything?"

"Don't think so. Not that they'd say, would they? Hey – have some more." And she loaded another spoonful on to Rayne's plate.

"Thanks, Tara. This is seriously delicious. Oh, I feel so much better for this."

"Course you do. You've got to *eat*, girl. So tell me – why isn't Ethan your man?"

"Urrrgh. Well, for a start, there's someone else he likes – Sarah."

"So kill her."

Rayne laughed. "Haven't got the energy. It's . . . complicated." *Understatement of the century*, she thought. She and Ethan were caught up together in this weird *thing* that sometimes seemed momentous, sometimes seemed so vague and unreal you could barely *think* about it, let alone talk about it. . .

"What do the fire people think?" asked Tara. "About who did the murder?"

"They've no idea either," said Rayne.

"Not even an inkling? What have they been saying?"

"Nothing." She glanced at Tara suspiciously. "Why d'you think they'd know anything? Do *you* think they're involved?"

"No. Let's change the subject. Let's have pudding. I bought chocolate."

"Brilliant. Tara – are you nervous?"

"What, of the murderer? Nah. I'm safe here with you!"

Now that the police search had gone further afield, preparations for the concerts that weekend took centre stage. The five musicians who'd taken over the top floor of the Keep continued their rehearsals in the library; their strange, haunting music permeated the mansion house and filtered out through the windows. Occasionally Rayne would see one of them crossing the forecourt, climbing the grand stairway, but they didn't acknowledge her.

"They're so *absorbed* in what they're doing!" Miss Skelton gushed. "Fifty per cent of the programme is completely new material – *they've* created it, together. We've got two music journalists coming on Saturday night – another critic, I hope, on Friday . . . this could be another string to Morton's Keep's bow! We could be part of the innovative folk music scene!"

Mrs Driver remained solidly unimpressed by it all.

Miss Skelton had costed outside caterers for the concert canapés – then ended up asking the housekeeper to provide them after all, despite the fact that the Keep was opening its doors to visitors for the first time that Saturday. The atmosphere was grim.

On the morning of the first concert Becky came running into the tearoom. She blanked Rayne completely and called out, "Where d'you want the mini quiches, Mrs D? Here or the Tudor kitchen?"

"Oh, the kitchen, dear, definitely. Have they worked?"

"They're fantastic. Fancy as hell. Even *she* won't be able to complain."

"Wonderful. Where's your mother parked?"

"On the forecourt."

"Take the trays across the courtyard, Becky, it'll be quicker. Rayne – here's my keys. Go and unlock the door, will you, dear? And give her a hand?"

Becky spun round and headed at speed out of the tearoom. Rayne, following, realized she'd have to break into a run to catch up with her, and decided not to bother. Becky pulled open the back door of the car, pulled out a foil-covered tray, and handed it back to Rayne without looking at her; then she took the two other trays herself, one on each arm. Becky's mum didn't say hello to Rayne; she didn't so much as turn her head.

As the girls crossed under the great archway, Rayne erupted. "What d'you want me to *do*, Becky? Hand in my resignation? You're still making *quiches* for Miss Skelton!"

Becky turned to face her, agog with indignation. "*Mum

might be. I haven't been employed since her *niece* got here!"

"I know! I texted you to say I'd had a *go* at her about it!"

"Didn't do much good, though, did it?"

"Oh, Becky, that's not fair. *You* know what she's like. Look – I know it's shit, but it's not my fault!"

"Maybe not, but now you're sharing *rooms* with Tara!"

"I had no choice. She got moved in."

"Well, you had a choice on whether you went into town with her! Sarah said she saw you, all cosied up, shopping! And you were seen in The Goat with her, on Saturday night!"

"Oh, God, what *is* this? Some kind of spy network? Look – I can't stand being treated as a traitor just cos I'm prepared to give Miss Skelton and her niece a *chance*! I've got to get *on* with them, haven't I? I can't just walk out – I've got nowhere else to go!"

Becky snorted, and stamped on ahead again. "Open the *door*, will you?" she snapped.

Balancing her tray on one arm, Rayne went up to the church-like door. The brass knocker, which had been made over two hundred years ago from a cast of Sir Simeon Lingwall's hand, glinted menacingly. She had the sudden thought that there was something different about it, and that unnerved her, but she couldn't think what it was. She pushed the key hurriedly into the lock, and shoved the door open.

Becky pushed past her and flounced along the stone-flagged corridor to the Tudor kitchen. In the utility room she efficiently made room for all three trays in the giant fridge. "Look, I don't like what's happening here any more than you do!" Rayne said, as Becky slammed the fridge door shut. "The atmosphere's awful, especially after that dreadful murder. And actually, Becky – don't you think the *murder* has put all the other stuff into perspective?"

Becky folded her arms, and looked down at the floor, chastened. "I know," she said. "It's awful. Everyone's talking about it. All the parents have got together, they're always on about it – they give us lifts everywhere now, it's awful."

"Well, it shows they *care*."

"Yeah, but it doesn't half cramp your style," Becky said, and she pulled such a comical face that Rayne laughed.

"Oh, *Becky* – I wish you were still working here – I miss you! I *know* it's bad you're not working here any more. But your mum is, still—"

"For *now*," said Becky. "She says Skeleton's a real cow to her. Acts like she wants her to leave."

"Oh, I'm sure that's not true. And maybe if things keep on improving like this, they'll need you as well as Tara!"

"I'm not bothered." Becky shrugged. "I'm in Ciara's Clothes on Saturdays now."

"Are you? I love that shop! D'you get a discount?"

"Twenty per cent. Like this skirt?"

"It's fantastic. It really suits you."

Becky looked down at the floor again. "I was more bothered about you dropping me for Tara than the job," she mumbled. "I thought we were friends."

"We *are* friends! It was *you* who didn't reply to my text, Becky!"

Becky smiled. "I know. I'm sorry. Look – I'd better go before Mum starts blaring her horn. Just tell me one thing." Her eyes gleamed. "Are they sleeping together?"

"What, the bosses? I don't know. Probably. Mr Stuart seems pretty smitten."

"Mum says they are. She saw Skeleton coming out of his bedroom. She says she's absolutely turned his head, and she's making all the decisions now. Oh, Christ – I'd better *go*!"

"OK, *go* – I'll lock up behind you." Becky hurried out of the door and Rayne called after her, "Hey – if I hear any solid gossip, I'll give you a ring, yeah?"

"You do that!" Becky called back. "Let's get together soon!"

Rayne felt more cheerful as she headed out into the courtyard again. She felt like Becky was her friend again. Somehow to have her as a mate was really important.

She tried not to look at the severed hand as she locked the door behind her, but it drew her eye like a compulsion. Why don't they get *rid* of it? she thought.

And then it hit her, what had changed about it. Before, most of the hand was unpolished, black, and only the fingers and the strange, jagged-looking ring had shone.

Now all of it shone. Eerily, powerfully, in the thin winter light.

Chapter
Twenty-six

It was Friday night, the night of the first concert. The overnight guests had arrived during the late afternoon and been shown to their imposing bedrooms, and now they and the rest of the audience were sitting in the library in five rows in an elegant, uneven semicircle round the grand piano. Great vases of hothouse flowers ravished the air with their scent. The log fire and the candles on the diamond-shaped mirrors were alight; the glass teardrops cascading down scintillated against the oak panelling.

The musicians were on their second song and already the audience was rapt, captured.

Rayne and Tara, in their dark and light Gothic dresses, had gathered compliments and admiring glances as they took the coats and showed everyone to their seats. Then they'd lined up champagne flutes and canapés on the long side table in the Great Hall, ready to be carried through in the interval. The evening was on full course to be another triumph for Miss Skelton.

After the fifth song, as arranged, the girls slipped out from the library to collect the ice buckets of champagne from the kitchen. They were halfway down the narrow corridor when they stopped dead in their tracks and gazed at each other wide-eyed, listening.

Some kind of fight had broken out in the library.

"Don't be *absurd*!" a woman was shrieking. "Don't act as if I'm the one causing the fuss – *he's* the one causing the fuss, pushing past everyone like that!"

"Come on!" breathed Tara, and the two of them scurried back to the library. A singular scene met them as they looked round the door. Miss Skelton and Mr Stuart were standing in front of a red-faced, gesticulating woman, trying to calm her. The musicians had stopped playing; everyone had twisted round in their seats, staring, glaring.

"I *won't* be sworn at, when I'm not the one at fault!" the woman ranted.

"Please, madam," murmured Miss Skelton, soothingly, "no one swore at you."

"*He* did!" She pointed at a man in the second row.

The man got to his feet. "I apologize," he said. "But I was enjoying the music, and your sudden – *outburst* – quite ruined it for me."

"But – that man just *pushed* past me – I thought he was going to hit me in the face, the way he was waving his arms about. . ."

"*What* man?" asked Mr Stuart.

"There you go again, *what* man? For Christ's sake – didn't anyone else see him?"

"I did," called out a fey-looking young woman in the front row. "I saw him go out. He was in costume . . . period costume . . . he must be employed here, surely?"

Mr Stuart hit his head with his hand, and let out a bark of laughter. Then he drew himself up to his full height, and said loudly, "Ladies and gentlemen, I think what this dear lady has just experienced is the ghost that haunts the library!"

Loud exclamations – of excitement, horror, disbelief – filled the room. Mr Stuart turned back to the red-faced woman. "Madam, tell me – was he in dark clothing? Was he thin?"

"Yes," she croaked, and she sank back, dazed, into her seat. "Very thin. And he was wearing a fancy sort of jacket. He looked a bit . . . literary. But he was no ghost, he was *real*—"

"Oh, he's real all right. But he's also a ghost." He turned back to the room. "It's Sir Philip Musgrave, ladies and gentlemen. He died in 1682!"

"Oh, how *thrilling*!" gasped Miss Skelton, theatrically, clasping her hands prettily to her chin. "He *came*!"

"Yes, he likes to come to our concerts in the library," Mr Stuart went on, proudly. "He sits at the back – he's fond of string quartets. I've never heard of him *leaving* before, although they do say he's less keen on singing. . ."

"I'd say that's an understatement," said the fey young woman at the front. "He looked really upset to me. I thought he was ill. He was stumbling."

"*Really* distressed," added the red-faced woman. "Actually, I thought he was angry. That's why I reacted the way I did. When he nearly hit me with his arm."

The room filled with excited conversation once more. Mr Stuart, though, was silent. He gazed, frowning, at the carpet.

Miss Skelton shot him an impatient look, then she swept forward through the lines of chairs and stood in front of the musicians. "Ladies and gentlemen!" she cried, clapping her red-nailed hands twice. "I do apologize on behalf of our . . . *ghost* . . . for the interruption to the concert! But I hope you feel – as I do – that the experience has been an absolute thrill and worth the inconvenience!"

The noise level rose again, and now some of the audience were smiling and laughing, and one man had switched on his phone and was eagerly calling someone.

"Perhaps Sir Philip Musgrave just feels it's time for a wee dram!" Miss Skelton went on, gaily. "Perhaps you agree with him!" She turned towards Rayne and Tara and nodded, pointedly. "Let's have the interval now, and resume the concert afterwards. Many thanks, ladies and gentleman!"

"Oh my *Go-od*!" squealed Tara as she raced down the narrow corridor after Rayne. "Was that for *real*?"

Rayne stopped in front of the portrait of Sir Philip Musgrave. He looked just the same: alert, and knowing. "I had this thought once," she breathed, "that the frame would be empty when his ghost walked."

"Oh, for *Christ's* sake!" Tara laughed, giving her a shove. "Get *going*!" They ran down to the Tudor kitchen and grabbed the four heavy ice buckets from the huge fridge.

"I can't believe you believe in crappy *ghosts*," Tara said, as they headed back, more slowly this time, dripping freezing water on the flagstones.

"OK, what was it then?" Rayne retorted. "*Two* people say they saw him!"

"Hysteria. It's infectious, you know. Or – you know what? Aunt Louisa slipped both those women a tenner to do it. To say they'd seen him. That'd be just like her. She *staged* it."

While Tara was handing round the champagne, Rayne hurried out to the Great Hall again to fetch the canapés. The fey young woman was waiting for her there, standing on the bottom step of the grand staircase. "I was looking for my coat," she said, agitatedly. "Where did you put my coat?"

"Oh, are you going?" Rayne asked. Her voice sounded high, thin, in the cavernous hall. "What's the matter – don't you feel well?"

"It was seeing . . . it was the ghost. It's . . . it's really disturbed me."

Rayne felt something cold trace up her spine.

"It wasn't that it was a *ghost*," the woman went on, wringing her hands. "I've seen ghosts before, I'm susceptible. I *like* being susceptible. Usually. But this was . . . I can't forget the look on his face. It was . . . it was *dread*. I thought he was ill or something at the time – but his face keeps coming back to me and it was *dread* that I saw on his face, absolute dread and horror. And now it's making *me* feel that way too. I've got to go, I've got to go! *Please* – get my coat for me, will you?"

Chapter
Twenty-seven

Early on Saturday morning, Miss Skelton posted the sighting of Sir Philip Musgrave up on Morton Keep's new website. Then she placed an old leather-bound book on the chair that the ghost had supposedly sat in, to keep it for him for that night. Anyone who phoned Morton's Keep that day got told the story. She wanted word to get round.

Rayne had the opposite instinct. She didn't even want to think about the ghost – or more particularly, about what the fey young woman had said, about how it had made her feel. She threw herself into her work. Breakfast had to be got for last night's guests, then the rooms made up again for the new guests. Then she manned the busy tearoom with Tara, while Mrs Driver and Becky's mum prepared a fresh batch of canapés.

Miss Skelton told the girls that they shouldn't have come back to the library when they'd heard the commotion – it had been unprofessional. But she did compliment them on how speedily they'd served everyone after that. This night, though, there was to be no rushing, even if, as she hoped, there was another "spectral interruption to the programme". It must all run smoothly and to plan.

And the night did run to plan. The guests were in a state of high excitement over the possibility of a ghost among them. They loved the music, and applauded it wildly. A storm broke out halfway through the third piece, but the musicians played on despite the thunder, earning them even louder applause.

Mr Stuart had a subdued air about him, but Miss Skelton's showmanship made up for that. At the end of the evening she gave a witty speech about the unpredictability of spirits, and apologized beautifully for the non-appearance of Sir Philip Musgrave.

On Sunday morning Rayne had to call Tara three times before she got out of bed. "This is a real *bitch*," she moaned. "Working at the weekends!"

"Well, we'll get Monday off," said Rayne. She minded less than she thought she would about weekend working. It filled the time.

"Monday – *big* deal! Honestly, Rayne, I'd *leave* if I was you! It's horrible here – worked to death, and that murderer still on the loose . . . the police are no closer to getting him, did you hear?"

"I know. They've ruled yet another suspect out of their enquiries. Are *you* going to leave?"

"No. It's even worse at home."

Rayne laughed, mirthlessly. "I feel the same." The last time she'd phoned her mum, she'd had the usual toxic brew of complaints, blame and resentment poured into her ear. Plus a report that her ex-boyfriend Damian had a new girl and they seemed really, really happy and in love. . .

"OK, not home maybe – somewhere else," said Tara. "Anywhere rather than here. I feel I kind of owe it to Aunt Louisa to stay, since she rescued me – at least for a *while* – but *you* don't owe her anything."

"Tara, are you trying to get rid of me?"

"No! Of course not. I'm just thinking of what's best for you. I'm like that. I'm *sweet*."

Rayne laughed, but Tara's words stayed with her during the day. Seriously, why *was* she staying on here? She was restless, gloomy, anxious . . . but somehow, she couldn't think of going, of leaving Morton's Keep.

Ben called by the tearoom around three for tea. Usually Mrs Driver handed him a mug through the kitchen-end window but this time she told him to come in, because the tearoom was nearly empty. Rayne, toasting crumpets for an elderly couple, thought it was another of their little acts of insurrection against Miss Skelton, and smiled.

"Weather's still unsettled," said Ben, as he sat down. "Black clouds and rain one minute, sun the next. No rainbows, though, I've looked."

Mrs Driver smiled bleakly. "No, no rainbows. I wish another storm would break, get it over with. I'm closing up in a minute. We won't get anyone else through the doors, not today."

"Funny thing earlier," Ben went on. "I was working down

at the far end of the estate, and I heard stags bellowing, in the woods."

"Bellowing? But the rutting season's over now, isn't it?"

"Well over. They stopped squaring up to each other weeks ago. But here it is, all flared up again."

Mrs Driver didn't answer, just shook her head as though it was yet more evidence of the wrongness of things. The elderly couple left, and she ushered Ben and the girls out and locked up.

Tara said she was going back to the Sty to crash and listen to her iPod. Rayne took in a deep breath and said she was going for a walk.

"You're mad!" scoffed Tara. "It's going to start chucking it down again any minute and it'll be dark in an hour or so!"

"I'll be OK."

"Well, stay in the grounds then, won't you? Don't go anywhere you might meet the *murderer*."

"Oh, shut up, Tara! Of course I will."

Rayne didn't stay in the grounds, though. She walked fast, and her feet just seemed to take her forward. She went down past the lake, through the woods, then climbed over a stile into a gloomy, tree-lined lane. In the distance, she could hear a stag bellowing, and without really making the decision to, she walked towards the sound. She was remembering the first time she'd ever heard a stag make that primeval roar.

It was during her first weeks at Morton's Keep, and St John had taken her into sprawling Fleet Woods for a picnic. They'd settled in a clearing, by two great, flat boulders, one laid on top of the other, with the remains of a fire on top. He'd been winding her up about the creepy reputation of the woods, how the fire men went there to worship the devil, and he'd told her the two huge stones were a sacrificial site. A witchy mobile made of twine, twigs, pine cones and feathers was hanging from a tree – he'd snatched it down and whipped it across the boulders, scattering the ash. He'd – she thought the word carefully – *desecrated* it.

Then they'd heard the bellow, deep, ominous, unreal – super real – from the depths of the woods. She'd been terrified, not knowing what it was. And then it had stalked forward through the trees.

She remembered her first sight of the wonderful stag, with its soaring antlers. She'd been filled with an urge to drop down on her knees in front of it, in worship and in fear.

She walked on. Overhead, the sky was dark with thunderclouds, then vivid with sudden streaks of red light from the setting sun. She walked into Fleet Woods.

Rayne had no idea where she was in the woods. Her sense of direction had always been poor; her mum used to laugh at her when she'd come out of a shop and turn back the way she'd come, instead of going on. A small voice at the back of her mind was telling her how insane she was, going into Fleet Woods at dusk.

But she kept walking, compelled.

The wind flowed like a river through the trees. She was caught up in its current, carried deeper into the wood. She knew the cause of it. She knew why she was being drawn on like this – *who* was drawing her. She'd felt this before, going down into Lingwall's dungeon, into his torture chamber.

"Leave me," she muttered, "leave me *alone*." Her breath was coming fast with fear but she couldn't turn back.

And then – Rayne felt as though all the breath had left her body. For a second, a second only, a towering pine tree ahead of her was woman-shaped. Great arms reaching, body swaying in the wind, green hair streaming all around her . . . then she was a tree again.

Rayne thought she might fall, fold up and fall to the ground, but she kept on walking. Past the giant pine tree, carried along on the flow of the wind through the trees. In the distance, she could hear the stags bellowing, answering each other.

She wasn't surprised when she reached the clearing with the two great stones. The watchers' altar. This time, though, it looked as though there were three boulders piled one on top of the other. She moved forward, peering in the half-light, her stomach churning with horror of what it might be.

The shape on top didn't move. She drew closer, and saw that it was the body of a stag.

She felt as though her heart had stopped. She moved closer still. Its head with the great arching antlers lolled back behind the boulders; the legs stuck out, stiff in death.

There was a thick rope round its neck and its throat had been cut.

Chapter
Twenty-eight

Rayne sank to her knees, crouching on the grass. "Oh no," she whispered. "*No*."

The wind seemed to boil in the trees, round and round, encircling her as she crouched in the clearing. The trees bucked and roared. "Oh, *God*," she whispered. "Please, no."

The stag's head was tragic. Its large, beautiful eyes were glassy and clear, as though they still had some kind of life in them. The rope was obscene.

On the boulders, Rayne could see the thick stain of blood. She leaned forward and retched, twice. Then she pulled out her mobile phone, and called Ethan.

When he answered, she could barely speak. "I'm at the watchers' place," she croaked.

"Rayne? Rayne, what's *wrong*?"

"Please come. Ethan, please come."

"*Where are you?*"

"Fleet Woods. The place with the two boulders, the altar. . ."

"Are you *safe*?"

"I don't know. But I can't leave. Please *come*!"

The phone went dead. She sat back, head bowed on her knees, curling her arms round herself protectively. The wind continued to circle the clearing, moaning softly.

Rayne had no idea how long it took Ethan to arrive, but she felt like she was waiting, crouched in the clearing, for ever. She felt like she'd been frozen there.

Then through the sad soughing of the wind she heard the pounding of hoof-beats, and she scrambled to her feet. Her first thought was that it was another stag, pounding towards her, and she ran over to stand behind a big oak tree for safety.

Then a black horse's head came through the trees, with Ethan's face bowed over its neck, stooping under the low branches. "Rayne!" he called. He reined the horse in, jumped down, rushed towards her, got hold of her arms. "Are you all right?" he asked. She nodded, and for a moment there was absolute silence as they met each other's eyes. Then he let go of her, and she pointed wordlessly at the stag on the stones. He turned, and cursed, then went to it. The horse, too, stepped carefully up to it and stared, his great head lowered.

"We didn't do this," Ethan said, hoarsely. "You know none of the watchers did this, don't you?"

"Yes," Rayne muttered.

"Why are you here? What made you—?" He broke off, as though he knew. The tall trees swayed in the wind all round them.

"I'm getting you out of here," he said, taking hold of the horse's reins again. "Hold easy, Hiker."

He lifted her up on to the saddle, and climbed up behind her. Then they rode out of the wood.

Within ten minutes, they were at the Green Lady inn. Ethan tethered Hiker in a little wooden lean-to at the back, and filled him up a bucket of water from the outside tap. Then he put his arm round Rayne and steered her into the pub.

The bar was almost empty, Sunday not being a night for heavy drinking, but the fire was lit. Its light flickered warmly on the dark walls and old oak beams. The large table by the bar had a group of men sitting at it; dazedly, Rayne recognized Will and several of the other watchers.

The old woman Patience, sitting gazing into the fire, looked up at Rayne and let out a piercing cry. "What's wrong?" she wailed, running a hand through her wild, white-grey hair. "What's *wrong?*"

"Mark!" said Ethan, urgently, to one of the men at the table. "Mark – can you take Patience upstairs, to her room?"

Mark frowned a query at Ethan, but he went over to Patience and gently helped the old lady to her feet. She was chattering and muttering, shaking her head as though to clear it. Talking persuasively, he steered her through a little door behind the bar.

"What's happened?" demanded Will. Rayne felt like all the men were scanning her face, scouring it for answers. She sat down at a small table under a window, her head in her hands.

"Get her a brandy, will you?" said Ethan. "She's had a shock."

A brandy was put in front of Rayne and she listened,

stone-faced, as Ethan described what he'd seen in Fleet Woods. The men heard the news in silence, grimly. "On our altar," muttered one of them. "Monstrous."

"First the murder at the Devil's Tankard – now this," growled Will. "They're linked, I reckon."

"Someone's trying to make mischief for us," said one of the younger men. "Pin these crimes on us."

"I think it's worse than mischief-making," said Will.

"What do you mean?" demanded the young man, but Will didn't answer.

"The police will be after us again if they get to hear about it," said another man.

"They won't get to hear of it," said Will. "John – Richard – you get along and bury the poor beast, will you?"

Rayne looked up. "Take the halter off," she croaked. "Take the horrible rope off, before you do."

"Aye," said Will. "Bury it with due rites and respect."

The two men left the pub, but as they left, three others came in, with two women, and the wind howled in through the door with them. One of the women said Mark had called her, told her something was up and she should call the others and get to the pub. The story of the sacrificed stag was repeated; the woman started crying.

"Why choose our places, eh?" said Will. "There's a reason to it."

"It could just be coincidence," said the landlord, nervously pulling pints for the newcomers.

"It's no coincidence. That poor girl, and the stag – they had their throats slashed on *our* places. On the places of protection."

"It'll be Martyr's Hill next," said an old man.

"And then – who knows where?"

"We don't know, so they don't know!" snapped the barman. "Whoever they are!"

"Oh yes?" said another man, rising to his feet. He had a short beard and Rayne thought she recognized him – from the fire dancing, and from Fleet Woods. "And how can you be so *sure* they don't know?"

"Sit down," said Will. "We've got to stay calm. Sit down."

Mark came back down into the bar, and the bearded man sat down again. "How's Patience?" asked Will.

"Not good," Mark answered. "Fearful. Unsettled. I'll go up again in a minute." The main door opened, and two more men and a red-haired woman came in. The story of the stag was told once more.

Rayne thought she might scream if she heard it again.

"That turns my stomach," said one of the men. "It's pure evil, that's what it is."

"The poor stag," said the red-haired woman. "How could they? Will?" She clasped her hands in front of her, wrung them together. Then she whispered, "Is it happening?"

There was a long silence. And suddenly Rayne heard herself bang down her glass and demand, "Look – can you tell me what's going *on*, please?"

Everyone turned to look at her once again. "What made you go there?" asked Will.

"I don't know," she snapped. "Ben Avebury was talking about the stags bellowing—"

"They were," said the woman. "I heard them all afternoon. Unnatural."

"And I just found myself . . . *there*, OK? By that poor stag."

"You were led," said the woman.

"Leave it," said Ethan. "Rayne asked a question, Will. You should answer it."

Will took in a deep breath, let it go again. "We're skirting round the edges of old myth and legend here," he said. "It's like the rings in a tree trunk – it goes deeper and deeper in, further and further back in time. . ."

"Oh, *what*?" snapped Rayne. "What are you *saying*?"

"I'm saying there's more to our fire festivals than tradition. More than just fun and games. It all goes back centuries. A millennium. It's all about protection."

"I know that," snapped Rayne. "I know all about what you think you do. But what did that woman mean? When she said – *is it happening*?"

"There's an old rhyme about Morton's Keep," said Will, heavily. "No one knows where it comes from, but it's never been forgotten.

"*Six cursed acts, the horror spreads free.*
Six fires to contain, to circle the bane,
Saved are we."

Several of the older men and women muttered *saved are we* along with Will. Rayne felt a rush of fear at the weirdness of their chanting, at the intensity of it. "Groovy!" she said sarcastically, to stem the fear. "Aren't you *containing* it anyway, with all your fire festivals? I thought that was the point of them."

174

Will turned his piercing eyes on her. "Our festivals, our dances and fires – we hope they keep the old evil subdued at Morton's Keep. We hope to stop reoccurrences of the terrible things that happened in Sir Simeon Lingwall's time—"

"Or what happened to poor Patience," said the red-haired woman.

"Or what St John Arlington tried to do," added Ethan, pointedly.

"Aye," said Will. "All that. But this rhyme, this ditty, it talks of something even worse. The old stories say there are six sacred sites all round the outskirts of Marcle Lees. They were set in place when Morton's Keep was built; they have it as their centre. Their purpose was to contain the evil within the town."

"Six sites," said an old woman seated next to him. "It's why the fire men make the six-pointed star, in their dances. The six points of the star mark the circle of containment."

"The rhyme tells how six profane acts on those six sacred places . . . will break the ring of protection. Let the evil flow free, beyond the Keep, beyond Marcle Lees itself . . . unleash it into the world."

"Which would make Lingwall's atrocities," said the old woman, quietly, "look like a child's brief game."

There was silence in the inn, only the sound of the wind mourning against the windows. Rayne picked up her glass and finished her brandy. It had gone to her head, a little. "It's just an old *rhyme*!" she muttered.

"Maybe," said the bearded man, heatedly. "But it seems now there are *others* who think it's more."

"*Six fires to contain*," said Will. "Six fires set all on one night, on the six sacred places, before the last cursed act takes place."

"But we have knowledge of only three sacred places," said an old man, who hadn't spoken up till now. "The Devil's Tankard, Martyr's Hill, the great stones in Fleet Woods where you found the stag, Rayne. The others . . . knowledge of their whereabouts has been lost to us, over time."

"Seems we may reap the negligence of our forefathers now," said the bearded man.

"That's why we keep to the rituals," said Will, looking hard at Ethan. "*All* the rituals, not just the lively ones. That's why we remember. That's why it *matters*."

Ethan's face was set as he stared down at the table ahead of him.

"There's been differences in the fire group," Mark said, "among ourselves. Young against old, mainly. But we all need to pull together now."

The door to the pub banged open again; the wind skirled round the bar. Rayne looked up as three more people came in. She saw the red-haired woman go over to them, and tell the dreadful story once more. The bar was full of faces now, staring at her; the fire had grown hotter, and now the door was shut again it seemed to suck the air from the room as it flared shadows on to the wall.

"Some say it did happen once," said the old man. "There's old stories about the rhyme, of course, just fancy mostly, but one of 'em has a ring of truth about it. It relates how in the eleventh century robber barons from beyond the border wanted to release the power of Morton's Keep and harness it for themselves. They rounded up six poor peasant lads and lasses, and began slaughtering them on the six sites."

"What happened?" asked Ethan.

"Fire happened. Six fires, simultaneously, burning round the fresh corpses, saving the life of the last of the victims. Some stories make out that the green lady caused them, others that the owner of the Keep rode out with his men to set the fires and the lady lit the last, in the nick of time. At any rate – the dark power was contained."

"The green lady," said the old woman. "She goes back to the start of all this. She knows where the sites are. Some say she created them."

"Yes," said Will slowly, looking straight at Rayne. "And if Patience was in this room still, she'd be saying you're needed now, girl. You have a link to *her*, you know you do. You saw her, didn't you. In the fire, that night up on Martyr's Hill."

Rayne shuddered, and closed her eyes to shut out their faces. But inside her eyelids was the mighty face she'd seen that night, the green lady's face, burning, roaring at her . . . the terror she'd felt then filled her again.

"She's chosen you," Mark said. "She'll show you the way to . . . to sort this."

"Like she showed you the stag," said the red-haired woman.

Something inside Rayne ripped open.

She sprang to her feet, pushing her chair back with a raucous scrape. "*You can't put this on me!*" she cried.

"Calm down," said Will. "Seems to me it's *on you* already."

"Not if I don't want it to be, it isn't!" She glared round at them all, wild-eyed. "*God!* You're all *raving*! You should hear yourselves!"

"If you'd just listen – if you'd let us explain—"

"*No!* You're all sick! I don't *want* to know!"

Ethan pushed his way through to stand beside her; he got hold of her arm. "Rayne, *please*," he said. "You remember! You remember what happened when St John got down in the basement – the hideous *feeling* there – imagine that magnified, imagine that *free*—"

She looked at him. She hated him. He wanted her just like St John had wanted her, for some twisted, ancient thing in Morton's Keep. . .

She yanked her arm away. "*Leave me alone!*" she spat.

And she ran out into the wild night.

Chapter
Twenty-nine

Rayne punched the local taxi firm number on her phone as she ran. "I'm on the road that leads to The Green Lady," she panted. "When can you get there?"

"Grant's in the locality now," she heard. "If you go back to the pub—"

"*No*. No way. I've turned left out of the pub, there's a road up ahead—"

"It's not the weather for waiting out of doors, love!"

"I don't care. I'm not going back."

"OK, OK, I hear you. Grant can pick you up on the corner. Five minutes."

Rayne didn't want to stop. She could hear running behind her, one pair of feet; she knew who it was.

Ethan caught up with her on the corner. "Rayne, *don't* run out on us like this! I know it's weird, I know it's scary—"

"Too right it's scary! And *you* – you're as bad as the rest of them! You told me to steer clear of the watchers. After the fire in the dungeon, you said all their rituals and stuff weren't *real*. And now you're a fully-paid-up member, aren't you – one of them!"

"I was wrong," he said, urgently. "I thought they were just messing around, wallowing in the past – not seeing where the real danger was coming from. But tonight has shown me different. Rayne – trust me! I was *wrong*!"

"Ethan, I'm not *listening* to this! St John's sick and mad and you lot are sick and mad. I can't stand it any more. I feel like I'm in some insane horror film. I'm going."

"Don't. *Please.* You can help us, you—"

"I'm not just here to *help*. That's all people think I'm for, isn't it – *helping*. I've been used all my life, Ethan – I'm sick of it."

"This is different."

"Too right it's different. It's insane." The anger racing through her felt wonderful, it made her strong. "I've had a basinful. I'm out of here!"

He took hold of arm, glared into her face. "Look – you can't just think about *you* now—"

She snatched her arm away. "Oh, I think you'll find I can!" she snarled. And then a car swerved to a stop beside them, and the driver looked out. "Ace Taxis?" he said. "You all right, miss?"

"I'm fine!" she snapped. Then she wrenched open the back door and slid into the seat and didn't look round as the cab drew away.

Rayne was almost completely packed by the time Tara, who'd been dozing, realized she'd got back to the Sty. Tara wandered, yawning, through the kitchen, putting the kettle on to boil as she passed. "Sweetheart!" she cried, as she saw the open case, full to the brim, on the bed. "What are you *doing*?"

"I'm taking your advice," Rayne said. "I'm getting out of here."

"*Tonight?*"

"First thing tomorrow. I've booked a cab for seven-thirty – there's a train at eight-fifteen. I'll be back in London well by midday."

"Oh my *God*! Has something happened?"

"Yes. No. I dunno. I've just – had enough."

"I don't blame you. I can't believe we only get one day off. I can't bear the thought of turning up at that poxy tearoom again. *Exhausting*."

Rayne looked at her. She has no idea, she thought, what's happening here – what's really happening. Any more than her aunt does. They're all caught up in the day-to-day and making profits and they don't let the darkness touch them, the crucified pigeons or the ghosts or even the *murder*. . .

"Will you do me a favour?" she asked, abruptly.

"Sure," said Tara.

"If I write a note to Mrs Driver, and Mr Stuart – and your aunt – will you give them to them tomorrow?"

"Of course I will. Hey – I'll make you some hot chocolate, yeah?"

At half past ten the next day, Rayne arrived at Paddington Station. She called her mum again; she'd got no answer from her last night. But once more, she couldn't get through, so she left another brief message and headed for the underground to make her way back to Cramphurst Estate.

When she'd woken up with the alarm that morning, the

glorious energizing anger had disappeared. She'd lain for a minute listening to the birds, and thought of the beautiful stag, dead on the stones, and grief to be leaving had seeped into her, filling her. But she knew she had to go. She had to make a shift, she had to wrench things out of the insane pattern they were in.

Tara had said goodbye to her last night, and taken the three letters she'd handed her. Rayne, writing them, had been vague and dramatic, hinting at some kind of illness, even a breakdown, not being clear if or when she'd be back. She knew it would probably mean she'd lose her job, but that was too bad.

Tara had kissed her and told her again that she was doing absolutely the right thing. It hadn't made her feel better.

On the underground, she felt as though she was in a mad dream. The noise of the train was like a great machine, processing her. Everyone looked dead, zombie-like. No one made eye contact – everyone was in their own little bubble of separateness. She thought that she could suddenly turn green, and no one would stare. The thought was oddly comforting.

After she'd surfaced from the underground, she made her way on to the bus and off at the stop by Cramphurst Estate. It was both terribly familiar and utterly alien.

At home – except it felt weird thinking of it as home – one of the heavy glass doors to the entrance hall had been replaced by hardboard, but apart from that the block of flats looked the same. Same graffiti, same stained concrete.

She took the nasty-smelling lift she usually avoided up to the fourth floor, because of her heavy case. Her arm was already aching from hauling it on to trains and escalators and the bus.

As she let herself in, she thought she'd say hello and then tell her mum she was ill and then she could shut herself into her old crowded bedroom and *sleep*. . . She heard her mum's voice, calling out from the kitchen. "That you, Dave?"

"It's me, Mum," she called. Her voice sounded strange in the cramped living room, against the noise of the television in the corner. The flat was overheated; she breathed in stale air.

In seconds, her mum was in front of her. But there was no kiss, no hug – not even a smile. "*Rayne?* What the hell are you doing here?"

"I called! I left a couple of messages. . ."

"*When* did you call?"

"Last night. And this morning."

"Oh, my phone's been playing up." She wasn't looking at Rayne as she spoke. "I'm always having to recharge it – Dave's getting me a new one. What's wrong? Have you got the sack?"

"Not exactly. I just thought it was about time I came back, that's all."

"Well, thanks for the *notice*, love."

There was a pause. Rayne could feel tears itching behind her eyes. She and her mum had never exactly been affectionate, they'd never really been close, but—

"D'you want a cup of tea?" her mum asked, abruptly. She looked better, Rayne thought. Her clothes were less worn. She'd put a bit of weight on and it suited her. Her hair, which used to look over-dyed and dusty, was a soft russet red.

"Yes, please. I'll just get rid of my case, OK?"

Her mum didn't answer. Rayne lugged her case across into the skinny hallway and pushed open the door to her bedroom.

It was clear that it wasn't her bedroom any more.

Her little brother Jelly's cot had gone. Her posters and soft toys and teddy bears were gone; her make-up and bangles and beads that used to strew the dressing table were gone. A duvet with savage-looking robots on its cover was sprawled across the bed; Jelly's cars and monster figurines were all over the floor.

She went back to the kitchen. "Jelly's got my room then," she announced, flatly.

"He's three now, Rayne," her mum said, as she pulled a box of tea bags from a cupboard. "He's started nursery. He needs his own room. Especially as—" She turned round, but she still didn't look at Rayne, not directly. "Dave's moved in with me," she said breathlessly. "He's left his wife. They're sorting out the divorce, then we're going to move away from the Estate. Together."

"That's great," Rayne said.

"I would've told you. But you were behaving so strange – the way you finished with Damian and everything – it was hard to get hold of you for a proper talk. Dave told me to just go ahead and do it, give Jelly your old room. It was like a – *reward,* for Jelly being grown up and not minding that Dave moved in."

"Oh. Did it work?"

"Yes. He's so much better, Rayne. He never wakes in the night now. Dave says it's nursery wearing him out."

Rayne thought that if she heard the name *Dave* once more, she'd start screaming. "Where shall I leave my case, Mum?" she asked.

"Well – behind the sofa for now. You'll have to sleep there, I suppose. It'll be OK for a day or two, won't it?"

Rayne hauled her case across the living room, and shoved it behind the sofa. Her mum had seen the case, she must know she hadn't come just for a day or two. . . She could feel tears niggling again. She had to get out.

"I'll see you later, Mum, OK?" she called, and ran out of the flat.

Chapter Thirty

Dave wasn't happy about Rayne sleeping on the sofa. He barely said hello to her. Rayne's mum smoothed things over by saying Rayne would babysit Jelly and they could go out to the pub.

Jelly had grown up in the few months since she'd been gone. He was less affectionate and more assertive. He insisted on having the telly on and he flew into a rage when Rayne wouldn't let him have a second chocolate biscuit, so in the end she gave way. She sat in the living room with him as he squatted on the floor, glued to his inane cartoons, the jangling music up far too loud, and she longed for the silence of the woods.

As soon as she'd managed to get him into bed – her old bed – and she could hear from the snuffling sounds that he was asleep, she pulled out the sleeping bag and pillow her mum had got out for her and got herself ready for bed. She wanted to be asleep – or at least pretending to be asleep – when Dave and her mum got back, so she wouldn't have to talk to them.

She felt like she was trying to sleep by the side of a

motorway. The room was full of artificial light: blinks and blips and flashes from the computer and the telly and the music centre. Car lights streaked across the ceiling; wheels squealed, horns and music blared. The couple next door still seemed to hate each other. Rayne could distinguish every insult, every curse. But eventually she drifted off into some kind of sleep, restless with snatches of dreams.

To be jerked awake again by the front door slamming open and the overhead light coming on, scorching her eyelids. "Oh, *please. . .*" she groaned.

"This is our living space, Rayne!" said Dave, indignantly. He refused to be shushed by her mum; he stomped into the kitchen and put the kettle on, grumbling loudly about not being able to watch telly while he drank his before-bed cup of tea.

This way of living – only it wasn't living, to Rayne it was a desperate kind of survival – went on for three days. On the third night, she met up with her old crowd at a local pub in the desperate hope that one of them might know of somewhere she could live. No one seemed to know of anywhere, though. One girl mentioned the small possibility of the top bunk in a narrow bedroom with her cousin – just the thought filled Rayne with claustrophobic horror.

Everyone was agog to hear why she and Damian had split up, and the reason why she'd suddenly come back to Cramphurst Estate. Rayne bluffed her way through all the questions. Then, at the end of the night, Damian himself and his new girlfriend dropped in at the pub. Someone must have texted him. He made everyone laugh by saying how he couldn't understand why Rayne wanted to be out in the stinking muddy countryside – how he'd concrete it all over if it was left up to him. And he was very keen to show Rayne how loved-up he and his new girlfriend were, how great a boyfriend he was, how much she'd lost by dropping him.

She wasn't sure if she felt regret or not. She just felt numb.

On the fourth day, desperation set in. Her mother greeted her that morning with a little chat about how sleeping on the couch could only be temporary. *Very* temporary. Then she'd asked her to make sure she put all her things away in her suitcase in the daytime and tuck it well out of sight behind the couch because Dave hated the living room to look messy.

Rayne had choked down some toast, and left the flat. All she could think to do was go down to the local social security offices to sign on, and see if they could help with accommodation, too. Going back to Morton's Keep was there at the back of her mind, but she couldn't begin to imagine how she could do that, not now she'd run out on them all.

As she pushed her way out of the heavy doors to the flat entrance hall, she saw a boy standing twenty metres away, against the garages. He was tall and broad-shouldered; he had a backpack on and he was studying a piece of paper he held in his hand.

Something about the boy was very familiar.

She walked a bit closer and saw that it was Ethan.

Chapter
Thirty-one

Ethan looked so out of place against the graffiti-covered concrete wall that it seemed to Rayne there was something magical about him being there, as though he'd been transported straight from the woods. She felt like her heart was beating again, after days of being pinched and tight. She ran over to him, grinning, not bothering to hide her pleasure at seeing him.

When she was in front of him, his face split into a wide smile too. "*Rayne!*" he breathed.

"What the *hell* are you doing here?" she choked out.

He reached out a hand, touched her arm, let his hand fall down again. "I've come to get you," he said.

"*What?*"

"*Jesus*, I'm glad you're here. I didn't fancy going into that place." He jerked his head at the flats.

"My home, you mean?" she laughed. Except it wasn't her home, not any more. But all that didn't matter, not now he'd come to get her.

"Sorry," Ethan said. "I'm not used to this. The *tube* – it

was *mad* – and people get so close to you, I've nearly got into a fight *twice*—"

She moved closer to him, smiling. "Ethan, is this the first time you've been to London?"

"No!" he said indignantly. "I just haven't been . . . recently, that's all."

"You mean your dad took you to the zoo when you were ten?"

"Actually it was the Natural History Museum."

They laughed, eyes meeting, then she looked down and said, "What do you mean, you've come to get me?"

His face grew serious. "Rayne – is there somewhere we can go and talk? And . . . eat, maybe? I'm starving."

Ten minutes later they were sitting opposite each other in the corner of an old-fashioned greasy-spoon café that was almost empty now the truck drivers and workmen had had their full-fried breakfasts and left. Ethan ate ravenously; Rayne watched him, and drank coffee, and felt full of peace.

When he'd cleaned his plate he ordered coffee for himself and said, "Rayne, I know that was hideous, what happened at The Green Lady. I don't blame you for freaking."

"Don't you?"

"No. I know they can come on like . . . well, like you said, a horror film. But . . . look, however weird and mad it all sounded . . . I think they're right. What they said was right."

"So what made you change your mind?"

"The murder, the stag. Things they said."

"Ethan – you warned me off the watchers."

"I know I did."

"You told me they'd turn me into an icon, I remember you saying it . . . you said they'd stick me up on a maypole with a crown on, it made me laugh. . ."

There was a silence, both of them remembering that night, how he'd gone back to the Old Sty with her and they'd had their one and only disastrous kiss. . .

"So you're with them now, are you?" she demanded.

He didn't answer. The intimacy between them, the draw, was immense. The table was no kind of barrier. She had to concentrate to keep on talking.

"You believe in that creepy rhyme now, do you?" she asked.

"That rhyme has been around for a thousand years, Rayne. There's got to be something in it. Look – I know I sneered at some of the stuff Will and the others did. I thought they put ritual before action. They were too busy disappearing into Fleet Woods, making fires and hanging up pine cone mobiles, to recognize the threat from St John. But . . .Will and I have talked. *Really* talked. We've buried our differences, and God knows we needed to, because. . ." He picked up his coffee mug and drained it.

"Because. . ?" she prompted.

"Something else has happened," he said, abruptly.

"What?" she asked.

He sat up straighter, as though he was steeling himself for something, and said, "A young couple were abducted."

191

For a second, Rayne could feel the room spinning. "Oh, God!" she croaked. "Were they . . . were they *killed*?"

"No – no, it's OK. They got away."

"What happened? Tell me what happened."

"They were out late, coming back from the pub, a bit pissed, walking along with their arms round each other. A big car drew up beside them and two people jumped out, wearing masks. Pagan-type masks, they said – one was like a bird, the other a goat, with horns, curly horns. The driver was some kind of dog, or wolf, with long pointed ears."

"*Jesus.*"

"One of them had a knife – a short knife."

"Oh, God." Horror streamed into her. "A dagger. St John's dagger. *Lingwall's.*"

"Maybe. They held it up against the girl's throat. The boy said that's why he didn't dare fight back. They got bundled into the car and driven to the outskirts of Marcle Lees. They said the one in the bird mask was a woman. They heard her give orders – directions." Ethan paused, looked into Rayne's face. "You've gone white – are you OK?"

"Yes. Go on. *What happened?*"

"Well, the car stopped on the edge of a field, behind some old farm buildings. As they were being hauled out of the car the boy broke free and knocked the dagger away from the girl. Then he spun round on the man who'd been holding him – and laid him out flat."

"*Brilliant,*" breathed Rayne.

"Yeah. Apparently he does mixed martial arts. And the girl was no slouch either. She went for the man who'd had the dagger, screaming blue murder, till her boyfriend took over. *Then* she went for the woman. Then they both *ran*. Down to the road, where they flagged down a car, and went straight to the police."

"And have the police got any leads?"

"No. They went back to the farm buildings, scoured the land – no clues. No dagger."

"So they've no idea who did it."

"Oh, they've an idea, all right. Us. The fire people."

"*What?*"

"The pagan masks, see? They think that's all one with our hawthorn crowns and antlers. They're *desperate* to nail someone for the Devil's Tankard murder, and now they're trying to link that up with this abduction and pin them both on us. They refuse to entertain the idea that we're being set up again, put in the frame by the real villains. And they wouldn't say who, but *someone* pointed the finger very firmly in our direction. They've had 'other information'. We've all been hauled in for questioning again. DNA swabs, the lot. They've got swabs and stuff from this young couple's clothes, and their hands and nails where they hit out . . . nothing's been stuck on us, though. Yet."

"It won't be. You lot didn't do it." She ran her hands through her hair, pushing it back from her face. Then she blurted out, "D'you think *he* was there? St John?"

"No way of knowing from the couple's descriptions. They were terrified, disoriented – they couldn't remember stuff, only the masks, a woman's voice. . ."

"Thank God they got away," she muttered.

"Yes. Thank God."

"I think I need another cup of coffee now, Ethan. Please."

Ethan smiled, got to his feet, and went back up to the counter again. He came back with two steaming mugs, and sat down.

Rayne took a sip of hers, scalding her tongue, wincing. Then she said, "Do you know the place where they were taken?"

He looked up at her, knowing what she was asking. "No. Nobody knows anything about it, it's got no history as far as we can tell. But Will and Mark and a few of the others went there, when they'd got out of custody. At the back of the farm buildings, in the field where those masked creeps had parked their car, there's this . . . it's like a huge circle of big old stones. Sunk into the ground, all overgrown, you can only just about still see it. Will and his men dug down, and found the stones go three deep. They're foundation stones."

Rayne took in a sharp breath. "A ruin."

"Yes. We don't know of what, but it's old, it's ancient – it could be one of the sacred sites. Rayne—" He leaned eagerly towards her. "We sketched out the six-pointed star, on a map of Marcle Lees, with Morton's Keep as the centre. Martyr's Hill is the top point. Go clockwise round – the second point is unknown, but these *stones*, they could be the third point. The Devil's Tankard is the fourth point of the star, the bottom point. Then the fifth is unknown and the *sixth* – that's the altar in Fleet Woods. It works. We can't rely on it, of course – it's not going to be a perfect mathematical star, is it, all regular and even. But on the map, this ruin *works*."

194

"How do we check it? How do we find out what the stones are?"

If Ethan registered her use of the word *we*, he didn't show it. "They're all looking into the old records now, but no one really knows how to go about it. We need a historian, someone used to sniffing the facts out."

"Have you asked Mr Stuart? He knows a lot about the history of the area."

"We thought of him right away. But Mr *Stuart* was dead evasive when Will turned up to talk to him. He fobbed him off with a lot of chat about not stirring up trouble, leaving the police to do their job. Practically shut the door in his face."

"He's always been . . . I dunno. *Wary* of the fire men. Hasn't he?"

"Yes. He seems to want to deny what Morton's Keep is all about. Mind you – if I lived there, maybe I would, too. Anyway, his manner got Will's dander up and he proper banged on the door again, and that bloody woman answered."

"Miss Skelton."

"She had the nerve to say the police had told them not to speak to us. Well, maybe they had. The thing is, we're just floundering about in the dark here, Rayne, and we can't see our enemy. We only know for sure about three sacred sites. There's been two definite 'cursed acts' – the murder in Devil's Tankard, and the stag in Fleet Woods. We're too late there. Will's put a twenty-four-hour watch on Martyr's Hill but we can't keep that up for ever. We need to find out if the foundation stones are the fourth site. It could all be just a fake, part of pointing the finger at the fire men. If it is the fourth site, we need to find where the last two sites are – fast – and set the six fires. Complete our circle before they complete theirs and *the horror spreads free*. Right now it feels pretty bloody hopeless, I can tell you."

Rayne put her coffee mug down on the table. "And you're completely convinced of the . . . the *reality* of all this, are you?" she said.

"No, Rayne! No, of *course* I'm not. Yesterday I woke up and thought – this is some psychotic mass hysteria, it's delusion. I wanted to run, like you'd done. But then I thought – I haven't got a choice. I'm a watcher and I dare not take the risk of thinking it's not real. Even though it looks completely hopeless, finding the lost sites – even though we haven't got a clue where they might be – we've got to *try*."

"I s'pose you have," said Rayne.

He leaned across the table towards her. "That's why I've come to get you, Rayne," he said urgently.

Rayne felt a stab of hurt when she heard this, that this was his reason, but she didn't let it show on her face.

"We need you to help," he went on. "*She* might show you – she might *take* you to the other sites. The green lady. I know it's mad, it's freaky – but. . ."

"Yes, it is mad and freaky," Rayne said, firmly. "And I know who could help in a much more practical way." She sat back from the table; her chair made a loud scrape. "We can call her now."

Chapter Thirty-two

Ethan watched Rayne as she called Mrs Driver and asked for Ms Barton's phone number. Mrs Driver passed it on with no comment about Rayne's sudden departure, no question about her whereabouts or welfare. Rayne assumed the old housekeeper was angry with her for the way she'd just upped and left, but she didn't waste time worrying about it. She called Ms Barton and held the phone away from her ear as Ethan leaned across the table, so he could hear. He was so close to her that she could smell the outdoor scent of his hair, like the smell of autumn.

Ms Barton said it was lovely to hear from Rayne again. Rayne asked after her mother and Ms Barton said that unhappily, she was no better, but it was a good time to chat because she'd just gone upstairs for a nap.

Then Rayne said: "Ms Barton, you were there when we burnt out the dungeon. You heard what St John's plans were for Morton's Keep. And right afterwards you had to leave to take care of your mum, and I never got to talk to you about it, to find out how much you knew about Sir Simeon Lingwall. . ." The name seemed to hiss down into the phone.

"I wanted to talk to you, too, Rayne," Ms Barton said, slowly, "I was sorry I never got the chance. Is there a . . . a reason you're asking about it now?"

"There might be," said Rayne, guardedly.

"Ah. Right. Well, I'd pieced together this and that, from old stories and records and books – I know quite a bit, actually. Definitely more than Mr Stuart wanted me to know. I asked him about Sir Simeon Lingwall once and he said it was a topic quite inappropriate for my guided tours of the house."

"Did he say anything to you after the fire in the cellar?"

"Only to make it clear that the subject was absolutely closed."

"Ms Barton." Rayne breathed in, breathed out again. "You always seemed very interested in the tradition of paganism in the area. The fire festivals, the dancing. . . Did you think they were in any way linked to . . . to the bad history of the house?"

There was a silence. Then Ms Barton said, "Yes, I did think that. There was . . . there was kind of a *pattern*. A reoccurring theme of the festivals being there for protection against . . . against something evil that had its focus, its *being*, at Morton's Keep. But that was another topic that naturally made Mr Stuart uneasy, that he decreed off-limits."

Ethan nudged Rayne, and she blurted out, "Do you know anything about six sites on the outskirts of Marcle Lees? Kind of . . . sacred, protecting sites, around the Keep?"

They could hear Ms Barton's sharp intake of breath. "Is

this about the murder at the Devil's Tankard? It was in *The Times* yesterday, how they still haven't convicted anyone."

"Yes. It's about that."

"Oh my lord. Those six sites – they were hinted at in some old records I found. There was a parallel with the six-pointed star shape that the fire men create in their dances."

Rayne leant her head closer to Ethan's as they listened. She felt as though her breathing had synchronized with his.

"People were very cagey when I asked about the sites," Ms Barton went on. "But if they *do* exist, it's certain the Devil's Tankard is one of them. Did you know that the early church would rename sacred pagan places with something to do with the devil, to put people off gathering there. . .?"

"Ms Barton, a beautiful stag was found with its throat slashed on an altar made of two great boulders in Fleet Woods."

"*Oh my God.*" Ethan's eyes were locked into Rayne's as they listened to Ms Barton's small voice from the phone. "The *altar in the woods* – I know it, I tracked it down, I've been there. It's well over a thousand years old, that altar. I heard all these rumours about it, mostly about the fire men doing devil worship there, but that's nonsense, and *typical*, it's all one with the early church renaming pagan sites devil's this and devil's that. . . Oh, *Rayne*. A stag, you say? How *horrible*. That's two of the sacred sites, desecrated. Oh, dear lord. There's an old rhyme, you know. I heard it from a strange old lady in a pub.

"Six cursed acts, the horror spreads free.
Six fires to contain, to circle the bane,
Saved are we."

"I've heard it too," said Rayne.

Ms Barton talked fast then, because Rayne warned her that her battery was going dead. Some time ago, she too had sketched out a map of where she thought the six sites were. It roughly followed the shape of the fire men's six-pointed star, with Martyr's Hill at the top and the Devil's Tankard at the bottom. Diagonally opposite the altar in Fleet Woods was a circle of old stones behind some farm buildings on the outskirts of Marcle Lees. The stones, she said, were the ruins of an old watchtower built by landowners in the Dark Ages to keep an eye on the robber barons in Morton's Keep.

Both Rayne and Ethan seemed to freeze when they heard this, and they didn't interrupt.

Of the final two sites, Ms Barton had no clear information, just an idea of location. One was a strange little flat-topped hill, which was actually an ancient burial mound – Peak's Barrow. The other was a valley called Wildhern that had pagan significance. Both fitted on to the star shape. She remembered something, too, about an old stone carving of a woman, a pagan goddess maybe, but she couldn't be sure it was linked. She promised to look into her copious notes and photocopies of old records, and see if there were any clues she'd missed, and get back to them right away. As she called out *"Keep in touch,"* the phone went dead.

Ethan sat back again in his chair. "There's no doubt, is there?" he said. "A tower that was built in the Dark Ages to keep an eye on the Keep. It must have been built on one of the six sites of protection."

"No doubt. The only doubt is whether it was enough of a *cursed act* just to drag that couple there – to have the intention."

"The intention was pretty evil, so I bet it was enough. At any rate, it makes no difference. We know four sites now; we're guarding the one that hasn't been desecrated; we have to find the exact location of the two lost ones. One on Peak's Barrow, one in Wildhern Valley."

"Ms Barton'll help us, I know she will. She'll be thumbing through her notes right now."

"Good. Because we have to find them quickly."

"Taking up residence here, are you?" the burly man behind the counter called out, bad-temperedly. "You two want anything else?"

Ethan got to his feet. "No," he said. "We're just going."

Out on the street, Ethan walked fast, looking around all the time. Rayne thought he was like an animal, on edge, alert – longing to get back to the woods. Well, she felt the same.

"So," he said, as they hurried along, "will you come? Will you come back with me?"

She knew she was going to go, but she said, "I can't just swan in and take up my job again, can I? Not the way I left."

"You could always stay with us," he said gruffly. "We've a spare room at the farm."

"Oh yeah? And what will I do for money?"

"You won't need money. Not if you're with us." He stopped walking, glared at her. "Rayne, don't you *get* it? This is bigger than jobs or money or where you stay. This is – I was going to say *bigger than both of us*, but you'd laugh, wouldn't you. Yes, it could all be crazy, superstitious crap. But more and more I don't think so – and you of *all* people ought to understand the power of it, the danger."

She turned away, started walking again.

"There's been such storms since you left," he said. "And the lake's flooded again."

"Fire, flood, fury," she murmured.

"Yes. Patience sings that all the time now. And *you've* felt it. You know."

They'd reached the flats where Rayne's mum and Dave and Jelly lived.

"I'll get my case," she said.

Chapter
Thirty-three

To Rayne's relief, the flat was empty when she let herself in. She got her case and left a note for her mum with five pounds for Jelly. She wrote *See you again soon* and she knew they'd be glad she'd gone.

On the bus on the way to the underground station, Ethan phoned Will, to tell him Rayne was with him and what Ms Barton had said about the foundation stones. On the underground itself he seemed tense, uncomfortable, and Rayne took over, leading the way. As soon as he was on the train back to Marcle Lees, he slept. He said he'd got up before six that morning and crossing London twice had knackered him.

Rayne found herself just studying his face as he slept. She wanted to reach out her hand and stroke the lovely line between his cheekbone and his jaw; she wanted to kiss underneath his eyebrows, and full on his mouth. But she just sat there, looking.

Outside the train windows, the landscape turned increasingly green. Fields and woods streamed past. Rayne felt a pulse start up in her, of wanting and knowing. She thought of the people she'd left behind on Cramphurst Estate, all the hours they spent in front of TV and computer screens, how "outdoors" for them was just something to be hurried across between home and work and the pub and shops. A kind of anguish filled her. "The human race is screwed," she thought. "We're becoming an indoor species. It'll *destroy* us."

Ethan's eyes sprang open. "Whaaa?" he mumbled. "What did you say?"

"Nothing," she said, embarrassed. "I was just thinking."

He checked his watch. "We'll be there in ten minutes," he said. He leaned forward, and stared out of the window. "I think I need to go round to St John again. Pay him another visit."

"You still think he's involved, then? Him and Flora and the others?"

"I don't know. Murder – abduction – slashing a stag's throat – it's a bit full-on for him, isn't it?"

Rayne nodded. "When we went round to see him – he was *wasted*. Not even capable of killing a pigeon."

"I bet he's got something to do with it, though."

"He could have brought in other people, I suppose. He could be connected. But what good would it do going round to see him again? This link to Lingwall . . . it's everything to him, it's his *life*. You could smash him to a pulp and he wouldn't tell you anything."

Ethan grinned. "It'd be satisfying, though," he said.

Ethan had borrowed his dad's old Land Rover again, and parked it in the station car park. As they got in he announced his intention to drive her to Morton's Keep, and "see what's what".

"Is your dad. . .?" Rayne began.

"Is he part of it?" Ethan said, as he put the car in gear and lurched out on to the road. "Is he a watcher? Not exactly. But he knows enough, and he's said I can have the car when I need it. And – well, I should be at school. But the teachers aren't on at me. It's weird, Rayne. It's like people *know*. Without really understanding it. It's weird."

They turned into the long, gloomy drive of Morton's Keep. "What d'you want to do first?" he said. "Go to the tearoom, or check out the Old Sty?"

"Maybe – go to the Sty," she said. "Drop my case off. Maybe if I just move back in, they won't kick me out again."

He swerved into the bushes and parked near where St John used to hide his motorbike. Rayne got out of the car and took in a great breath of sweet, fresh, earthy air. Together they walked through the shrubs and trees and into the medieval garden. Ethan was carrying her case, and she trailed her hands over leaves and grasses as she walked, loving the touch of them.

The door of the Old Sty was standing ajar, and someone was singing.

It was a high, thin voice that would have been sweet if the song hadn't been so eerie, drifting out across the ancient garden. Rayne, trying to hear the words, realized they were in a foreign language that she didn't recognize.

She decided she didn't like the song; it made her uneasy – threatened, somehow. She took a few steps closer to the Sty, and Ethan followed her.

The song ended, and a shrill laugh rang out. Then Rayne heard Tara call, "Excellent, my love! You'll shrivel their souls with that one!"

Then the door was pulled wide open and a slim, sharp-featured girl with dark hair coiled on top of her head stood looking at them. "Who are you?" she demanded.

In seconds, Tara was beside her at the door. "*Rayne!*" she gushed. "Oh my God, how *are* you? You never answered my texts!"

"I never got your texts," Rayne said.

"Really? I sent at least three. Rayne – this is Sessie. Short for Cecilia. She's a singer."

"Another singer?"

"I *know!* Aunt Louisa's gone potty, she's really getting into her concerts, there's another planned for this weekend. . ." She paused, took in a breath. "Sessie, this is *Rayne*, well you know that – and that's her friend Ethan."

Ethan was silent, Sessie too. "Have you come back then?" carolled Tara.

"Yes," Rayne said.

"Only . . . *well*. . ."

"Sessie's got my room. I can see that."

"There was no room *left* at the house! Not even a couch for her to sleep on – absolutely chock-a-block!"

Sessie's shoes and bags and clothes were all over the place. The table had been pulled out at right angles to the window and two more chairs put round it.

"You've taken the antlers down," Rayne said. "From over the stove."

Sessie lifted her chin, looked straight at Rayne, and said, "They were horrible."

"Oh, *oh*, Rayne – I feel *terrible*!" squealed Tara, putting out her arms as though to hug Rayne, then, thinking better of it, dropping them down by her sides. "We thought you'd *gone*! For *good*! That note you wrote to Aunt Louisa. . ."

"Just said I needed a break," said Rayne. "Asked her to understand I needed to get away for a bit."

"Yes, but you sounded *desperate*! What was it you said? 'I don't know what's wrong with me, but I can't stay here any more, I have to get away' . . . it sounded so *final*!"

"OK, well. I need to see your aunt, I suppose. And Mrs Driver."

"Do you *want* your old job back?" said Tara. "Are you sure it's the right thing for you, coming back? You don't look well, Rayne."

Ethan got hold of Rayne's arm and pulled her gently backwards, away from the two girls standing in the door. "Come on," he muttered. "Let's go."

Rayne found she had tears in her eyes as she climbed back into the Land Rover. "That was *my room*," she said, fiercely. "The only room I've ever had just for me. And they handed it over to that snotty, singing bitch without even asking—"

"Hey," Ethan laughed, "calm down!"

"How long have I been gone? Not even a week! And they kick me out, move the next one in. . ."

"Maybe they'll let you have your room back. If you want

it. Personally, *I* wouldn't want to sleep next door to that white-haired creature."

"*What?* Tara's OK. She's a good cook, for a start."

"I don't trust her."

"OK, she's a bit phony, and I've no doubt she's a bit two-faced. . ."

"You said it. She's all over her new best friend now, isn't she? And what was it she said? *You don't look well, Rayne.*" Ethan imitated Tara's high, rather affected voice, and Rayne smiled.

"You look well," Ethan said, angrily. "You look *really* well."

There was a silence, both of them taken aback by what he'd blurted out. Then he said, "You know what? I'm starving. Are you?"

"Ravenous."

"OK. Let's—" He broke off as his mobile sounded, and he answered it. "Yes, she's here," he said. "She's sitting next to me in the Land Rover. Why, what—"

Rayne watched Ethan as he listened to the tinny little voice from the mobile. His expression didn't change but his breathing was coming quicker. Then he said, "We'll come now. It's OK. See you in ten minutes." And he rang off.

"*What?*" asked Rayne, searching his face. "What is it?"

"Something's happened," he said, slowly. "Nothing – no death, no victim. But they're afraid . . . they think something might have happened on another site."

"Oh my God – *what*?"

"He wouldn't say. Rayne – we've got to get to The Green Lady. They're waiting for us there." He started up the engine.

Chapter Thirty-four

Rayne felt completely different as she walked into the ancient inn this time. Her suspicion and panic had evaporated and she felt as if she was just waiting to see what would happen next. Somehow she knew she'd be able to deal with it.

A phrase her old English teacher had used, trying to get the class to accept tricksy literature, came back to her. *Suspend your disbelief.*

That was what she was doing now, she thought. Suspending her disbelief. And waiting. And watching.

Watching all of them.

Will and Mark and a few others ("the inner circle," thought Rayne) were there, grouped as usual round the large table by the bar. They all looked up as Rayne and Ethan walked in. "Before anyone says anything," Ethan said, loudly, "we're hungry."

"No problem," said the landlord. "Cottage pie do you? It's grand."

"Perfect," said Rayne. Without being invited to she

pulled out a chair at the table and sat down, smiling round at everyone, and they smiled back.

"Welcome home," said Will.

"Thank you," she replied.

Patience wasn't in her usual place by the fire, but she decided not to ask about this.

"Well," said Ethan, sitting down just across from Rayne, "what's happened?"

Will laid his hands flat on the table and examined them for a moment. Then he said, "After you'd told us the place those kids were taken to was an old watchtower, we got out our map and looked at what would make up the top triangle, as it were, of the star, with that and Martyr's Hill. There's a funny little hillock there, Peak's Barrow, we thought might be a likely spot."

"It is," said Ethan, "according to Ms Barton. Sorry, I didn't get round to telling you that. It's an ancient burial mound."

"Ah. There it is then. Well – five of us went along for a recce, and we found . . . well. Traces."

"Traces," echoed Ethan.

"Traces of a . . . well, a party. It's flat on the top, Peak's Barrow. It struck me it looks a bit like a stage. And up there right in the centre the grass was all flattened and bruised, as though a lot of people had been there, moving about, lying down. There was broken glass, too, but not from a bottle – fine glass, it was."

"And there was bottles, too," said the old man sitting next to Mark. "Wine bottles. And corks."

"Bones," said the red-haired woman. "Pheasant bones and feathers, all thrown about. And grape stems – you

210

know, what's left when you eat all the grapes. And pretty golden cake cases, crumpled up."

"Aye," said Will, "they'd had a good time. There was a bit of torn cloth on some briars lower down, soft blue silk it was, as though a woman had walked by and caught her dress . . . and near that, some pale blonde hair, just a few strands of it, on a thorn."

Rayne shuddered.

"And that was it?" Ethan demanded. "Nothing else?"

Will put his hand in his pocket, withdrew it, and threw something small on to the table. It rolled a little, then lay there on the wood, glittering.

It was an earring. A single, silver drop earring, with a dark red stone like a drip of blood.

The landlord came over and put a plateful of pie and vegetables in front of Rayne and Ethan, but they didn't start to eat.

"It's not much to go on," said Ethan, at last. He picked up his knife and fork.

"It wasn't just what we found," said the woman. "It was . . . it was the *feeling* there. It was horrible. It should have had a nice festive feeling, with the silk and wine bottles, but it wasn't. I don't know what they'd been up to, with their party, but it was . . . horrible."

Rayne and Ethan were eating steadily now, as they listened.

"We told the police," said Will. "Told them we thought it was connected to the abduction. They didn't want to know, of course. Accused us of wasting police time and haven't even been out to look."

"Well, why should they?" said Mark. "No crime was committed. Last I heard they'd decided the abduction of that couple was just drunken foolery, and they'd got a new lead on the murder up north."

Will grunted, then turned to Ethan. "Have you been out to see that lad again, the twisted one?"

"St John Arlington? Not since that first time I told you about. And if it is him – he must have others working with him this time."

"You going to pay him another visit?"

"I think so."

In the silence that followed, Rayne finished her cottage pie. She scraped up the last bits of gravy-covered carrot and put them in her mouth. "Will you get your job back?" asked Will.

"I don't know," she said. "If it's up to Miss Skelton, probably not."

"They've moved someone else into her room," said Ethan. "She can stay at ours tonight, and after, if need be."

Mark nudged the old man next to him, who started chuckling. Ethan glared and clattered his knife and fork down on to his plate.

"You need to see Mrs Driver, girl," said Will. "Soon as you can. See her and get your job back."

It was already dark when the two of them drew up outside Ethan's farmhouse and got out of the Land Rover. The moon was bright and nearly full and stars were prickling the sky like splinters of ice. "They're gaining on us," said Ethan, gloomily, as they walked over the rutted ground towards the house.

"Whoever *they* are."

"That's the fourth desecration."

"You don't *know* that. You don't know that that wasn't just an . . . an incidental party."

"Outdoors, in November? Come on, Rayne. I know it, and you know it, and *they* – they know where all the sites are. We can't watch Martyr's Hill for ever. It's just a matter of time."

"Stop being such a misery. We'll find the last one. *No* problem.

"Six fires to contain, to circle the bane,
Saved are we."

She glanced up to catch him looking at her with such a fierce, open look on his face that she looked away again, fast. And gasped, "What's *that*?"

"What?"

"That black shape on the ground – it's moving – *two* shapes – right by our side – *why are you laughing*?"

"Rayne, have you really never seen your own moon shadow before?"

She looked up at the moon, and down at the ground, and then she laughed too.

"You can only really see your moon shadow when there's no other light," he went on. "You'd never see it in the city."

"I love it here," she said.

Chapter
Thirty-five

Ethan's parents were welcoming and matter-of-fact. She was shown into the spare room, a box room where there was just enough space for an old wooden bedstead with a fat mattress and a little chest of drawers with a round mirror on a china stand. The bed already had a big, slightly worn blue towel laid on the end of it, as if they'd known she'd be coming to stay.

"Weather's been dreadful," said Mrs Sands, as she pulled the curtains at the window. "I hope you'll be warm enough."

"I'm sure I shall," said Rayne. She pushed her case under the bed, where it fitted neatly; she thought she'd unpack tomorrow.

"Bathroom's just across the hall. Call if you need anything. You sure you're not hungry?"

"Honestly, Mrs Sands, I'm full up of Green Lady pie."

Ethan's mum laughed. "Goodnight, dear. Sleep well." She went out, shutting the door quietly behind her.

Rayne turned off the light, walked round to the window and pulled back the curtains again. The trees were thrashing, leaves whirling in the moonlight. "I know you're out there," she murmured. "Calm down. I've come back, haven't I?"

There was a tap at the door.

"Yes?" she called.

The door opened; Ethan was silhouetted against the landing light with a large mug in his hand. "Sorry!" he said. "Are you going to sleep already?"

"No, I just wanted to look out at the moon."

"I brought you some cocoa. Dad makes great cocoa. Hot milk and everything." He took a step into the room. The door swung to behind him. "You going to be all right in here?"

"Of course I am. It's a lovely room. And your mum's lovely too." She took the mug from him, smiling.

"So – you want a lift tomorrow? To the Keep?"

"I suppose so. Thank you." She took a sip of cocoa. "Too hot," she said, putting it down on the chest of drawers, "but delicious, like you said."

There was nothing between them now. Nothing to stop them taking hold of each other in the little dark room. She could see his eyes glittering in the moonlight from the window, hear him breathing, sense him moving almost imperceptibly closer.

"E-*than!*" called Mrs Sands, from the big kitchen below.

He let out a sigh, and turned to the door. "I'll make you breakfast," he muttered. "When you get up."

And he vanished.

Rayne slept as she used to sleep in the Old Sty, deep and still, waking with the birds, then dozing off again. By nine she was sitting at the big farmhouse kitchen table drinking coffee, dressed in the black skirt and white shirt she wore to work in the tearoom. Ethan was frying eggs and bacon for them both, with flat field mushrooms his mum had gathered from a nearby field an hour earlier.

They didn't talk much, just the odd comment about the breakfast, and the farm, and the weather, which was still wet and wild. Last night, when they'd stood facing each other close in her dark room, was still between them.

Ethan drove Rayne over to Morton's Keep and dropped her off at the top of the drive. She told him not to wait; she'd run over to the old dairy tearoom to see if she still had her job. He said he'd go straight round and pay St John another visit. Unless she wanted to come with him, that was.

"No," she said. "No – once was enough for me."

"OK. Call me, then, yeah?" he said. "I can pick you up. Let me know what happens."

"I will," she promised.

He drove off, and silence descended. Ancient energy seemed to hum all around her. The rain had stopped but bleak pools of water puddled the gravel; the stone basin of the ivy-choked fountain was filled with water and each gust of wind skimmed a spray on to the ground.

She looked up at the two looming towers behind the ancient wall, wondering if they had the money to fix the roof on the west tower yet. Miss Skelton had said it needed major repairs before the winter set in. Well, winter was setting in with a vengeance now.

Rain started falling again, thin and relentless. She shivered, and ran across to the tearoom. The door was unlocked; she opened it and went in.

The ivy had been cleared from the window in the vestibule, and the lovely green light had gone. She heard voices from the tearoom, and went on.

The place been transformed. The newly whitewashed walls had been hung with huge black and white photographs of historic details from all around Morton's Keep. A griffon from the grand staircase. A window from the Old Stone Hall. A gargoyle's leering face above a doorway. A cherub's fat hand holding the fairground crown over the mad-smiling woman in the Great Hall.

It was stunning, and stylish, but it ruined the clean, white space of the old dairy. As Rayne stared, a kind of fear traced its way up her neck, and she turned, slowly, somehow knowing it would be there.

It was behind her, on the wall by the entrance way.

A huge photograph of the brass door knocker. Sir Simeon Lingwall's severed hand, blown up to thirty times its real size. The light in the picture made it look alive; the strange ring shone.

"Like it?" Tara called out. She was standing behind the kitchen counter at the end, next to Sessie. "Aunt Louisa's idea. They're cool, aren't they? Dead Gothic."

"Dead Gothic," said Rayne.

"We get people in asking where they're all located. It's almost like a quiz for them."

"Was that why the door knocker got polished up? To have its picture taken?"

"What? Oh . . . I expect so."

Rayne took a couple of steps towards the counter, and asked, "Is your aunt here?"

"Look at you, in your waitress uniform," said Tara. "You want your job back, don't you?"

"Well . . . yes. I do," said Rayne.

"To be honest, I don't know what she'll say. Sessie's been helping out, and another of the musicians – they fit it round rehearsals easy-peasy."

"Is your aunt here?" Rayne repeated.

"She's doing a tour," Tara said. Sessie continued to stare at her without expression.

"Where's Mrs Driver?" asked Rayne

"Oh – she hasn't been well," said Tara. She sounded more and more offhand as she spoke, and now she turned away and started pulling bread rolls out of a bag and laying them out on a cutting board. "She's been up in her room for days. To be honest, they're talking of pensioning her off. I mean – it's not as if she's any use now. And – you know what? We could really use her bedroom."

Without another word, Rayne turned on her heel and walked out, passing the first of the visitors as they came in for coffee. She heard them exclaiming over the drama of the massive photographs as she shut the door behind her. Thunder was rumbling at the edges of the woods again; the rain fell.

She walked quickly round to the back of the house. A coach and three cars were parked on the newly gravelled car park to the side of the house, which meant that the great baronial doors to the Great Hall would be unlocked, to let the tourists in. She hurried forward, and twisted one of the huge rings that served as handles.

The door swung slowly inward. She crept through, and shut it quietly behind her. The door to the Old Stone Hall was open; Miss Skelton's musical Scottish voice floated through it.

"Hundreds of young men – and women too – have been sentenced to death in this chill hall. They would stand on that gallery, looking down at the men who had the power of life and death over them, no doubt grasping that wooden rail to prevent themselves collapsing in mortal terror. . ."

She's milking it, thought Rayne disgustedly, as she tiptoed across to the grand staircase. She could still hear Miss Skelton as she made her way upwards, her tale measured out by the tick of the one-handed clock on the landing.

"We used to tell people they were taken out to the courtyard to be hanged, but that's untrue. Do you see that narrow window at the end of the gallery? Do you remember me asking you to take note of that strange dark beam protruding from the wall as we crossed the courtyard? That beam would have a rope round it. The noose would lie on the sill. Once the death sentence was pronounced, the noose would be thrown round the prisoner's neck, and he or she would be thrust from the window. . ."

Rayne shuddered. St John had told her that. He'd loved the idea, and he'd said it wasn't widely known. Where had Miss Skelton found out about it?

She hurried upwards, past the glass case with its creepy exhibits of mourning rings with hair from the dead, and the comb Anne Boleyn wore when she was beheaded. She reached the main landing and speeded down the corridor with its lowering portraits, to Mrs Driver's door. It was the first time she'd ever been to the housekeeper's room. Softly, she knocked.

Silence.

She knocked again, a little louder. The door opened.

Chapter Thirty-six

Mrs Driver's expression didn't change when she saw Rayne standing there. "Hello, dear," she said, almost in resignation. Then she stepped back, and Rayne walked into her room.

It was dark in there, darker than the corridor. The sky was now so overcast that barely any light came through the long, narrow window with its half-drawn, blue velvet curtains, and no lamps were on.

"Are you OK?" Rayne said, awkwardly. "Tara tells me you've been ill."

"Not ill exactly, dear. Just – not up to working in the tearoom."

The bedroom was very simply furnished. Two easy chairs by a little stove, cupboards in the wall, a bed, a table. It was a room to retreat to.

Rayne looked at the old housekeeper hopelessly, not knowing what to say. Then she blurted out, "Mrs Driver, have you heard what's been going on? With the watchers?"

Mrs Driver looked down, didn't answer her. Then, breaking eerily into the waiting silence, there was a noise. It came from over by the window – a strange, muffled noise, like soft laughter – like someone giggling into the long velvet curtain.

Rayne stared at the window in horror. "Who's there?" she breathed. The curtain moved, swayed. "Oh, *God*," she cried, "who's *there*?"

Mrs Driver sighed. "It's all right, dear!" she called, as though she was calling to a child. "It's all right. You can come out now. You don't have to hide."

The curtain swayed, swished, and out from behind it stepped a thin, dishevelled woman with mad eyes and long, wild, white-grey hair.

"Patience!" whispered Rayne.

"The sweet dark girl!" sang Patience, coming towards her, arms outstretched and clutching. Her hands with their long cracked nails looked like claws. "The sweet one *she* loves!"

Rayne took a step backwards, heart quickening in fear.

"Now be calm, Patience," said Mrs Driver, laying a hand on the old woman's arm. "Be calm."

"She's come to help us!" sang Patience. "*Fire, flood, fury, she is fire, flood, fury. . .*"

"Please don't let her come any closer," hissed Rayne.

"Patience, dear, you must be calm," said Mrs Driver. She was holding on to Patience now, stopping her from reaching Rayne.

"I'm sorry," muttered Rayne, "she's just freaking me out, that's all. . ."

"Sit down, Patience, dear. That's right, on the bed. Or you'll frighten the sweet girl, and she'll go away, and you don't want that to happen, do you. . ."

222

Patience's mouth trembled. "Stay!" she breathed. "*Stay!*" Then she plunked herself down on the bed, and sat very upright, her eyes never leaving Rayne's face.

"She's been with me for the last few days," Mrs Driver said, softly. "Sleeping here. Ever since . . . things have started to accelerate. She was growing increasingly distraught and they couldn't cope with her at the Green Lady inn. And we're old friends, aren't we, Patience? I haven't seen much of her in recent years, but – she knew I'd look after her."

Patience nodded, her eyes still on Rayne's face.

"I'm glad you've come back, Rayne," said Mrs Driver. Then she sighed again, and walked over to the window and stood there looking out, as the rain came down.

"Ethan came to get me," Rayne said. "It was horrific back at home, I can't tell you. I felt wrong, I felt out of place. It's not my home any more, I don't know why I called it that." She took a step towards Mrs Driver, hands lifted, almost pleading. "Look – it sounds mad but I think I've come back to help. I know you hate hearing about this stuff, but *dreadful* things are happening, and—"

"I know all about them," the old housekeeper said. She was still staring at the rain. "Will's been to see me. He told me what was going on."

"Will? He told me to come and see *you*."

"He would do, dear."

"But I thought you . . . I thought you didn't like the fire festival men. You always seemed to want to keep away from them."

"Did I? Well, that was then. This is now. And I've realized

223

I . . . I can't sleep through all this any longer. I can't *hide* any longer."

Then Mrs Driver turned round.

She was different.

Quite how, Rayne couldn't put her finger on – but she was different right down to the bone.

Her old expression of worried vagueness had gone. Gone, too, the anxious, elderly hunch to the shoulders.

Now she stood up straight. She seemed taller. She looked Rayne directly in the eye and Rayne realized she'd never really noticed her eyes before – they were deep blue, like the sky in summer. Her arms, which used to wrap round each other for comfort or warmth, hung loose by her sides as though she was ready.

"None of us can hide now," she said.

Even her voice had changed. It was deeper, surer.

"Mrs D, what's happened to you?" whispered Rayne. She felt scared, excited. "You're different."

"I've woken up," the housekeeper said. "To what I've known deep down all along."

"Will told you about the six sites? The old rhyme?"

"I already knew about the sites, and the rhyme. When I heard about the murder at the Devil's Tankard, I knew it was happening, but I was . . . frozen. Unable to act. Then Will came and told me about the other *cursed acts*. He got through to me – he said there's no time to be lost." She paced across the room, wringing her hands, and stood right in front of Rayne. The energy from her was so powerful Rayne had to fight to hold her ground, not to take a step back, away from her. "I'm . . . *so ashamed* of myself!" Mrs Driver cried.

"Ashamed? Why?"

"Ashamed of my *denial*. I knew from the start we were all under threat. You remember that lantern I made you, out of a turnip, at Halloween?"

"Yes, of course I do. You kept saying it was just an old tradition, just a bit of fun, but you seemed so urgent about it, so *serious*. . ."

"It is an old tradition. But this year I felt I really *needed* to make those lanterns, and I needed to give you one. And you put it in your window, didn't you? You lit it night after night. I saw it in your window. I . . . came down to the Sty, to check. You felt the same compulsion that I did."

"It looked to me like the green lady's face," said Rayne, nervously. Just saying the name made her nervous. "The open mouth, that – roar of breath."

"Yes. The face is always carved like that. Traditionally."

"But, Mrs Driver . . . when you gave me the lantern . . . nothing had happened! The pigeons with their throats slit . . . the murder . . . *nothing* had happened."

Mrs Driver lowered her head. "Miss Skelton had," she said.

Chapter Thirty-seven

"Miss *Skelton?*" echoed Rayne, in disbelief.

"Yes," said Mrs Driver, in her new, clear voice. "Our wonderful new manager. The one who was going to *save* Morton's Keep."

"But – oh my *God*. I remember you *saying* it was dangerous, all her plans to make money out of the dark side of the Keep. I thought you were over the top at the time, but . . . oh, God, d'you think *she's* stirred something up, *she's* somehow caused. . ."

"There's no *somehow* about it," said Mrs Driver, sharply. "This isn't an accidental effect, Rayne. I think she *is* the cause. I knew as soon as I saw her face, but I wouldn't admit it to myself. She's the danger, she's the threat."

Patience let out a little cry and pulled her legs up on the bed, then lay down all curled up. Mrs Driver went over, and in a sure, maternal movement, covered her with the blanket that was folded at the bottom of the bed.

Then she turned to Rayne, a finger on her lips. "She's exhausted," she whispered. "She knows everything is coming to . . . to a resolution. Come, sit by the fire."

Rayne sank into one of the little armchairs in front of the stove. Her mind was reeling.

"Miss Skelton has come here just as St John Arlington did," said Mrs Driver, sitting down very upright on the other chair. "In fact, I'm convinced she came here *because* of him, because of that wretched perverted website he was running. Have you seen it?"

"The Hidden History site?" muttered Rayne. "Yes, I've seen it."

"St John came to tap into the old evil, to draw on it, to gain power from it . . . she's come to do that and more. She's come to increase it, and release it. *Six cursed acts*. She's behind them."

Rayne stayed silent, staring into the small flames. It was too frightening to look into Mrs Driver's eyes.

"These things, they work on different levels," Mrs Driver went on. "And my sin was in not letting the levels connect. I pushed that initial terror down, that *fear* that made me carve the lanterns – I told myself I was irrational. I told myself I was seeing things in a distorted way because I'd taken an extreme dislike to the woman. My mistake was in not recognizing that that dislike was entirely *justified*." The housekeeper took in a deep, resolute breath, then went on. "I didn't trust her and I didn't like the way she was bringing all these changes to Morton's Keep. Trading on the grim history of the place, stirring old horrors up. Ben Avebury and I would talk about it together. We didn't think it was decent. But underneath – more than that – we were profoundly *worried* by it. We should have been more brave – we should have woken up. We should have let that worry *surface*."

"I knew you were worried, but I thought you were just put out," murmured Rayne. "You know – your nose was out of joint. This glamorous new broom coming in. . ."

Mrs Driver laughed. It hit Rayne that she'd never heard her laugh before. "Oh, there was a bit of that in there as well. I've been housekeeper at the Keep for over thirty years and no other manager has trespassed on my territory the way that woman did. And I didn't like the way Mr Stuart's head was so turned . . . 'Louisa this and Louisa that'. . . she could do no wrong and I was. . ."

"Hurt," said Rayne. "Jealous?"

"If I'm honest, I suppose a bit of both. And *cross* with him – that he could change his tune so much! Before, whenever Ms Barton had asked questions about Sir Simeon Lingwall, he'd been very starchy with her, told her it wasn't a subject for guided tours. But Miss Skelton just got round him. She convinced him it was the grim and the gory that would bring the tourists in and he . . . well, quite against his finer side, I believe . . . he went along with it."

"So you had all these feelings – milling around."

"Indeed. Utter confusion. And on top of all that Miss Skelton was, after all, very good at her job. So I tried to ignore my feeling of unease and *be positive*, fit in with her, as the profits soared."

"And could you? Ignore your feelings?"

"No."

Rayne leaned forward on her chair. "Mrs Driver, what happened? What made you . . . let the levels connect?"

"It suddenly came to me, what she was doing. It was the day after the first grand dinner. I'd gone into the Old Stone Hall to help clear out the flowers. Oh, Rayne. Such decadence – such waste. The sight of all those glorious blooms, the smell of them, all bundled into rubbish sacks. I looked up and saw myself, arms full of exotic flowers, in that wretched new mirror she'd put up – and it was then that it hit me. Miss Skelton wasn't just bringing the house back to life, as Mr Stuart insisted, she wasn't just making money to keep it afloat. She was *taking it back to Sir Simeon Lingwall's day*. The musicians up in the gallery, the rivers of champagne, the overnight guests in the state bedrooms, and most of all that great mass of flowers in the Stone Hall – she was recreating it all. Recreating how it was in *his* day."

Rayne stared at her, silently, and the sound of the ghosts dancing on the night of the first grand dinner came back to her so vividly it was as though she could actually hear them again. On the bed, Patience stirred a little, and muttered something in her sleep.

"It was a terrible realization, Rayne. You know, we never have flowers in the Stone Hall, but I'd . . . let myself forget the reason. They were banned because *he* used to fill the Hall with flowers, great expensive exotic blooms, when he held his diabolical parties."

"Did you tell anyone?" Rayne whispered. She felt as though her throat was closing up in fear. "What you'd realized?"

"No. Not even Ben Avebury. I was terrified, unsure how to act. Looking back, I think Ben was feeling the same way. I think *he* knew too. He kept a fire burning in the

Old Stone Hall, day and night, for protection, until that woman stopped him. And we avoided each other, in fear of what the other would say. But I watched *her* like a hawk. I saw how she was with Mr Stuart, how she lulled him, seduced him. I watched the musicians she'd moved into the house . . . they're not just ciphers, Rayne, they're *knowing*, part of it. The music they play – it makes your blood run cold. The way they all are together – we could be back there, back in Lingwall's day, when the house was full of these . . . *creatures*."

"Mrs D, that's . . . terrifying. To think the house is full of them. . ."

"Sharing bedrooms, doubling up. Oh, they're after this room too, but they won't get it. She's calling in new people all the time. They visit, they're drawn to the dark energy here . . . they make contact. She *recruits* them. The photographer who took those photos for the huge pictures that *ruined* my tearoom – I've seen *him* here again."

Mrs Driver leaned forward and jammed a log in the fire.

"And Tara?" muttered Rayne.

"Part of it, part of it. Sessie too."

The room lapsed back to silence, just the little fire in the stove clicking. Rayne couldn't speak. In her mind's eye she saw Tara diving through the back window at the Sty, arms reaching, fingers splayed. She remembered how afraid she'd felt when she'd seen her; how she'd shrugged it off as irrational.

And all the other little instances of fear. The Gothic dress, floating like a woman in the Old Sty. Miss Skelton and her niece talking in the darkening Spanish room, their features sharp in the half-light, laughing after they'd heard about the murder.

Maybe her fear had had deep roots. The thought terrified her.

"Louisa Skelton may not have *personally* murdered that poor girl in the Devil's Tankard," Mrs Driver said, "but she's behind it. The six cursed acts – it's *her*. I know it. In my bones, I know it. Mr Stuart – he's told her . . . everything, I think. *Everything*."

Rayne thought about what Mr Stuart could have told her. What he could have *shown* her. "Just before St John broke in and we burnt out Lingwall's cellar," she began slowly, "Mr Stuart told me about the old papers he'd found in the library. Lingwall's papers – accounts of his monstrous experiments. And the later reports of the . . . you know, the *reoccurrences*. . ."

"He kept them locked up in a safe in one of the attics."

"You *knew* about them?"

"Of course I did. I know everything about this place. Rayne – I'm the house *keeper*. I just . . . got scared, and . . . *lazy*. Lazy about my real role here. I wanted a quiet life. I didn't want to think about it, or talk about it. You'd try to get me to, sometimes, wouldn't you, dear? You'd ask me things and I'd brush you off. I wanted to keep it all tidily tucked far down in my mind. If you see what I mean."

"Yes," said Rayne. "I think I do."

"He will have shown her those papers. Without a doubt. And anything else he has. Miss Skelton now knows everything there is to know about this place and all the myths and legends surrounding it. Let us just fervently hope she doesn't know where the last lost site is. Before *we* can discover it."

Rayne had started trembling, despite the warmth of the fire. Wave after wave ran through her, and to try and protect herself she said, "OK, OK, you're convinced, Mrs Driver, but what *proof* have you got? All this is just about feelings, isn't it? Hunches? The flowers – they could just be a horrible *coincidence*. The events, the musicians – they're such a success. It could still all be about Miss Skelton making money for the Keep."

"Rayne—"

"No, I *mean* it. Her urgency, her drive – even her enslaving poor old Mr Stuart – it could all be because she's so desperate to make money to save the Keep. Look – she made me swear not to say anything, because she said it would humiliate Mr Stuart – but the west tower roof is in bad need of repair, and if it isn't fixed soon it could collapse, even bring down the side of the house next to it."

"The west tower was fixed four years ago," Mrs Driver said, firmly. "It's absolutely fine."

Rayne stared at the logs burning, mind churning. "She lied to me," she muttered. "She was so . . . convincing."

"When did she tell you?" demanded Mrs Driver.

"It was right after we'd had that awful meeting in the library, when she came on like a bull at a gate, telling you to cancel the Advent Craft Market and everything. She asked me over for supper – she was really nice to me."

"There you are then. It was pure damage limitation, getting you on her side so you wouldn't object to all her money-spinning schemes. So you'd think they were *just* money-spinning schemes, when really they were so much more. She knew that you were a threat – St John will have told her what you did, that night in the dungeon. And she could sense your power, Rayne. She was tying you to her side with bribery, with secrets."

"That night was when she gave me . . . it was when she gave me that long black dress."

"More bribery. And seduction, into her ways. She may even have hoped to win you over . . . recruit *you*. That would be just like her arrogance."

"It makes me feel sick, looking back. That I wore it."

"Yes. I never liked you in that dress, Rayne. It wasn't *you*. You left it in the Old Sty when you went back home, didn't you."

"I didn't see the point of taking it."

"Sessie wears it now. There was another big dinner when you were away, even more decadent than the first. Oh, we've wasted so much time – I should have trusted my instincts from the first! And trusted the *ghosts*! My little serving girl on the stairs – she knew what was up. She tried to warn me, bless her. As did Sir Philip Musgrave – remember? The way he rushed out of the library, hating the music. And Ben tells me you heard dancing. *Dancing*."

Rayne shot to her feet. She felt like if she heard any more she'd start screaming. She put her hands to her head and scrubbed at her hair. "Mrs Driver – I need some air, OK?" she blurted out. "What you're saying about Miss Skelton – it implicates Mr Stuart too! Are you saying he's just standing back while . . . while she takes the Keep back to Lingwall's day?"

"I'm saying she beguiled him. An attractive woman, twenty years younger than him – of course she beguiled him."

"It's so much to take in. And *you're* so different – it's all too much to take in."

"I understand, dear," said Mrs Driver, gently. "Off you go. Close the door quietly, we don't want to wake poor Patience. And . . . Rayne?"

"Yes?" said Rayne. She was already at the door.

"Come back any time. I'm staying here. I'm still the

house keeper. I'm staying. To find out what I can, to spy, to . . . to *watch*."

Rayne made her way hurriedly back down the grand stairway. Her thoughts careered, desperate to find a solution, desperate for safety. It terrified her to think that the threat was coming from inside the house. Somehow that seemed so much worse than from the outside. It was so much more *dangerous*. So much harder to fight.

Images, memories crowded in on her again. Times when she, like Mrs Driver, had not let the levels connect. Had known – but not let herself know.

Then in her mind she was back at the beginning, back in Ms Barton's flat, cleaning it up for Miss Skelton's arrival. She remembered the feeling of panic in it, all Ms Barton's belongings strewed about. Then the feeling of . . . the feeling of *waiting*.

She let herself out of the great double doors, and ran round to the woods behind the Old Sty. The Sty might not be her home any more, but the woods – they were still hers. She sat down on a moss-covered tree stump and pulled out her mobile phone. The trees shushed around her, dropping copper-coloured leaves.

Ms Barton's number was there, recently called.

She called it again.

Ms Barton was glad to hear from Rayne, although she had no news to tell her. She said she was afraid she'd not uncovered anything new about the sixth site.

"Can I ask you something?" said Rayne, abruptly.

235

"Ask away."

"Right after you left, I cleaned your flat out, and you'd left all this stuff—"

"Yes, I'm sorry about that. I do appreciate you packing it all up to be sent on."

"Oh, that wasn't a problem. I just – I know you were worried about your mum and everything, but you seemed to have left in such a hurry . . . a *panic*. . ."

There was a silence from the phone. Then Ms Barton said, "Yes. It wasn't very pleasant."

Rayne took in a breath. "What happened?" she asked.

"Oh, nothing definite. Nothing you could *see*. I was worried about Mum, of course I was, but I had my train booked, there was no need to rush . . . and then I just felt this extraordinary need to *go*. As you say – it was like panic. A panic attack. But I've never had one before or since – it's just not *me*. I fought it for a while, then I phoned the cab company and got them to come as soon as they could and I just – *got out*. I said goodbye to Mrs Driver. She thought I was upset at leaving, which I was, in a way, but more than that I was just . . . I don't know. Just panicking. Desperate to leave."

"How awful," murmured Rayne.

"I got to the station about two hours early, it was ridiculous. I just sat there drinking coffee, trying to calm down. Which I did of course, eventually. But I was shaken, really shaken. I'd never felt like that before."

"And your mum," Rayne said, "how is she?"

"Not very good. It's a strange illness – the doctors still haven't diagnosed it properly. Some form of neurological degeneration, they think. But it leaves her helpless and . . .

and very dependent on me. It's awful, the way she's deteriorated – and it came on so suddenly."

Another silence. Rayne could hear Ms Barton breathing, quick, sharp, breaths, as if the thought that had just hit Rayne had hit her too.

That her mother's illness had been caused, somehow. . .

That she'd been cursed.

That something malevolent, and powerful, had engineered Ms Barton's exit from Morton's Keep.

So that Miss Skelton could come in.

Rayne couldn't put this into words, though. She muttered a few platitudes about hoping her mother got better, and Ms Barton, voice bright and tight, thanked her, and then they said goodbye.

Then Rayne called Ethan. Relief coursed into her as she heard his voice, answering. He said he'd seen St John. He said he'd pick her up from the forecourt in about ten minutes' time. She scrambled to her feet and hurried over there.

Rayne had only been waiting for a couple of minutes when she heard voices from the courtyard. Miss Skelton, talking loud, and Tara, answering, and another voice, a man's, she didn't recognize. . .

There was nowhere to hide. She had to brazen it out. She heard Miss Skelton's heels clicking over the cobblestones behind her, heard her exclaim, "*Rayne!* What on earth are you doing, still here?"

Rayne turned and faced them, sullenly. "I went to see Mrs Driver," she said. She recognized the man as one of the violin players. He was tall, elegant, sneering at her. "Tara told me she was ill."

"Oh. I see," said Miss Skelton crisply. "And it was necessary for you to wear your waitress's clothes to visit her, was it?"

Rayne didn't answer. Miss Skelton let out a sarcastic little laugh. "I'm sorry, Rayne," she said, "but you can't just pick up your job where you left off when you ran out on us with no notice. Mr Stuart and I are quite in agreement about that. We need staff who are *reliable.*"

"That's OK," said Rayne. "I don't want my job back now."

"Hmm. Enlighten me – why are you standing here?"

"I'm getting a lift."

Miss Skelton tossed her head, as though utterly dismissing her, then walked on across the courtyard, with Tara and the violinist. "As I was saying before the *interruption*," she said, "I'm beginning to give up hope of ever finding it again. I've looked everywhere."

"Poor you," said the man. "*So* unbelievably irritating."

"Tara," Miss Skelton went on, "did you check in the library?"

"I combed it," said Tara. "And I went up the grand staircase, stair by stair. It's not there. Are you sure you lost it in the house?"

"No. I've no idea when I lost it. For the life of me, I can't remember taking only one out."

"After a party, maybe?" the man asked, silkily. "After a bit too much to drink?"

"Probably. *Damnation*. They really were my favourite earrings. They've been in our family for generations. I wonder if I can get the other one copied?"

238

Chapter Thirty-nine

"You look like someone's hit you on the head with a sandbag," said Ethan, sticking his head out of the ancient Land Rover window.

"I feel like they have," Rayne muttered.

"So you didn't get your job back."

"No way. And . . . oh, *Christ*, I can't think straight, Ethan." She pulled open the passenger door, got in beside him. "Did you see St John?"

"Yes. No joy, though, like we thought. Did you see Mrs Driver? Did she tell you anything?"

"Yes. Lots. Look – can we go back to your place and talk? I want to get out of here."

"Sure." He started up the car, and headed back down the drive.

"Ethan?" she murmured.

"Yes?"

"What about the pigeons? I meant to call in to the dovecote . . . they won't have been fed since I went away. . ."

"Oh, they have been. Ben's been on it."

"Are they OK?"

"No more crucifixions, if that's what you mean. The tower roof's sprung a leak in all this rain, but they can still get out of the wet. And Ben says he'll fix it."

"Are they . . . OK?"

"I doubt Ben's that good at judging a pigeon's emotional state, Rayne. But he says they're OK."

She sat back on the seat and closed her eyes. The Land Rover turned out of the long drive to Morton's Keep and sped off down the road.

Mrs Sands had left lunch out for them, at the farmhouse. Cold roast chicken and potato salad, with sliced tomatoes. Rayne devoured it all hungrily, almost matching Ethan. The two of them washed up together, then they went through into the chill little back parlour, to be alone to talk.

"Can we light a fire?" asked Rayne, rubbing her arms.

"Chimney's blocked. Here, put this round you." He handed her a black fringed shawl, and she huddled it round her. "Now. Tell me."

"No. You first. Did you learn anything from my ex?"

"Urrgh. Don't call him that. No – not a sausage. Flora was there, all curled up on the bed with him. They were just sneering and laughing and stroking each other. . . I didn't stay long. They gave me the creeps. One thing I did think, though. . ."

"What?"

"He's looking better. More energy. *Happier*. Now you, Rayne. What happened?"

Slowly, reliving it, Rayne explained everything. About

Patience being there in the room, and Mrs Driver's transformation. About the house keeper's sense of shame that she hadn't "woken up" sooner, and her belief that Miss Skelton was returning the manor house to how it had been in Sir Simeon Lingwall's day. About Miss Skelton's lie about the west tower needing urgent repairs, and Mrs Driver's certainty that it was Miss Skelton behind the cursed acts.

Ethan barely interrupted her as she spoke, only to check a detail, make sure he'd understood. When she ran out of words he said, "No one ever thought the cursed acts would come from *inside*. In all the stories, it's from outside – a stranger, an enemy just wanting to wreak havoc on the town. . ."

"It feels more dangerous this way."

"Yes. Skelton's *in* there, living there, she's moved in all her lackeys, she's got Mr Stuart under her thumb – she's already achieved what St John only dreamed of. She's . . . *nurturing* the dark power of the Keep. And at the same time – if it's *her* doing the desecrating on the six sacred sites – she's setting out to free it."

"That's what Mrs Driver said. *She's come to increase it, and release it.*"

Ethan stretched his long legs out in front of him. "And Mrs Driver just plans to stay there, does she?" he said. "In her room?"

"Yes. She said she'd find out what she could, she said she's *watching.*"

"She's a brave old girl. There on her own. You know – I always thought there was more about her than met the eye, even though she could be a bit stand-offish about the fire festivals. Is she getting food?"

"Oh, I think so. You should see her now, Ethan, she's strong, she's so different – I wouldn't challenge her if she came into the kitchen for food! She said she was still the house keeper and when she said it – it was like it was two words now. The keeper of the house."

"Rayne – we need to tell Will. He's called me twice already. We need to get to The Green Lady."

"There's more stuff you should know, Ethan. I phoned Ms Barton. And—"

"Tell everyone, Rayne. At the pub."

"OK, OK, give me a minute. I'm just – I don't want to move, I feel safe here. And this shawl – it's like it's electric! It's so *warm*!"

Ethan grinned at her. "City girl," he scoffed, but his voice was kind. "It's pure wool, that's all. Ten times as warm as those fake fabrics. Keep it on. We've got to go."

"OK," she said, and stood up.

"Mind if we take Hiker this time?" said Ethan, as they left the farmhouse. "He's been stuck in his field for the last few days, and he's sulking. He likes an outing."

"Won't he mind the extra weight?"

"He won't even notice you."

"In that case – cool!"

Chapter Forty

Hiker had a big old saddle that just fitted two if they sat very, very close. Rayne loved riding Hiker; it felt so natural, being on his back. She loved sitting behind Ethan even more. Fitting up against him, legs, arms, body. She wondered if he felt the same and if that's why he'd suggested they go on the horse. She tightened her arms round his waist as Hiker started to trot, feeling his muscles move as he guided the horse.

Weird, she thought, to be caught up in this fantastic cosmic crisis and still feel . . . what she was feeling for Ethan. She thought about Sarah, Becky's friend, the girl who really fancied him – she wondered if they had got together, and what Sarah thought about her moving into Ethan's farmhouse. Maybe she was OK about it because Ethan had made it clear to her that he just wanted Rayne for her role in this weird, ancient battle.

But that couldn't be true, could it. Not after what had passed between them in the box room, just before his mum had called him down. Not the way their bodies were fitting together now.

She leant her cheek against his back as the horse cantered on.

They reached The Green Lady. It was still too early for the pub to be open for the evening, but they tethered Hiker in the stall at the back with his bucket of water, then Ethan took her through an unlocked door next to the stall. A walk down a low-ceilinged corridor brought them into the bar. The same group that had been there the night she'd fled was at the same table, worried expressions on their faces. And Rayne sat down with them, and began to tell her story again. No one interrupted her; she finished by describing her phone conversation with Ms Barton, and their strong sense that her departure from Morton's Keep had been planned, engineered.

The watchers seemed as dazed by the idea that the threat would come from inside the Keep as Rayne and Ethan had been. "It *can't* be that Skelton woman, desecrating the sites," said Mark. "If she is taking the Keep back to Lingwall's day, she's got all the power she needs right underneath her. . ."

"Maybe she wants more," said Ethan.

"But why *release* it?"

Will, who'd been silent up to this point, sighed. "Remember the first line of the old rhyme? *Six cursed acts, the horror spreads free*. Spreads – not leaves the Keep like a wolf, but *spreads*, like an infection. And no doubt stays festering in its original place, too. It will increase. More than we can imagine."

There was a silence, then a plump woman piped up, "I can't believe it's Louisa Skelton, though. Not at the root of it."

"No, not all that witch-energy malarkey," said one of the men. "Cursing Ms Barton's mother, Mrs Driver talking about just *knowing* she's the one—"

"Well, I trust Mrs Driver," said Will. "I've known her since childhood and I trust her instinct like I trust my own."

"But I've *met* Louisa," said the woman, "several times, and she seemed really nice. And *really* dynamic – just what the town needs. Lots of the local people think so. And my cousin, Amy, she's just got a job there at the Keep, cleaning and so on . . . they need more staff with all those guests. . ."

"That's why *Louisa's* been firing people, too, is it?" asked a young man, sharply. "Becky Brook's mum – she's been given the push."

"Doesn't prove anything," snapped the plump woman.

"I wish we *had* proof," said Mark. "I wish we *knew*."

"Will," said Rayne, suddenly, "that earring you found, up on Peak's Barrow – have you still got it?"

Will nodded, stood up, and went behind the bar. He pulled open a drawer and came back to the group with a tiny cardboard box. He tipped the earring out on to the table. It lay there, silver and blood red.

"It's hers," said Rayne, in a flat voice. "It's definitely hers. Earlier today I overheard her talking about losing one of her favourite earrings. And now I see it I'm sure. She was wearing them, with her hair up, on the night of the first grand dinner. She was dressed all in red. She looked stunning."

"As she no doubt did at that cursed party, on Peak's Barrow," said Will.

There was a long, long pause. Ethan exhaled, long and low.

"You want to have a word with your cousin Amy," said the old man, to the plump woman. "She either needs to get out from the Keep – or you need to cut her clear off from you."

"And we'd better get on with it," said Ethan. "With finding the last site. With setting the six fires."

"Are they still guarding Martyr's Hill?" asked Rayne.

"Yes. Louisa Skelton isn't the only person drawing people to her cause. We've already built the bonfire there, a huge one – I've got no lack of volunteers. I've put young Cory in charge, with Jack Lewis, they're doing a great job. Word is spreading – people are feeling it. It's worse now – worse than we dreamt, with that monstrous base at the Keep. But at least now we know our enemy."

"And we know the rough position of the last site, don't we?" said one of the men. "Wildhern Valley."

"Wildhern is nearly a mile long, and pretty wide across. You going to set fire to all of it?" snapped Mark.

And then, as she knew they would, everyone seemed to be staring at Rayne again. "I know," she muttered. "I know you think the green lady will . . . she'll tell me. But it feels so *weird*. And I've no idea what to do. How to go about it."

"Go to the valley," said Will, gently. "See how it takes you."

"I'll go with you," said Ethan, quickly.

Chapter Forty-one

It was four o'clock and growing dark when Rayne and Ethan arrived at Wildhern Valley, dismounted from Hiker, and started walking. Wildhern Valley was a local beauty spot, used by farmers to graze their sheep. Two gentle slopes stretched beyond the horizon; the bottom of the valley was some thirty metres wide. Rayne looked at it and felt despair nudge at her. "It's hopeless," she muttered. "It's huge. And we don't even know it's the right spot, do we? We're just assuming it because of the star shape. Which – as you said – is not going to be all symmetrical. Maybe the sixth star point is way out. Maybe it's bang up against another point. Maybe it *overlaps* it. Maybe. . ."

"Oh, shut up, misery!" groaned Ethan. Then he put his arm round her and gave her a squeeze, so hard her shoulders crunched, and then snatched his arm away again, and walked on, fast.

The only happy member of the party was Hiker. Ethan had taken his saddle off and dumped it behind some bushes, and let him run free. He trotted about, sniffing the air, then dropped to the ground and rolled blissfully in the long, damp grass.

"I mean . . . what's supposed to happen?" said Rayne. "The green lady's going to suddenly appear and point the place out to me? I don't think so."

"Well . . . maybe you have to . . . get in the mood," Ethan said, uncomfortably. "Open your mind. Clear your mind."

"Oh, God. OK. Let's walk."

"And we'll just check it out. Keep our eyes open. We might see something that . . . you know, that looks likely. Stones, like the altar in Fleet Woods, or a group of very old trees. . ."

"OK, OK. Let's split up and walk."

They each took a slope of the valley and meandered slowly forward, up and down, looking all around themselves, trying to sense the place. Sheep bustled away from them, baaing indignantly, as if annoyed that they weren't keeping to a straight path. Hiker trotted cheerfully behind, chomping up mouthfuls of grass, sometimes breaking into a canter and overtaking them.

All was tranquil, harmonious, and night was approaching. Rayne tried to relax and clear her mind but she grew more and more tense as the shadows deepened and nothing caught her eye. "That's the end of the valley," said Ethan, gloomily, pointing. "By those woods. Let's go on just a bit, then we'll turn back."

On the way back, they walked fast, along the bottom, barely bothering to look about. "I'll phone Ms Barton again," said Rayne, morosely, as Ethan saddled up Hiker.

"She said she'd keep on with her research. Maybe she's had a breakthrough."

Ethan didn't answer. Rayne felt like she was a fraud, a failure. She'd found nothing – she'd failed.

They clopped away in silence, away from the valley, and didn't see the three dark figures rise up against the skyline, come over the eastern slope of the valley, and stand there unmoving, as though they were staring after them.

Rayne couldn't sleep that night, at the farmhouse. At three in the morning she got out of bed and looked out of the little casement window. The weather was calmer than it had been, and the moon was bright.

She was suddenly filled with a need to get out into the night. It was madness; her brain told her to get back into bed again. But she put on her coat over her pyjamas, and pulled open her bedroom door.

The farmhouse was silent, everyone sleeping. She crept down the stairs to the kitchen. The three farm dogs, sleeping by the cooking range, lifted their muzzles and stared at her, then closed their eyes and dropped their heads down on their paws again, as though she was an irrelevance. She found her wellington boots in the line by the door, and pulled them on. Then she drew back the bolt and went out.

What kind of guest *am* I? she thought. Leaving the door unlocked when there's murderers about? Ah well. The dogs'll sound the alarm.

She walked down the tree-lined lane that led to the farm. Large birds roosting in branches above her head clattered into the air in panic as she went by, and whirled off into the darkness. At first this scared her, then she got used to it. Her moon shadow went with her, skidding bright and black along the ground in front of her.

She'd ceased to think, to analyse what she was doing; she simply walked, unfrightened, and let the night fill her up.

She knew the green lady was with her. In the shadows, in the trees stirring, in the cries of owls. She walked on in her company.

After about half an hour, she was back at the farmhouse door. When she opened it the dogs shot to their feet and wuffed, but she said *shhhh* firmly, and they settled back down again. She took off her wellies, bolted the door behind her once more, went back up to bed, and slept deeply.

If Ethan, or anyone, knew she'd been out, they didn't mention it the next morning. Breakfast passed uneventfully. Then Rayne got a call on her mobile. It was from an unknown number, but she answered it.

"Rayne?" said Mrs Driver's new, clear voice. "Can you come to see me, dear? As soon as possible. I've something to tell you."

Chapter
Forty-two

Ethan was not at all happy about Rayne going to Morton's Keep on her own, but she insisted he shouldn't come with her. "I can just slip through the doors to the Great Hall again," she said, "and run upstairs. If anyone challenges me, I'll say I'm visiting Mrs Driver. If *you* come – they'll see it as an act of aggression, won't they?"

"And knowing Ethan it could well turn into an act of aggression," said Mrs Sands. She sounded quite proud. "Fists first, think later. He's been like that since he was eight." She pushed a paper carrier bag into Rayne's hands. "Take this to Mrs Driver. It's just some jam, and biscuits, and some cold beef I've packed up. If anyone stops you, wave that at them. Say you've got her a present."

"That's kind of you," said Rayne. And she thought: Ethan's right. Everyone's part of this. Everyone *knows*.

"I'll give you a lift to the end of the drive, at least," said Ethan.

"Thanks. But no further."

*

No one saw Rayne as she crept up the grand staircase and on to the landing. The door to the Red Queen's room was open; she could hear laughing from inside, and several voices, musical and light. She couldn't hear any words but they had a teasing, gloating sound that made her quicken her pace. She sped along the corridor to Mrs Driver's room and knocked, turning the handle as she did so. It was locked. "It's me!" she called, softly, looking anxiously back over her shoulder towards the Red Queen's room. "Rayne!"

Almost immediately the key turned and the door was open. "Come in, dear," said Mrs Driver. Rayne stepped inside and the housekeeper locked the door again behind her.

The room was more cheerful this time; the curtains were pulled back.

"I've brought you a present," Rayne said. "From Ethan's mum."

"How lovely." Mrs Driver peered into the bag. "Her home-made jam is wonderful. We've got treats for tea, Patience!"

Patience was sitting on a stool at the window. She waved eagerly to Rayne, then went back to gazing outside again.

"I'm pleased you're staying at Sands Farm," said Mrs Driver. "You're safe there. Sit down, dear." They sat opposite each other by the little stove, and Rayne held out her hands to its warmth. "I'm so glad you could come. And I'm sorry I sounded melodramatic when I called you, but I was using the phone in the library, and I didn't want anyone to overhear."

"The library? I'm glad you're still moving about the house, Mrs D."

"Indeed I am. They don't dare challenge me. Patience and I walk in the grounds, too. But Miss Skelton and her houseguests are getting . . . less pleasant. It's only a matter of time before they confront me." She looked down at her hands, and sighed. "I bumped into Mr Stuart as I was leaving the library. He seemed . . . well. Very embarrassed and distressed to see me. He was just asking me how I was when Miss Skelton appeared and took him off. He seemed to have no say in the matter."

"I'm glad he was embarrassed, at least."

"Yes. Although – poor man, too. Anyway, Rayne. I overheard something. About the sixth site. I was in the utility room, getting some food from the fridge, and several of those . . . *creatures* came into the Tudor kitchen. So I laid low and listened. One of them said something about *trying again tomorrow night.* Another grumbled about the amount of ground they had to cover. Then the first voice said, *At least we know she's on the ridge.* It's not much to go on, I know, dear. . ."

"*She's* on the ridge."

"Yes. She. If they're talking about the sixth site, and it's Wildhern Valley, then it might cut your search down a little. . ."

Rayne pulled out her mobile. "You should get one of these," she said, smiling, then she called Ms Barton.

"Oh, Rayne," said Ms Barton tiredly, when she answered her phone, "I'm afraid I've nothing new for you. I've had very little time. Mum's been having more tests and they're still not finding anything. . ."

"Oh, I'm so sorry. And I'm sorry to hassle you. I just – I remembered you saying something about an old stone carving, when I phoned you first of all. Of a pagan goddess maybe. . ."

"Oh, yes. I found the paper that related to that. Among some early church records from Marcle Lees. Nothing to link it to the sixth site, I'm afraid – no clues at all about where it was. Just a letter from a bishop to his priest, saying . . . hang on, I'll fetch it. I filed a copy of it."

Rayne held the phone out so that Mrs Driver could hear, too. "It's dated sixteen hundred and thirty-two," said Ms Barton. "Lots of stuff about parish matters, money and the lack of it . . . here it is. *As for the matter we discussed, I urge the destruction of this stone with all possible dispatch. Whomsoever this lady might be, she is not of the True Faith.* There, that's all it says. I couldn't find any other mention of the stone."

"A mysterious lady of stone that has nothing to do with the church. . ." said Rayne.

"Yes, you can just *feel* the fear and suspicion, can't you? The seventeenth century is rather late to be demonizing the pagan still, but it may be connected to the widespread fear of witchcraft that was around at that time. I thought of the myth of the green lady right away, of course, but I've nothing to back it up."

"Thanks for reading it to me, Ms Barton. Well – I won't take up any more of your time."

"Goodbye, Rayne. Keep in touch, won't you."

"I will. I hope your mum gets better. Goodbye." She rang off.

Mrs Driver smiled at her. "*Letting the levels connect,* Rayne?"

"A bit. If Skelton's lackeys know more than we do – and they say it's a *she* on a ridge – well, it's worth another visit to Wildhern Valley, to scour the high edges. Looking for stone this time, maybe fragments of broken stone if it was a statue and it's smashed. . ."

"I'd say it's definitely worth a visit. You'll know it when you find it, I'm sure of it. And this time . . . let yourself be guided."

Rayne hung her head. "I wish I could. I wish I knew how to. It's all so . . . freaky. Why should she contact *me*?"

"She already has, dear, freaky or not, hasn't she? You've seen her several times. She's led you, she's guided you. You just have to open up to it. You don't want to be guilty of doing what I did – of burying your head in the sand. Oh, it costs so much to confront it and step up to the line and own it – no one knows that more than me! You have a link with her, a strong one. I know it. Why do you think I gave you the job in the tearoom? On the spot? I knew that you were . . . *needed*. But I was too lazy and scared to own it to myself at the time."

There was a silence. Rayne was wondering how Mrs Driver knew quite so much about the green lady guiding her, but she didn't know how to ask about it.

Then Mrs Driver said, "Have you ever wondered, Rayne, how Patience got away from the tower dovecote? How a young girl got away from Peter Saul, the monster who'd abducted her?"

"Well, it did seem a bit weird. I thought maybe he'd just let her go."

"No. Help came for her. The green lady helped her. I'm not sure how, but sometimes Patience talks about being *lifted up* – floating above the trees. She was found, you know, in the middle of a wood with twigs and leaves in her hair. To be honest, to this day I don't know whether it was Peter Saul's atrocities or the green lady's rescue that made poor Patience lose her mind."

"Great. And that's supposed to make me want to open up to her, is it?"

"Rayne, you're infinitely stronger than Patience. Have some faith."

Rayne stood up. She felt she needed to get out into the air again. "Thanks, Mrs Driver. I'm going to go now."

"All right, dear. Good luck with your search. I'll keep watching here, keep monitoring. Stay in touch, won't you? Let me know how you get on." She smiled. "Mobile or no mobile."

Rayne slipped out of the great doors to the Hall without being seen, and made her way down a little pathway on the edge of the estate. She needed to walk to clear her head, before she called Ethan. A wind had got up, with a spattering of cold rain in it. She skirted some trees and saw Ben Avebury in a clearing, sawing wood, but she didn't call out to him. She hurried on with her head down. At the end of the path she climbed a stile into a field. She crossed it at a pace, stomping along the ruts made by tractor wheels, not making detours round the puddles, just ploughing straight through them. The wind suddenly grew stronger, so sudden and fierce that Rayne stopped in her tracks. The trees at the end of the field reared and bucked under its force, long branches thrashing, leaves roaring. Then, as Rayne watched, a great stream of yellow and brown leaves soared upwards, whirled together, streaming through the air. . .

An extraordinary terror came over her.

"Oh, no," she whispered. "No, *please*. . ."

A dozen crows rose from the trees and flew fast at the leaves, circling them, screaming with their harsh, raw cries. Rayne, transfixed, stared as the leaves formed a head, streaming hair, flowing robes, long arms reaching out towards her. . .

Awe filled her. "Please," she whispered. "*Please.*"

The green lady swooped closer, leaves whirling, circling, hair streaming . . . she was so close now that the great open mouth filled Rayne's vision. The crows flew with her, screaming, cawing. And now the green lady was so close that Rayne could feel her breath on her face, a great *haaaa* that smelt of earth, fire, growing things, dying things. In absolute fear she slammed her eyes shut. She could hear the roaring of the wind, feel the leaves whipping her face, enveloping her, covering her . . . she trembled as she stood, eyes forced shut.

The wind softened.

The leaves were dropping gently now, pattering all around her, falling soft as snowflakes. She stood there for long, slow minutes as the leaves covered her with a thousand tiny touches. At last it stopped, and she opened her eyes.

She was standing in a great drift of leaves, half covered by them.

"It's OK," she whispered. "It's OK. I know what you need me to do and it's OK."

She pulled out her mobile and called Ethan.

Chapter Forty-three

Dusk was settling on the top of Wildhern Valley. Rayne and Ethan had parked the Land Rover on the road that ran alongside it and headed up to the high ridges. They'd been walking for over an hour, scattering the sheep, searching, peering, prodding and poking the earth. They'd found nothing.

They sat down on the ground, tired and dispirited. The wind blew through the trees behind them, taking the last of the dead leaves off and scattering them over their heads. A patch of long grass at their feet rippled like a woman's hair.

Rayne looked down. She'd told Ethan about her visit to Mrs Driver, but not about the green lady appearing to her. She couldn't talk about it – she couldn't think about it without shaking. And yet it was real, she knew it was real. Leaves still clung to her jacket and her hair.

"It might help," she said, "if we knew exactly what we were looking for."

"I know," grumbled Ethan. "What was it Mrs Driver said? *You'll know it when you find it*. Fat lot of good that is."

"We've been over this whole area. There's nothing."

"Maybe if we just set the fire here, at the highest point—"

"But we could be way out. We've got to find the exact spot, Ethan. We've got to find the stone."

"I don't think it's still here."

There was a gloomy silence. Then Rayne got to her feet, and paced forward, frowning, concentrating. Let yourself be guided, Mrs Driver had said, but how did you *do* that?

All right. Show me. Come on, show me.

She walked on, further away from Ethan. *Use me like a divining rod. I'll know. Help me.*

She tried to clear her mind, empty it of all thoughts. She shut her eyes; she tried to move intuitively.

Is it here, is it over there? Guide me, guide me!

Her head was spinning with the effort of focusing. She knew she was trying too hard, straining; nothing would happen like this.

She stood stock-still, eyes still shut, and let the wind flow over her. Into her mind she brought the image of a bonfire. She saw it, on this hill, beautiful, burning, keeping the town safe. The image filled her, seemed to set light to her body. And then she turned to her right, and began to walk, eyes open now.

After a few moments her left foot hit a rock. She looked down. It was a flat rock, buried in the turf that had crept over it. She fell to her knees, and started to tear at the turf, pulling it back. Hundreds of years of creeping soil and tough hillside plants had covered it, made it theirs.

"What is it?" shouted Ethan. He got to his feet and started to run towards her.

"Probably nothing," she said, through gritted teeth, still scraping at the soil. "I'm probably ruining my nails for *nothing*. Just a hunch." But she kept on frantically digging at the stony soil.

Ethan picked a sharp-edged piece of flint up from the ground. "Here," he said, "use this." He found another piece of flint for himself, and started a little way away from her, digging deep into the turf and tearing it back in strips. "Here's the edge of the rock," he said, after a few minutes' hard work, "here, I'm clearing it now. . ." Something made him stop and look up at Rayne.

She'd stopped scraping. She was very still, staring down in front of her.

"I've found her eyes," she said.

Chapter Forty-four

Ethan was at her side in a second, peering down too. "Oh my God," he breathed.

In the rock were carved two simple eye shapes, each the size of a fist. The pupils were visible as deep holes in the centre. He reached out a hand and started to clear the earth away around them.

"Careful," breathed Rayne. "Be careful. Don't hurt her."

"You do it," said Ethan, gently.

She worked slowly, only using her flint when the turf was too tough to shift by hand. She loosened a thick wedge of soil and grass below the eyes, then peeled it down. A nose appeared, a simple two-line etching into the rock face. Then the mouth. Rayne felt a shiver as she cleared it, saw that it was open – open like the mouth in the Martyr's Hill bonfire, like the lady of leaves who'd flown at her. She moved up, and began to clear above the eyes. The head was surrounded by a halo of wild hair, like branches radiating out.

"Well," muttered Ethan, "looks like Mrs Driver was right. We'd know it when we found it."

"It's ancient," said Rayne. "It looks medieval." Less solemn now, less awed, she cleared faster, down below the face. "She's wearing a medieval sort of dress. High-waisted. Look."

Ethan joined in, clearing above the head, all round the edge of the rock that he'd uncovered. "Hey," he said. "There's writing here." He scraped eagerly, carefully, pulling up tough little plants rooted into the rock. "Look. Roman letters. Look."

The letters were faint, worn away by hundreds of years of rain and soil. But they could still be read: *MCCCXIII.*

"Thirteen hundred and thirteen," said Rayne. "That's right, isn't it? Thirteen hundred and thirteen."

Ethan was copying them on to the back of his hand with a biro he'd found in his pocket. "Not sure," he said. "But Ms Barton will know. We should call Will. Call everyone."

"Not yet. Let's finish this first. It's *important.*" She'd cleared the whole of the top of the stone, and was starting to work down the side. Ethan worked down along the other side. A great, smooth slab, like a large tombstone, emerged.

But, as Ethan found when he dug down beside it, it went deep into the earth. It had been there since the hills had formed. It couldn't ever be moved. "So they carved it here, in place," he said. "And they carved it deep, so that even after all this time, we could still see it."

"*God,* I'd love to know what happened," said Rayne, fervently. "Why they chose this stone."

"Maybe they didn't choose it – maybe they were shown it. Maybe they saw *her* here."

"You're right. She showed them where the sacred place was. Where the fire should be."

"And then over the years, as the threat grew less. . ."

"It got forgotten, and buried under the turf. Until we came along." Rayne turned to look at him, and smiled, and he smiled back, and their faces grew close.

"You found it," he said, admiringly.

"No," she said. "I was shown it, too."

They worked for another half-hour on the stone, clearing the turf well away from it, so that by the time they'd finished it sat raised on a sort of platform of earth. Rayne brushed at the surface of the stone, clearing dirt from the face and dress, digging it out of the eye sockets and roman numerals.

"They'd have to have been pretty secretive about this," said Ethan, thoughtfully. "Back in thirteen hundred and thirteen. If the priests found out they were conducting some kind of pagan ritual up here. . ."

"That's why there aren't any records, I suppose," said Rayne. "Just that letter from the bishop to his priest, over three hundred years later, telling him to destroy it."

"He didn't, though, did he. I wonder what happened."

"They were risking their lives when they carved it. All of them, all of the townspeople who came . . . their belief in her must have been so strong."

Suddenly, Ethan sat back on his heels. "Oh . . . *shit*," he muttered.

"What's the matter?" Rayne asked, looking up at him.

"See what we've *done*. We've *exposed* it. Totally.

However we try and hide this now, Skelton's lot'll find it. They're already looking in the right place."

"Oh, *God*. I didn't think of that. It just felt right to . . . to clear it, to clean it up. . ."

"Yes, it did feel right. But – *Jesus*, I have to call Will."

He pulled out his mobile. Rayne saw that his hand was shaking.

Once he'd described what they'd found and explained that it couldn't now be hidden, Ethan listened. Rayne tried to hear what Will was saying but Ethan seemed oblivious to her; he kept the phone clamped to his ear. Then he said, "That's fine, take Hiker. We'll see you here. Hurry up, OK?"

He rang off and said, "They're bringing wood now, to all the sites except Martyr's Hill, where it's already built. Will's had it planned like a military campaign. We're lighting the fires tonight."

"And what do you and I do?"

"Stay here to guard the stone. And hope like hell that Skelton's lot don't turn up before our lot get here."

They'd been waiting for fifteen minutes, sitting on the turf. It was growing cold up on the ridge, and darker with every minute. The sheep had settled for the night, but the moon hadn't come out yet. They peered into the dusk, constantly looking all around them, alert for every movement.

"Did Will say how long he'd be?" Rayne murmured, for the second time.

"Shouldn't be long now – *what was that?*"

They froze, breath held. Two roe deer trotted out of the

woods, then seemed to sense a human presence, and fled back again.

"I wish they'd hurry," Rayne muttered.

"I know." He shifted a little closer to her.

"Ethan – you know the Devil's Tankard? Are they having two fires there, like they did at the festival?"

"No. Just the one in the pit. The other's just for show."

"So you lot can show off racing and chucking your torches."

"That's right." He shifted on the ground, and said, "Rayne – can I ask you something?"

"Course."

"When you said you were shown the stone, did you mean. . ."

"She showed me. Yes. I just cleared my mind and imagined a fire and. . ."

"So you believe it again now. You're back with us now."

"What d'you mean?" she asked, sharply.

"Oh, come on – you changed. You were amazing, you were this heroine, blasting into the dungeon – you were the one the green lady showed herself to. But then you cut off. Even though you came back here with me, and you were practical, phoning Ms Barton – you still doubted it all. You didn't want to think about it, or talk about it."

"That is *so* not true!" Rayne sat up straighter, spiky with indignation. "*I* didn't want to talk about it? You were the one who clammed up, right from the beginning! You wouldn't talk about what had gone on, you wouldn't tell me about being a watcher. . ."

"I was messed up about it, back then. And anyway, you didn't want to hear."

"Oh, *rubbish!*"

"Rayne – I tried to talk to you! *And* I bought you those pigeons."

Rayne took in a breath. She felt like she wasn't going to hide any more, she felt like she could say anything now, up on the ridge with the night thickening. "Those pigeons weren't for me," she said.

"*What?*"

"They were for *her*. The green lady. You were only interested in me because of her – because of what I might mean, just like all the other watchers. . ."

"Crap, Rayne. That is such crap."

"You pushed me away."

"*You* pushed *me* away. That night – when I tried to kiss you—"

"Oh, *what?* How can you blame me for that? I was shaking, I nearly passed out, it was right after St John and everything—"

"Yeah, St John. Who kissed like an angel. How could I ever compete with him?"

There was a huge silence. It vibrated like a gong. Rayne stared at him, mouth open – then she burst out laughing. "Oh, you idiot," she gasped, "you *idiot!*"

"Don't call me an idiot!" he said, but he was smiling now, smiling right back at her.

"Is that for real?" she demanded. "Were you skirting round me cos you thought you wouldn't compare to that hideous creature?"

"No. Yes."

"Yeah? Well, what about Sarah, Becky's mate? Going after you at the fire festival, up by the Devil's Tankard? You pulled her that night, didn't you?"

"No. Yes. OK – she pulled me. But I only let her cos *you* were being such a stand-offish cow, siding with Miss Skelton and trying to get a load of outsiders into Morton's Keep to make money out of the fire festivals—"

He broke off, because Rayne had reached out and shoved his shoulder, hard. He grabbed her hand, pulled her up against him. Their faces were inches away from each other, laughing at each other, waiting to kiss.

And then a gloating, sarcastic voice came out of the darkness.

"What an *adorable* scene!"

Rayne and Ethan sprang apart, hearts hammering, and peered desperately at where the voice had come from.

The moon hung above the woods. St John stepped forward, with Flora, two men and a young woman, and all of them were grinning.

Chapter
Forty-five

Rayne and Ethan were on their feet in seconds. "Oh, *God*," he muttered, distraught. "Oh *God*, we weren't *watching*. . ."

"It's OK," breathed Rayne. "It's OK, we'll hold them off. Will'll be here in a minute."

St John came closer, the others following. The sailing moon glittered on the dagger in his hand. "Oh, you've *found* the stone!" he cried. "She's wonderful – how can we thank you? You've saved us so much bother!"

"Don't come any closer!" Ethan snarled.

"But we only want to *see* her! The green lady stone – how marvellous! We've been looking for ages – however did you find her?"

Rayne stared at St John. The air of weary sickness that he'd had when they'd visited him at his home had vanished. He stood tall; energy emanated from him. He was back to the old St John now, back to how he'd been at the beginning of autumn when he'd besotted her, very nearly seduced her.

She felt bile rise in her throat.

The woman put her hand on St John's arm. "We need

to act fast," she said, urgently. "They've cleared the stone, they're guarding it – they must mean to set the fires tonight."

"Such haste!" said St John. "But you're right, Melissa – we must act. Roll on the fifth cursed act. And what a perfect platform for it. Look at her, ancient and true, shining under the moon. How *clean* you've made her. How *glorious*!" He raised the dagger; it flashed in the blackness.

"We need to phone Miss Skelton," Melissa rasped out. "They need to get to Martyr's Hill."

"Of course they do. The goat this time, yes? It seems a shame . . . we have Rayne here, and she's so much more emphatic and exciting than a *goat. . .*"

Flora let out an excited little laugh, and St John lovingly took her hand.

"There's no time," Melissa said. "I'll phone Miss Skelton. They need to get there in force – the place is watched, remember. And you – for Christ's sake – *hurry*!"

"Melissa, *please*," said St John, sounding pained, "no need for all this *tension*! You can't hurry our solemn ritual. But you're right – we must act." He took a step closer to the stone, then suddenly barked, "You two – *seize him*!"

The two men loomed out of the blackness, both of them older, taller, broader than Ethan.

"*Run*, Ethan!" cried Rayne.

"I'm not leaving the stone," Ethan gritted out, as he sprang backwards, avoiding the first man's lunge, "and I'm not leaving *you*!"

The second man ran at him. Ethan shot sideways – then forward again, leaping over the wide stone.

269

"You're going to have to move faster than that to grab hold of *dancing boy*," sneered St John. Ethan whirled away again, evading the men, then stopped in a stand-off across the stone. "Lordy," drawled St John, "this could almost be a Morris set, couldn't it?"

Melissa had finished making her call; she started moving towards Rayne. Something dark swung in her hand as she walked – a belt, or maybe rope. St John, grinning, advanced with her, Flora hanging on to his arm. "What cursed act would *you* like to enact, Rayne, my darling?" he purred, as he walked. "It doesn't all have to be mayhem and murder, you know."

Rayne turned and ran, racing across to Ethan, but one of the men swerved out and lunged at her, grabbing her arm. At the same split-second that Ethan sprang at him, fists flailing, St John launched into the air and landed on Ethan's back.

They fell to the ground. "Move and I'll *stick* you," St John hissed. "And then I'll stick your *girlfriend*." He scrambled to his feet, dragging Ethan with him. The dagger glittered by Ethan's neck.

"Take them to the stone!" he cried.

The seven of them started walking, two by two, an execution procession. *Help us!* Rayne prayed. *Help us!*

But the night was still, with no wind.

Then, two metres from the stone, the procession stopped. Froze.

Something huge was thundering over the grass, pounding towards them out of the darkness.

Chapter
Forty-six

It came nearer, blacker than the night.

"Hiker!" breathed Ethan. "*HIKER!*" he yelled.

The great horse charged, turf flying from its hooves, running straight at the group.

"*Up!*" shouted Ethan. "Hiker, *UP!*"

And Hiker reared up, neighing, hooves flying. In the pandemonium and panic, Ethan and Rayne broke free from their captors. St John and Flora stumbled backwards, tripped and sprawled on the grass. Melissa backed away, hands out in front of her in terror. One of the men made a grab for Hiker's reins; a flailing hoof struck the side of his head. He fell back, lay still, and the other man ran over to him and crouched on the ground beside him, talking to him, trying to bring him round.

"*Steady*, Hiker!" Ethan shouted. "*Easy!*"

The horse landed on all fours again and Ethan sprang into his saddle. St John scrambled to his feet; Ethan kicked the horse forward and faced his enemy.

"Stand still!" he yelled. "Stand still – all of you – or I'll run you down!"

St John stood still, arm round Flora. Ethan swung Hiker's head round at Melissa, and she froze where she stood. The two men stayed on the ground.

"Very impressive," said St John, and he took a slow, deliberate step forward. "But you're still outnumbered."

The man who hadn't been hurt stood up, and he too moved towards the horse, from behind. "You can't run us all down, not all at once," he said.

"I'm *warning* you!" Ethan shouted. Hiker's hooves drummed on the ground.

"How will your fine horse fare," said St John, "if I slit its belly?" And he took another step forward.

Then there was a shout from behind them. All seven of them spun round.

Eight silhouettes were coming over the brow of the ridge, running, all in line.

Rayne felt her heart wrench in terror.

Then she heard, "*Hold them, Ethan!*"

It took only three minutes' hard fighting before Will and Mark and the others were trussing St John, Flora and the two men up, back to back. They used the rope Melissa had dropped when she'd raced off into the trees. Two of the watchers had run after her but she'd given them the slip in the blackness and they'd come back without her.

"We're halfway along the valley," Will said, tightening a knot so fast that St John cursed in pain, "and Hiker starts whinnying and bucking like the devil's on his tail. We'd loaded him up with firewood and he's bucking so hard

272

it's half off his back. Mark goes to straighten it and Hiker lunges, loses the lot – and then he's off."

"So we drop our loads, too," said Mark. "We knew something was up."

"And by God we were right," said Will. "Weren't we?"

"Clever old Hiker," said Rayne, stroking his broad nose. "Clever boy." Then she looked up at Ethan, and smiled.

Ethan, grinning, went to dismount, but Will stopped him with a hand on his leg. "Go back for the firewood," he said. "You'll see it, down in the valley – we dropped it in a huge pile. Go on, all of you – get cracking. This fire's to be the first – it's the signal for them all to be lit. I'll stay here with the . . . *prisoners*. And the stone."

"You sure St John hasn't got his dagger still?" asked Rayne, anxiously. "He could cut himself free."

"I'm sure," said Will, pulling the dagger out of his belt and holding it up in front of him. "First thing I did was knock it out of his hand. Now go on. *Move!*"

They brought all the firewood to the ridge in one trip, Hiker carrying the load he'd ditched, and laid it on the ground. "Make a ring," Will ordered. "A wide ring round the stone. We'll not harm the lady by setting the fire on top."

Soon, a great pile of branches and brushwood circled the stone. "They'll see this from the watchtower ruins," said Will. "And light their fire. Then that will be seen from the Devil's Tankard. They'll have built that up high in the hollow to be seen from Peak's Barrow. Peak's Barrow will be seen from Fleet Woods. Maybe only the smoke from there will be seen from Martyr's Hill – but they'll see it, in this moonlight. And we'll all see the fire blazing from Martyr's Hill and know the six points of the star are alight and the circle has been closed."

Will stooped down and pulled two petrol-soaked torches out of a bag by his feet. He held them while Mark struck a match and lit them, one after the other. Then he solemnly handed one to Rayne and one to Ethan. "Either side," he said. "Either side of the ring."

Rayne could feel her blood racing as she took her position opposite Ethan, facing the ring of firewood that surrounded the ancient stone tablet.

"That's good," said Will. "Now – *light it*!"

The two torches were dipped as one, and pushed into the dry wood. The twigs started to crackle; the kindling flared as the fire danced outwards. It was only a matter of minutes before the two fires had reached each other and joined in a ring of flame. Everyone but the four prisoners cheered.

Rayne was conscious of the watchers staring at her and Ethan, smiling in approval. "Why did he give the torches to us?" she whispered.

"I guess he felt we'd earned it. It's an honour. I'd just assumed he'd light it himself."

"Well, he could've brought three torches, and lit it with us!"

"No, there's supposed to be only two. It's all part of the legend. Will gave me a long lecture on it all, on the meaning of the number eleven to the watchers. Six sacred sites, eleven watchers – two torches to light each fire."

"Maths not the strongest point of you fire people, then?" said Rayne, smiling.

Ethan grinned. "Guess who's the twelfth. Not that she needs a torch."

"Oh," muttered Rayne, and a kind of shiver ran through her, like leaves trembling. "Oh, I see."

The fire was mounting every minute; it was taller than a man now. Sparks flew into the dark sky and smoke billowed, silvered by the moon.

"They'll see that at the watchtower," said Will, in satisfaction. "No problem. But just to make sure. . ." He pulled out his mobile.

After that, it was just a question of waiting. One of the men had brought a backpack full of sandwiches and cans of beer, and handed it all round.

The four prisoners refused even water. They sat hunched forward against the ropes, staring bleakly at the ground. A few of the watchers wanted to call the police, and get St John and his henchmen taken in for questioning about the murder and the abduction. But Will said they must wait until the great circle of fires was complete.

"We don't want to get distracted by dealings with the police," he insisted. "We must keep alert, keep watch still. Those four have been out of touch with their mistress. I heard a mobile go a while ago, under those ropes. Skelton will know something's up. And the woman, Melissa – she'll be back at Morton's Keep by now. Reporting back. They'll try to get to the two sites they haven't desecrated yet. We must prepare for the second wave of them."

It was important not to let the fire die down – to keep it going at full strength until they could see the blaze from the top of Martyr's Hill. People kept wandering off to the trees at the end of the ridge and coming back with armfuls of wood that they'd throw into the blaze. As they walked, they'd scan the moon-washed horizon anxiously.

Rayne and Ethan sat side by side, hands held out to the circle of fire. They hardly spoke, but their shoulders were touching. Rayne felt like she couldn't wait for all this to be over, for them to be alone and ordinary together.

"Fires on the six points of the star," said an old man, ruminatively. "It's good the way it all works out, the way the next fire site in the chain can see the one before it. . ."

"Aye," said Mark. "Almost as if it's been planned."

"Every site should see the Martyr's Hill blaze, when it goes up," said Will. "It's the highest point of them all."

Rayne huddled closer to Ethan, and gazed into the flames. "No face glaring out at you this time?" murmured Ethan. His hand strayed on to hers.

"Nothing," she said, but again she felt a slight shiver, as though the leaves were falling all around her once more. "No sign of her at all."

Chapter
Forty-seven

Will was growing increasingly uneasy. Everyone could sense it, but no one wanted to comment on it, although they all knew they'd waited long enough for the chain of fires to link up. He kept looking north-west towards Martyr's Hill, as if willing a fire-glow to appear. In the end he drew his mobile out and called the man he'd put in charge there.

"No answer," he muttered. "Maybe he's too engrossed, getting the blaze going." But he didn't look reassured, and a few moments later, he called the woman in charge of the site at the stone altar in Fleet Woods, the site before Martyr's Hill in the chain.

His face was grave as he came off the phone. "She says they set their fire some fifteen minutes ago," he muttered. "She was worried the blaze wouldn't be seen from the Hill, so they put on lots of damp stuff, made a great plume of smoke that she says rose right above the trees, but there's no sign from the hill, nothing at all—" He broke off. His phone was ringing in his hand.

As he took the call Rayne thought she could actually see

the colour ebb from his face. He listened, but he didn't say a word.

Then he looked up. "Call everyone you know," he shouted, hoarsely. "Everyone who's not already involved in this. Call them and tell them to *get to Martyr's Hill.*"

Ethan shot to his feet, pulling Rayne up with him. "What's happened?" he cried.

"There's a stand-off there," said Will. "I could barely understand Cory, he was shouting – incoherent – talking as he was fighting. Seems Skelton's stolen a march on us. She's there with hordes of her people. Christ knows where they've all come from."

St John lifted his head above the ropes. In the light from the bonfire his smile was a skull's grin.

"They've overpowered the guards round the great bonfire we built," Will went on, his voice full of anguish. "They're stopping us reaching it."

"And the *cursed act*?" shouted Mark. "Has it happened?"

"*I don't know.* The call got cut off. We must get as many folk as we can – tell them to get up there. Bring weapons, farm tools – *anything.*"

"We'll get over there now!" said Ethan. He caught hold of Hiker's reins. "Rayne and I – we'll go. But most of *you* – you must stay here. Phone everyone, but *stay here.* If they've won on Martyr's Hill, if they've desecrated the site – they'll be on their way *here*, won't they?"

St John tipped his head back and let out a horrible gloating laugh. "It doesn't take long to slit a billy goat's throat!" he sang out. Flora giggled.

"Yes, Ethan, you go," said Will, urgently. "Complete the

278

fire circle before they get here to complete their vile ring. Lad – *don't fail.*"

Ethan vaulted into Hiker's saddle, then leaned down and put out his hand to Rayne. "Are you up for this?" he said.

"You bet," she answered. Then she took his hand and swung up behind him.

They rode fast, out of the valley and across open fields, heading north to Martyr's Hill. "Will Hiker make it?" Rayne shouted, into the back of Ethan's neck, as she held on tight to him. "Up that steep hill with both of us to carry?"

"Course he will," Ethan shouted back. The horse galloped on, and soon they were climbing the hill, Hiker panting but determined. "Oh, Jesus," muttered Ethan, as they got closer to the summit. "Oh, Jesus – *look.*" He reined Hiker in, and they trotted slowly forward.

The scene that met them was terrifying. Around the huge unlit bonfire stood a tight ring of people, some with long, evil-looking knives in their hands. They were grinning breathlessly, as though they'd only just secured their position. All of them were facing out, facing down the group of watchers, who were outnumbered and helpless before them. Four or five lay on the ground; four or five were tending to them, tearing strips off their clothes to act as bandages.

Ethan urged Hiker closer to the stricken group. "Mrs Lewis?" he called. "Mrs Lewis, is that you?"

A middle-aged woman looked up; Rayne recognized her. She'd been at the fire festival in this very same place, handing out flapjacks. . .

Now she was binding up a cut that gushed blood on the arm of a man.

"They got Jack!" she cried. "Oh, *God*, Ethan, it was horrible – they're *insane*. . ."

"Where's Cory?"

"He's hurt, poor lad. Slashed on the leg."

"We couldn't hold them," groaned Jack. "We failed."

"You didn't *fail*," said Ethan.

"They came out of nowhere," sobbed Mrs Lewis. "I recognize some of them – they're from the town. They've got knives, swords – they were slashing at us – we didn't stand a chance."

Rayne sat up straighter on the horse. She felt something like fire start up deep down inside her.

"*Where's the torch?*" hissed Ethan.

Mrs Lewis nodded towards a great wooden staff lying near her husband. It was topped by petrol-soaked wadding, bound with twine.

"Pass it up!" ordered Ethan.

Silently, she picked it up and raised it. Ethan seized it, then urged Hiker to trot on, nearer to the ring of Skelton's people.

Miss Skelton was in the very centre of the ring, vivid and glorious in her long red dress. She was climbing carefully and elegantly up on to the great flat pile of logs that formed the base of the bonfire. Tara was climbing up after her, with her friend Sessie, in their Gothic dresses. The vampire bride and the vampire princess, following the blood-red queen.

Tara held a long garland of exotic flowers, like the flowers that had decked out the Old Stone Hall. At the end of it, a small black goat with flowers twined crazily round its horns bucked and bleated as she dragged it upwards on to the pile of logs.

Rayne watched, and felt as though a great storm was building inside her. She felt it in her blood and her bones, and it mixed with the fire.

With one last scramble, Miss Skelton reached the top of the base-pile of logs, and stood upright, arms raised. It was as though she was on a stage, and the huge bonfire piled behind her was her backdrop. The great ring of her people had all turned inwards now, gazing at her, cheering her as she stood there. She was absorbed in her triumph, oblivious to the horse and its riders.

Ethan urged Hiker a little closer. "I can throw the torch from here!" he hissed. "I can reach the bonfire!"

A thin man appeared from behind the great pile of wood and branches, dragging someone. Dragging a girl.

Ethan struck a match on the saddle, he was putting it to the torch—

"*No!*" cried Rayne. And she knocked the match from his hand.

Chapter
Forty-eight

"What the *hell*—" snarled Ethan, turning round on her.

"That's Becky!" said Rayne. "He's got *Becky*! Look – her hands are tied, he's got a knife to her throat. He'll kill her as soon as he sees the fire start."

"*Jesus*, Rayne!" groaned Ethan. "OK, OK. So what do we do?"

"They're going to kill her soon anyway," said Rayne, her voice monotone. "Her and the goat. They want a really brilliant bloody grand finale. Ethan – *ride closer*. Ride round behind them. Ride towards those trees."

Something in her voice – some incredible intensity – made him obey. He urged Hiker on, towards the clump of low thorn trees.

It was then that Miss Skelton spotted them.

"Why – *Rayne*!" she cried. In her right hand she had a long, curved knife; she raised it now and pointed at them. "Rayne and her farm boy!"

"Let go of that girl!" yelled Ethan, as he pulled Hiker's head round and they faced them all. "Let go of Becky! You don't need her – you've got the goat!"

"Oh – reason not the *need*!" Miss Skelton sang. "*Becky* made a fool of herself! She broke through our circle, she ran at *me*. She wanted to be important – well – now she can be!"

"Do you really imagine you can get away with *killing* someone where we can all see?" Ethan shouted. "We'll go to the police. You can't kill all of us."

Miss Skelton threw back her head and laughed. "You have *no idea*, do you, farm boy? No idea what will be released – no idea of the *power* we'll have – once this circle of atrocities is complete?"

"You failed at Wildhern Valley!" roared Ethan. "St John and his henchmen – we tied them up!"

"Yes – Melissa told me. Sweet, fleet-footed Melissa. She evaded your lumpen fire men, didn't she? And called me. And I set – *all this* in motion. Eight fire men, Melissa said, guarding the green lady stone. Well, twenty of my best people are on their way there now. I shall let St John do the sacrifice, on the stone, with his little dagger. To salve the poor boy's wounded pride. And because he *enjoys* it so much!" Then she laughed again and, this time, her people joined in with her, all round the circle that ringed the bonfire. It was an eerie, hateful sound, circling in the darkness.

Then, softly at first, another noise joined it.

The noise of wind blowing.

It started low, moaning from behind them in the thorn trees, then it grew stronger. Leaves flew past Rayne and Ethan, and howled towards the bonfire.

Rayne felt her heart pound, and she thought, *This is it. This is when I succeed or fail.*

Then she scrambled up and stood on the saddle, balancing perfectly, her hands on Ethan's shoulders. The wind increased. Her hair whipped out from her head like a wild halo. The wind roared round her, and the leaves whipped by her, and she saw the absolute terror on the faces in the great circle in front of her, and in utter disbelief at what she was doing, she let go of Ethan's shoulders.

And she flew.

The wind roared her up and over the heads of the henchmen, whirled her across to land at the base of the bonfire. It was over in an instant and no one looked at her – Miss Skelton and her niece and everyone stared in horror at what was beyond her, behind her. She seized hold of the rope that held Becky, jerked it from the nerveless hands of her captor.

Then she ran. She ran at the other side of the circle and the whirlwind came with her, leaves skirling round her, and broke her through, with Becky.

On the opposite side of the circle she could see the glow of the huge petrol-soaked torch. Ethan had ignited it. He was ready.

"*THROW IT!*" she yelled.

It was the longest throw Ethan had ever made in his life. He urged Hiker into a gallop at Skelton's people, drew back his arm, and hurled it with all his strength.

His aim was true. It hit the bonfire three metres from the ground and almost instantaneously the twigs and brushwood caught; flames licked along the branches like snakes.

Miss Skelton shook herself out of her terrified trance. "*Put that out!*" she screamed. "Get *up* there – *extinguish* it!"

Men broke from the circle and ran at the wood pile, tearing their jackets off. Within seconds one of them had clambered up and was beating at the flames with his coat, then another joined him, flattening his coat over them, and then all that could be seen of Ethan's fire was a glimmer at the edges. . .

Rayne watched, holding on to Becky's hands, which were still tied with rope. Despair gripped her.

Then the coat smothering Ethan's torch suddenly exploded into flames. Miss Skelton and the two girls fled, screaming, as the men hurled themselves backwards away from it, only just in time to avoid what happened next.

The rest of the bonfire trembled, shifted. It shook and shifted as though it was alive – and then suddenly, instantaneously, it burst into great, glorious, leaping flames.

Flames a metre high, on all sides of the bonfire at once. Flames that blazed across the lines of watching faces, that lit up the whole hillside.

Flames that could be seen for miles around. That completed the sacred circle.

Rayne felt her face grow wet with tears. Relief flooded her. "*Saved are we,*" she murmured. Beside her, Becky was crying, too.

Chapter Forty-nine

All Rayne could hear was cheering. She looked about, dazed, ecstatic, and saw wave upon wave of townspeople, people who'd had the watchers' calls, making their way over the crest of the hill. They were carrying torches, baseball bats, pitchforks and chains, and they were cheering at the tops of their voices as they drew closer and closer to the great blazing fire.

Miss Skelton, Tara and Sessie, holding up their long dresses, were racing away from the searing heat. They broke through the ring of henchmen, which disintegrated and scattered. Soon, everyone was running, and the hillside became a battle scene. Cory, limping, his face smeared with blood, was marshalling the attack. Young men broke from the crowd of newcomers to join him, throwing themselves at Skelton's people, flailing out with fists and bats and chains, making them drop their knives.

Rayne saw the goat bucketing away from the fire and the battle, bleating in terror, trailing and tripping on its rope of flowers. She ran after it, caught the end of the rope and gently pulled the frightened animal to her, talking softly to calm it. Then she knelt on the ground in front of it, took hold of a curved horn in either hand and pressed her forehead to its brow. "It's over now, it's over," she murmured, "you're safe, you're safe, you're not a sacrifice."

"Thanks to you," said a small voice behind her. She looked up. Becky was standing there, face wet with tears, hands still tied in front of her.

"Oh, *Becky*. . ." breathed Rayne. "I haven't even given you a hug yet." She scrambled to her feet and flung her arms round her.

The battle seemed to be over. Another ring had formed, safely away from the great roaring fire, with the henchmen on the inside, and Cory leading the townspeople to pen them in.

"What *was* it?" sobbed Becky. "What *happened*?"

"Don't think about it," said Rayne, hugging her hard. "Don't think about it right now. Look – we've done it! It's over. You're safe."

"If it hadn't been for *you*. . ."

"It wasn't me, Becky. Did you see what it was?"

Becky shook her head violently. "I shut my eyes. I was *so scared*. . . They were going to slit my throat. After the goat. They told me. They weren't even going to clean the knife. They told me."

"Don't think about it, Becky," urged Rayne, and she started untying the rope that bound her friend's wrists. "You were brave. You ran at Skeleton."

"I was an idiot. I thought I could grab her knife."

"You were *brave*!" Rayne insisted. The little black goat

was standing next to her, leaning its weight against her legs, and she pushed back, to comfort it. "It's brilliant that you came."

"It was kind of accidental, how it happened," said Becky, her voice sounding clearer now, more normal. "Cory told us all about the massive bonfire being built – twice the size of the one at the last fire festival, he said – and then we heard about the fire men *guarding* it. All these rumours were flying about – it was exciting, you know? Me and my mates came up to see the bonfire and we all said we wanted to be there when it went up in flames. Then Chloe texted that she'd heard it was going to be lit tonight, and we all met up at the foot of the hill. . ."

"Just to see a bonfire?"

"No – OK, we *knew*," said Becky. With one last tug, the rope fell from her wrists and on to the ground. "Underneath we knew. Like everyone in the town knew, everyone who's come here today. And we were right. We got here and we saw Skeleton and her cronies, attacking the watchers."

"And you charged her!"

"She'd slashed out at my uncle, he was bleeding. I . . . I just saw red, Rayne. I *hate* her."

Rayne put an arm round Becky's shoulders, and a hand on the goat's woolly head. They stood looking at the scene in front of them. The police had arrived, with two small, cross-country vans, and with help from the townspeople were energetically bundling Miss Skelton and her niece and all her creatures into the back of them. Ethan circled on Hiker, watching in case one of the prisoners tried to break free.

When the police-van doors were slammed shut, he rode over to the girls, grinning. "She did it, didn't she?" he said. "Our lady. She was the twelfth."

"Yes," said Rayne, happily. "She did it."

Hiker leaned down and sniffed at the goat, who squared up to him, legs braced.

"I called Will," Ethan said. "They're all fine on Wildhern Valley. Still keeping the fire going in a great ring round the stone, and they can see *this* fire bright as a comet."

"Didn't Skelton's lot make it there, then?" asked Rayne.

"Yes – but so did a load of the townspeople, too. Just like here. It was all over in minutes."

"Oh, brilliant."

"Your ex never even got his ropes off."

"Don't call him my ex!" laughed Rayne.

"There won't be room in prison for all that lot!" said Becky. "They were packed in those vans like sardines."

"They'll let some of them go, they have to," Ethan said. "For most of them the biggest crime was just being here. But *we* know who they are now – we know who joined Skelton, and who came to help us. That's not going to get forgotten in a hurry."

"Hey, hero!" called a voice. Rayne turned round to see Sarah standing there, gazing up at Ethan. Lisa and Chloe were with her, and they swarmed over Becky, hugging her, asking her how she was.

"Hi, Sarah," said Ethan. "What a night, ay?"

"*Unbelievable!* We should celebrate our victory! You're a *hero*, Ethan! You coming over by the fire? Cory's there."

"Is he OK?"

"Mrs Parker, she's a nurse – she's stitching him up now. He's full of himself!"

"So he should be!"

"Well, come on, then! Let's party!"

"I ought to check if everything's OK at Morton's Keep. Skelton's mob must've all come up here with her, but I ought to make sure. You coming, Rayne?"

"Definitely," Rayne said, smiling up at him. Then she turned to Becky, and said, "Will you take care of the goat, Becks?"

"Of *course*," said Becky, as Rayne handed her its rope. The exotic flowers had nearly all dropped off by now, and been trampled underfoot. "We've a bond, haven't we, goaty? Fellow victims. Partners in survival. Though God knows what my mum will say if I try and take him home. . ."

"We'll come and get him later," said Ethan. "He can come to our farm. He'd love it there." Then, like before, he leaned down, holding out his hand to Rayne, and she took it and sprang up behind him on the saddle, and they rode off down the hillside with the fire at their backs.

Chapter Fifty

"Mr Stuart wasn't there, was he?" shouted Rayne, as they cantered into the long drive of Morton's Keep.

"No. And I think that's in his favour."

"I can't believe he was part of it all. I just can't. Ben Avebury wasn't there, either."

"He'll have stayed here, to watch—" He broke off suddenly, reining Hiker in. "Oh, *Christ!*" he cried. "What's going on?"

Through the great arch in the ancient wall, firelight was dancing, sending crazy shadows up on to the two looming towers and the walls of the Keep.

"Easy, Hiker," said Ethan. They trotted forward. Ahead of them, the archway glowed like the mouth of a great oven. They reached the forecourt and dismounted. Then Ethan led Hiker slowly forward.

The fire in the courtyard was much smaller than it seemed from the outside. Feeding it were eight great picture boards – the huge photographs that Miss Skelton had hung in the tearoom – stacked up against each other. Rayne took a step closer, staring through the heat haze.

The griffon from the grand staircase was blackening in

the flames. The gargoyle's face was crowned with fire. And as she watched, the cherub's fat hand ignited.

She moved round to the back of the bonfire. Patience was there, beaming with happiness, dancing about on the cobblestones. "She loves it!" she cried. "She loves it! She is fire, she is fire, she is *fire*!"

"Hello, Patience," said Rayne, smiling, then she turned back to the fire. Sir Simeon Lingwall's severed hand, thirty times life-size, was curling and twisting in the flames, then it fell to ashes.

Rayne laughed out loud, and Patience clapped her hands. "Where's Mrs Driver?" asked Rayne. "Is she inside?"

Patience nodded. "Cooking," she said, still dancing. "Cooking!"

Ethan tethered Hiker safely by the courtyard horse trough, well away from the dying fire. Then he caught Rayne up as she went into the house and along to the Tudor kitchen. Mrs Driver was in there, with Ben. Two huge pots were bubbling on the stove; Ben was kneading dough and Mrs Driver was laying out great slabs of cheese on a board, singing as she worked.

"What's going on?" cried Ethan.

Mrs Driver dropped the cheese knife she'd been holding and came over to Rayne. Then slowly, steadily, she put her arms round her and hugged her, hard.

It was the first time they'd ever touched.

"You did it," she murmured. "You saved us. I knew you would." Then she let go of her and beamed. "And we're having a party to celebrate!"

"At two in the morning?" asked Rayne, grinning, still glowing from the hug.

"What better time? I've told them all to come here, all who want to! The fires are dying down. They're on their way."

Ben advanced with two bottles of beer that he'd just knocked the caps off, and handed one to Rayne and one to Ethan. "Cheers!" he said, eyes sparkling.

"Ben – let's get that scone mixture in the stove, sharpish," said Mrs Driver. "It'll take twenty minutes."

"Aye, aye, ma'am," said Ben.

Rayne took a long, very welcome pull of the ale, then asked, "All those extra people – Skelton's followers – where did they come from?"

"Ah," said Mrs Driver. "There's a *coach* and about ten cars parked at the side. I imagine as soon as *that woman* heard you'd found the stone, she was on her nasty little phone, calling everyone to her. . ."

"She'd recruited people from the town, too," said Ethan. "It was a real shock, seeing their faces."

"They won't be able to stay here now," said Mrs Driver, smoothly. "There'll be a few houses going up for sale soon."

"How's Mr Stuart?" asked Rayne. "Is he coming down, is he coming to the party?"

"I don't think so, dear. He's . . . well, he's shaken, shaken to his core, and most of all he's ashamed. He thought he was safe from Lingwall's influence, that he could never be used as a tool in a reoccurrence. But it got to him all the same."

"Through a woman," said Ben. "He was lonely and starved of loving – he was her prey."

"I'd like to find out more about Skelton," growled Ethan. "It's pretty obvious she contacted St John through his sick website – but who *is* she?"

"Rayne, check the soup for me, dear," said Mrs Driver. "Don't let it simmer too fiercely."

Rayne went over to the stove, lifted the lids one at a time, and stirred the great pots of soup. A delicious savoury smell of chicken and herbs, celery and carrots filled the kitchen.

"Are you avoiding answering me, Mrs D?" asked Ethan, smiling.

"No, dear," said Mrs Driver. Then she reached up to the mantelpiece and drew a small, gold-framed, oval picture out from behind a stone jar. "Mr Stuart brought this down this evening," she said. "He brought it down and threw it on the table and said, *That's who she is.* Then he hauled down all Miss Skelton's clothes and stuff from his room – she'd been all but living with him for the last few weeks – and made a bonfire of them in the courtyard. Then he went off to the old dairy and pulled all those great photographs off the wall, one after the other, and threw them on the fire."

"Good for him," said Rayne.

Carefully, Mrs Driver laid the little oval picture on the table, face up. It was a delicate, well-executed portrait of a pretty woman with dark hair and a red mouth. Her hair was intricately looped and braided, and two blood-red drop earrings hung tantalizingly from her ear lobes.

"Oh God," murmured Rayne.

"It's her, isn't it?" said Mrs Driver. "It's Miss Skelton. Look at the shape of her mouth."

"And the *eyes*," said Ethan.

"Turn it over," said Mrs Driver.

Ethan turned it over. On the back, in gold paint, was delicately scribed a name.

Selina Lingwall.

Rayne drew back just at the sight of the inscription. Ethan let out a low whistle. "The twisted niece," he said. "The woman St John claims to be descended from."

"We have just his word for that," said Mrs Driver. "But as for Louisa Skelton's heritage, I think you could say the proof is staring you in the face."

"Especially as she inherited those earrings," said Rayne. "God, the artist has painted them perfectly. No wonder she was so upset when she lost one."

"And Mr Stuart *had* this portrait?" demanded Ethan. "He had it all this time, and he didn't see the similarity?"

"It was locked away, Ethan. Mr Stuart said he'd forgotten all about it. It was in the safe in the attic, with all Sir Simeon Lingwall's sadistic writings and the reports of the reoccurrences. Tucked at the back, wrapped in a red velvet scarf."

"Well, he must have *put* it there!" retorted Ethan.

"He did, but over twenty years ago. And he hasn't gone near that safe for years. Why would he?"

"He added his own report," said Rayne. "About the reoccurrence – St John and his cult. After we burnt out the cellar."

"You're right. But the portrait was under all the old

documents he'd found in the library. He wouldn't have seen it."

"Until he showed them to Miss Skelton."

"Indeed. He said he took her up to the attic to examine them. He didn't want to bring them back down into the house. And when he saw the little red bundle at the back of the safe, he couldn't even remember what it was. But some instinct made him leave it there, and not even mention it to her."

"Maybe the hideous look on her *face* – as she rummaged through everything looking for clues to the six sites – gave *him* a clue!" said Ethan.

"*Ethan!* Stop being so uncharitable to Mr Stuart! But perhaps you have a point. I think, deep down, he was starting to realize what was going on – what she *was*. Anyway, something made him shut the safe up with the red bundle still inside, while she concentrated on the papers. Then – two nights ago – he went back to the attic, alone."

"And came face to face with an image of the woman he was sleeping with."

"Crudely but accurately put, young man. Yes."

"So why didn't he act *then*? Why didn't he denounce her *then*?"

"Oh, Ethan. You're young, you're idealistic – you can't imagine how devastating it would be to find love after years of loneliness, and then discover it's a sham. And not only that, but to find that your infatuation has put the people you've dedicated your life to *protecting* – in mortal danger."

"No," said Ethan, gruffly. "I can't."

"Don't judge him, Ethan," said Mrs Driver, her voice rising. "Don't you dare!"

"Yeah, Ethan," said Rayne, "just lay off him, OK?"

"He was *destroyed*," Mrs Driver went on. "He went out and walked all night. I saw him the next morning, wearing the same clothes he'd gone out in. He looked like a ghost. I imagine he spent the whole night letting all the doubts he'd had about Miss Skelton – and pushed down, desperate for things to be *good* – just rise to the surface and confront him. He spent that whole night being forced to see that how he'd been living for the last two months was a great *lie*, a dangerous lie."

"Money and sex!" said Ben, suddenly. "Between them, they did for him."

"He so wanted to believe in her," said Mrs Driver. "And you're right, Ben, it was for Morton's Keep's sake, as well as for himself. He's in a state of shock and grief right now."

There was a silence, just the soup bubbling gently on the stove. "Shall I take him a bowl of that soup?" asked Rayne.

"I think he wants to be left well alone right now, dear," said Mrs Driver. "But it's a sweet thought."

Ethan's snort was drowned out by the sudden sound of happy, excited voices from outside the back door. Rayne hurried over and pulled the door open, then set it flat against the wall as Will and Mark and Cory and all of the watchers and a whole crowd of others streamed triumphantly into the kitchen.

Chapter
Fifty-one

The party went on until dawn came up. There were over seventy people in the great Tudor kitchen, pressed up against the walls, crowded round the ancient refectory table, spilling out into the corridor. The soup and scones and cheese disappeared in less than half an hour, but people had brought food and drink with them and it was all shared around and no one went hungry. Rayne and Ethan stood close together, so close that no one could see they were holding hands. They desperately wanted to be alone, but they couldn't leave the party. Not this party.

"A toast!" shouted Mark, raising his third bottle of beer to the ceiling. "A toast to our great triumph!"

Everyone raised their drinks; a woman started calling, "Speech, Will – speech!" and soon others had joined her, clapping in time, drumming their glasses on the table and calling for Will to speak.

Will took his place at the head of the long table, and began talking.

"During the Great Plague, one village not a million miles from here took a very brave decision. It knew that some of its people had contracted that foul and lethal disease, and it sealed itself off so it wouldn't infect others. We're a bit like that, here in Marcle Lees. We need to contain our infection. And tonight – we've done that. *Resoundingly*."

More cheering and clapping, and then Ben shouted out, "It's still here, then, is it?" and laughed wryly.

"I don't know, Ben. All I know – all I'm sure of – is that we stopped it getting out and growing. We dealt it a blow tonight. And I don't know if we're in for more trouble, or none, but I *do* know we completed our circle of fire before they completed their cursed acts and that means we've stopped it getting out and spreading. We're as brave as those villagers who kept in the plague. And when I say *we* – you all know that we were helped this night."

There was a kind of stirring in the kitchen, like a cornfield in the wind.

"The corrupted men who built Morton's Keep knew what they were doing," Will went on. "They knew a building raised on this place of ancient evil would become a stronghold full of dark power. They knew it would give them the strength to rule the whole area, and beyond – conquer into Wales, march on London – take over the crown, take over England. But before they could realize their dreadful ambition, something happened. Some greater sorcery."

"The green lady," whispered Rayne, and in the sudden quiet, her voice carried.

"Yes, Rayne. Your lady was at the root of it. We have no records, only old stories. But back then, over a thousand years ago, we know the tradition of the fires was started.

The six sites were sanctified. The power to protect was put in place."

He turned to Ethan and Rayne. "When you two young people burnt the dungeon, it stopped St John Arlington, but it wasn't the end. Evil was released just as gas is released from burning wood."

"We had to do it!" said Ethan, indignantly.

"Of course you did. But Miss Skelton was poised to soak it all up. She was there with her seductive ways and formidable organizing skills. And we didn't realize she was the one, the enemy, until it was nearly too late." He raised his glass towards them. "And it was you two again – you two with your courage and perseverance – who we have to thank. You believed, even though it all sounded crazy. You found the stone – you found the last site. You rode to Martyr's Hill, to stop the sacrifice and light the fire. Ladies and gentlemen – another toast. I give you *Rayne and Ethan!*"

"*Rayne and Ethan!*" cried everyone, and they swigged back their drinks.

"*Rayne and Ethan,*" murmured Ethan, his mouth very close to hers. "I like the sound of that."

Chapter Fifty-two

It was eight in the morning, only just getting light. The last guests were leaving, straggling out through the back door from the Tudor kitchen and away across the fields. Rayne and Ethan wandered tiredly out to the courtyard, hand in hand. Poor old Hiker had gone to sleep standing up by the water trough.

"I'll lead him for a bit," said Ethan. "Let him find some grass to eat. Then we can ride him back to the farm."

"Are you sleepy?" asked Rayne.

"No. I'm absolutely knackered, I feel like I can hardly walk – but I'm not sleepy, not a bit."

"Let's go to the dovecote. Check if the pigeons are OK. I'll run back to the utility room and get some seed for them."

"*Run?* You could *run?*"

"Crawl. I'll crawl."

"Go on then."

"Let go of my hand then."

"Oh," said Ethan. "Must I? Oh. OK."

*

When Rayne got back to the courtyard with the seed, Ethan was just walking Hiker through the arch. The three of them meandered over to the tower dovecote. Ethan dropped Hiker's reins, and the old horse started cropping the lush grass of the maze.

"I hope he doesn't trample the bushes," said Rayne. "Although I don't suppose it matters."

"No. He deserves it. Actually – you know what? I don't think Hiker's role in all this was properly recognized. He's been a star. If we hadn't had him, we might have had our throats slit."

"And we certainly wouldn't have made it to Martyr's Hill in time."

"You're right. I'll start a fund to pay for a statue of him."

"Or at least buy him some horse treats."

They were fencing round each other, dancing round each other, talking, talking, because all they really wanted to do was get hold of each other and kiss.

They went through the dark tower door together. The rising sun was shining down through a jagged hole in the roof. Rayne started tipping bird seed into the empty dish. The white birds were shifting and rustling on the rim of the old floor above them, not quite ready to stop roosting for the night. Then at last they flew down to feed.

"They're all here," said Rayne, counting. "Apart from – you know – the two that got crucified. They look fine, don't they?" She felt Ethan close behind her, his hands on her shoulders, sliding down to the tops of her arms. "They're going to breed in the spring," she went on, breathlessly.

302

"I know it. They're going to *fill* this horrible tower with beautiful white birds—"

"Oh, *Rayne*. . ." he muttered.

She turned round and put her hands up on his neck, on his face, and he pulled her close, and at last they were kissing.

It went on. And on, beautifully. All the last weeks, all the doubts and hopes, were absorbed into that kiss.

At last they moved apart, and she smiled up at him.

"You're not shaking," he said, smiling back, "this time."

"No," she murmured. "Although actually – I am a bit."

"So – did I make the grade? Did I come up to St John?"

"Stop fishing. You *know* you left him way back. Back where he belongs." Then she reached up for him and they were kissing again as the white birds hopped and fluttered around them.

It was wonderful walking back to the farm in the early morning. Hand in hand, Rayne leading Hiker. They talked about everything, skimming over all that had happened, following where their thoughts took them, not needing to talk about the fact that they were really together now because that was all there in their two joined hands, it was all there ahead of them.

"You know," said Rayne, "somehow I'm not surprised Miss Skelton and Tara are descendants of Selina. Something in me didn't trust them from the start, even though I got . . . sidetracked. Even when I was supposedly buddying up with Tara, when she was really sucking up to me, something about her creeped me out. That time I saw her kind of slither in through the back window in the Sty – it *really* freaked me but I told myself I was just being silly. . ."

"You should trust your instincts more. You *know* – deep down you know – you just need to trust it."

"You didn't trust them either."

"No. I think I knew, too. Like I knew Mrs Driver was more than just the old housekeeper." He stopped walking, turned to her. "Rayne – everything that's happened – it's going to change so much round here. Will's been going on and on about how Marcle Lees got lazy, forgetting where the sites were, not understanding the real meaning of the festivals. It's like . . . everything that was just a story, a legend, a superstition . . . it's got real. And what happened on Martyr's Hill tonight – *she's* real, and people know that now – the green lady is *real*."

There was a silence, and they started walking again. Rayne tightened her grip, just a little, on his hand. "Did you see her?" she asked.

"I don't know. I saw *you* – you . . . it was like you *flew*. And there was something behind you, like a storm, flinging you up, but it's like I can't remember it now, not like . . . *visually*. Just the feeling it gave me – just . . . amazement. *Awe*."

"Same for me. It's like the feeling's fading. I don't know if I flew, if I was thrown . . . it's unreal now, like a dream. Except. . ."

"What?"

"I remember her face. Her face in the fire that time. And later . . . in the leaves. It was terrifying, electrifying. I'll never forget it." They walked on in silence for a while, just the sound of Hiker's hooves clopping. Then Rayne said, "So will it change what the watchers do, d'you think?"

"Bound to. Let's just hope they don't try and . . . I dunno. Pin her down. *Rationalize* her."

"They can't. She's not *contained*, it's like she . . . flows in and out of things. She makes fire, she makes the wind fiercer, the storms build. . ."

"I think she's kind of dormant most of the time," said Ethan. "In the trees, in the weather . . . then when something's really wrong around Morton's Keep, she kind of gets focused, to warn us, and help us, and sometimes, you get a glimpse of something. . ."

". . . that is definitely a woman," said Rayne.

"Oh, yes. She's a *woman* all right."

Rayne laughed. They'd reached the farm. Through the open kitchen window, they could smell eggs and bacon cooking.

Chapter
Fifty-three

The first thing Mrs Driver did, after she'd cleared up after the party in the Tudor kitchen, was phone round and organize the Advent Craft Market that Miss Skelton had so callously cancelled. There were seventeen days to go until Christmas – there was plenty of time. Her regulars were delighted. They all promised to turn up to the old barn that Saturday, and most of them said they'd been busily knitting and stitching anyway, keeping the faith that, somehow, the market would go ahead as always.

Marjorie Blake shyly mentioned that she was adding a new line to her popular little Christmas tree angel ornaments. A green one, with wild flowing hair and a curiously wide-open mouth. It was to prove to be a best-seller.

There was time, too, to plan a Christmas week party, a grand one in the Old Stone Hall. Not one for select paying guests this time, but one for all the watchers and the townspeople, for anyone local who wanted to come. Mrs Driver planned to "roll out the barrel" of generosity. She said the Keep's bank balance was, after all, healthier than it had been for decades.

It was Mr Stuart who'd suggested the party. He spoke of wanting to open the Keep up to the townspeople and their good energies. He didn't get involved in its planning, though. When he wasn't taking long, solitary walks, he kept to his room. Mrs Driver told everyone he'd be fine, he just needed time to convalesce.

The house keeper was brimming with energy. She made a wonderful garland of holly and ivy and wound it all the way up the grand staircase banisters. She filled great jugs with ivy and holly, too, and set them on tables in the library and the Tudor kitchen and the Great Hall alongside bowls with glowing tangerines and shiny nuts still in their shells. Candles glowed; fires were kept burning in all the grates. Visitors came and went. Ben Avebury sang carols loudly as he came in and out, replenishing the log baskets.

The darkness had receded so far from Morton's Keep that it seemed almost festive.

Ms Barton – whose mother had made a full recovery and was moving into sheltered accommodation so there'd always be someone to keep an eye on her – was planning to come back to Morton's Keep. She talked of doing more research on the myths and stories around the green lady, and of producing a pamphlet on them, with the newly discovered stone as its cover, to "give our lady a higher profile".

Rayne was uneasy at this idea, but Mrs Driver told her not to worry, it would balance out all the gruesome stuff that had been emphasized by Miss Skelton. She was delighted at the thought of having Ms Barton back as manager.

The watchers were delighted, too, because they knew

Ms Barton was truly one of them. Mrs Driver was one of them too, of course, but the house keeper had gone back to avoiding discussing "all that", as she called it. She'd subsided a little now the need to fight was past.

Rayne took up her old job at the dairy tearoom, and Becky joined her. She said she knew she'd get laid off after Christmas at Ciara's Clothes, so she may as well leave now – especially as her mum was back working at the Keep again, so she could get lifts. They were kept very busy – Miss Skelton's website had of course been closed down, but visitor numbers were still up. It seemed word of mouth was now kicking in. Rayne and Becky liked it that way. In between the cooking and the serving, their easy friendship renewed itself, and thrived.

A week before Christmas, Rayne moved back to the Old Sty, because all the bedrooms at the Sands farm were needed for relatives, and also because it was time to go. Ethan, of course, started to spend more time at the Sty than at his home.

They were in love, but not talking about it. It was too huge and wild and important and wonderful to talk about.

As Ethan had predicted, Will held a big meeting at the Green Lady inn to discuss how the role of the watchers would change after all the drama of the recent weeks. Rayne and Ethan were there, legs pressed together under the large table. Patience was there, in her spot by the fire. She seemed happier than ever, clapping her hands whenever she heard the green lady's name.

First, Will confirmed that Miss Skelton and St John had been released from custody, as no proof could be found to pin the Devil's Tankard murder on to them or to anyone. And despite Becky shrilly insisting that she'd nearly had her throat cut, no one was charged in connection with the battle on Martyr's Hill, either. The police put it down to local fire festivities that had got out of control.

Miss Skelton had apparently slunk back to Scotland. St John was back at home. They and their creatures, Will said, must be monitored, tracked.

He grew solemn as he talked about how the watchers' work was more important than ever now. "We were half-hearted before," he said. "Half thinking it was just an old story, buried back in time. We got lazy, we got sleepy. We know different now. Yes, we stopped the last of the cursed acts, we completed the circle of fire. But the evil hasn't been destroyed, just prevented from *spreading free*. We all have to be vigilant. There could be yet more reoccurrences. We must all still *watch*."

An ambitious agenda was drawn up. There would be more meetings, more rituals by the stone altar in Fleet Woods. They'd continue to dance at the Apple Fair at Morton's Keep – and they'd be there at other times, too. Christmas, Midsummer – "The Keep will be sick of the sight of us," Will said.

The three rediscovered sacred sites – Peak's Barrow, the ruined watchtower and the great stone slab high up on Wildhern Valley – were all to have their own events at next autumn's fire festivals. The first fire festival, where they marched with torches to each corner of the town to protect the boundaries, followed by the party with the braziers in the square, would still happen – but the six sacred sites would be the main focus now. The events themselves would be more elaborate, more linked to their deep purpose – and this would inevitably need much more careful planning.

Ethan pressed his leg harder against Rayne's as they listened to Will lecture on. They were longing to get away together, to be on their own.

No one could agree how to manage the care of the green lady stone. Some of the watchers wanted to ring it with an iron fence; some others suggested placing another stone beside it, with the inscription:

Six cursed acts, the horror spreads free.
Six fires to contain, to circle the bane,
Saved are we.

But in the end it was Rayne who said the stone should just be left as it was, simple and free. She promised to tend it, to make sure it didn't get overgrown again. There was unanimous agreement at this.

She was aware that people were looking at her all the time; they'd smile if she caught them staring. She was embarrassed to be singled out like this but she understood why they were doing it. In her, they saw a kind of manifestation of the green lady herself.

The Advent Craft Market was a resounding success, with mainly locals visiting but lots of outsiders, too. Rayne and Becky worked flat-out in the tearoom to cope with them all. They worked flat-out at the Christmas party, too, replenishing the sausages and pies and other simple food laid out on the great cracked stone table, and going round with jugs of steaming mulled wine and icy punch. So many people turned up that for once in its thousand-year existence the Old Stone Hall felt too warm, and the great log fire in the pagan fireplace had to be damped down.

It was never really in Rayne's thoughts that she'd go back to Cramphurst Estate, to what used to be home, for Christmas. The flat would be far too crowded, with Dave living there now. At the Craft Market she bought a little toy wooden horse and rider for Jelly, and a beautiful embroidered make-up bag for her mum, and posted them.

She was going to the Sands farm for Christmas day. Ethan said he couldn't be apart from her then and she had to spend some time with the billy goat again and, anyway, his mum cooked the best turkey in the world.

Epilogue

It was the morning of December the twenty-eighth, that quiet, gentle, slightly tired time between Christmas and New Year's. Rayne woke in the Old Sty with the thin winter sun streaming on to her face, and got out of bed. The air smelt fresh and beautiful; she pulled on her warm, raspberry-coloured dressing gown, a Christmas present from Mrs Driver, and opened the door.

At first she thought there'd been a heavy frost. The ground was white and glinting, soft and sparkling. But the air was too warm for frost.

She stepped out of the door, barefoot.

The ground was covered with snowdrops. Snowdrops, everywhere. They'd just appeared, and flowered, overnight. A great gorgeous carpet of them, lapping at the threshold, leading into the woods.

She laughed out loud in sheer pleasure, and started to walk. Snowdrops covered the ground all the way through the medieval garden and down to the lake where the three white geese sat on their island, bemused. She went into the woods, and the flowers dwindled a bit where it was darker under the trees – but when she stepped out on to the wide lawn behind the house, she gasped. It was covered, every inch of it, with the pretty white flowers, like a sudden explosion of spring.

There was a face at one of the bedroom windows, at the far end. She recognized Mr Stuart, and waved furiously. He opened the window and leaned out, and she hurried over and stood right beneath it.

"Has this ever happened before?" she called up.

"Never," he answered. His face was soft with pleasure and wonder. "*Never.* We have a few snowdrops round the edges, usually, and not till well into January. And anyway – they've just *appeared*, haven't they? No shoots, no leaves – just the full flowers."

"It's a sign," said Rayne firmly, and she laughed out loud. "It's a sign from *her*. What else could have done this – what else can it be?"

"I think you're right, Rayne. All's well at the Keep."

"Yes. And *you*, Mr Stuart—" She pointed up at him, suddenly bold. "You've got to forgive yourself. You've got to come down from your room and join in the life here again. It's not your fault. That Lingwall power is hard to resist when it's focused on you. I should know."

To her delight, he burst out laughing. "You should see yourself," he said. "Bundled up in that pink dressing gown with your lovely black hair, against this amazing sea of snowdrops!"

Then he pulled his window shut, but before it closed, he called out, "Thank you, Rayne."

She smiled, and as she turned away, there was a flash of

white up above her. She gazed upwards, and saw a flock of white doves and pigeons, wheeling free in the air, then soaring back to the tower dovecote. She laughed, her throat tight with the pleasure of it. They'd be building nests soon.

Then she waded back through the flowers to the Old Sty, to get dressed. Ethan had said he'd be round before eleven.

She couldn't wait for him to see it all. She couldn't wait to see him.

Kate Cann

*P*ossessing
Rayne

We've been watching you